Desperate
Times

By

Ethyl Smith

TP

ThunderPoint Publishing Ltd.

First Published in Great Britain in 2018 by
ThunderPoint Publishing Limited
Summit House
4-5 Mitchell Street
Edinburgh
Scotland EH6 7BD

Cover Image © Ethyl Smith
Cover Design © Huw Francis

ISBN: 978-1-910946-46-6 (Paperback)
ISBN: 978-1-910946-47-3 (eBook)
Printed and bound in Great Britain by Clays Ltd, Elcograf S.p.A

www.thunderpoint.scot

Acknowledgements

Those men and women who lived in 17th century Scotland and provided a history worth remembering.

Seonaid & Huw Francis of Thunderpoint Publishing for continued support and belief in my series about Covenanting times. Thank you.

My family for support, patience and willingness to accompany me on research trips to strange places.

I gained insight into this period from James King Hewison *The Covenanters*, John Howie *Scots Worthies*, Robert Watson *Peden: Prophet of the Covenant*, Andrew Murray Scott *Bonnie Dundee*, Magnus Linklater & Christian Hesketh *For King and Conscience*, Dane Love *The Covenanter Encyclopaedia*, David S. Ross *The Killing Time*, Rosalind K. Marshall *The Days of Duchess Anne*, Ian Whyte *Agriculture and Society in Seventeenth Century Scotland*, John Greenshields *Private Papers*, Robert McLeish *Archivist of Lesmahagow Historical Association*, Newsletters *Scottish Covenanter Memorial Association*, Dr. Mark Jardine *Jardine's Book of Martyrs*. Culpeper *Culpeper's Complete Herbal*, J.H. Thomson *The Martyr Graves of Scotland*, Elizabeth Foyster & Christopher A. Whatley *A History of Everyday Life in Scotland 1600-1800*, Ecco *The Laird and Farmer*, Maurice Grant *The Lion of the Covenant*, Maurice Grant *No King But Christ*, W.H.Carslaw *The Life and Letters of James Renwick*, Maurice Grant *Preacher to the Remnant*, Thomas McCrie *The Bass Rock*, Ann Shukman *Bishops and Covenanters*, Charles Sanford Terry *John Graham of Claverhouse Viscount of Dundee 1648-1689*.

Dedication

For Simon and Karen Smith

Faithfu unner tyranny

'In the world ye shall have tribulation; but be of good cheer,
I have overcome the world.' John Ch16 *

Oot on the moss, Brown lifted his heid tae a soond
as he cut peat efter faimly worship. In simmer mist,
he wis hainin wairmth agin sair winter. But it wisnae
a peesie-weep welcomin the morn, it wis sodgers.

They kent him, a guid man and a lang marked yin.
Excited, the Dragoons steekit him, nae argie-bargie,
an taen him tae his ane door. But fir aw the swords,
guns an threats, he couldnae, wouldnae abjure.

No fir his ane skin, no fir the bonnie bairn
tae come, no fir the wee laddie hidin his big een
in his mither's petticoat. No fir his guidwife
standin bricht as faith in the saft May sun.

Oh she kent his thochts oan attendin the curate,
she'd seen flocks o fowk flutterin oer the muir
tae pray. Sure hadn't she been warned tae keep linen
by hir, fir his windin-sheet? She wis aye ready.

The angels may luve sic shinin peeity
but it wisnae enuch. No strang enuch airmour
agin the winnowin mesh grippit bi Bluidy Clavers,
fyle he raged ravenously oer the land.

From the chapter read by John Brown on the morning of his death

Poem specially written for Desperate Times
by award winning poet Finola Scott

'Under certain circumstances profanity provides a relief denied even to prayer.'

Mark Twain

Chapter 1
Friday 23rd July 1680

Lucas Brotherstone sat at the kitchen table of Westermains Farm and stared at the black covers of his Bible. John Steel sat opposite, watching his tormented expression.

Twenty four hours ago they'd been in the village of Douglas witnessing Richard Cameron's mangled head being pulled from a filthy sack and swung in front of a horrified crowd.

A platoon of troopers had finally caught up with him on Airds Moss near Cumnock. Only a few weeks earlier on 22nd June, the anniversary of that fateful defeat at Bothwell Bridge, a defiant Cameron had ridden into the town of Sanquhar with twenty armed men to pin up a declaration on the Merkat Cross, denouncing the King's rule and warning of war against all royal supporters. The government immediately condemned this as treason and offered a 5000 merks reward for Cameron's arrest, dead or alive. For months this young man had been a real thorn in the government's side, tramping the countryside speaking to large gatherings of people, persuading them to stick to the Word of God, taking an ever more forceful stand against the so called rule of law. Already he was known as the Lion of the Covenant and one to be feared.

The temptation of informing for such a huge reward worked. His whereabouts was whispered and troopers arrived to deal with this rebel. One minute Cameron and his sixty followers were on their knees praying for the peace of heaven the next minute their swords spoke out as they slashed and hacked at the armed platoon, killing at least twenty-eight. Cameron and his closest allies had been cut down while others turned to flee across the moor. Cameron's hopes and aims were over. The sight of his swinging head confirmed it. John hadn't been surprised but Lucas still seemed traumatised as if the reality of the situation was beyond him.

A long time passed before Lucas looked up. "I need tae luk for guidance but – " The words faded into a whisper.

"Ye're a meenister. Ye're supposed tae be the guide. Whit's

stoppin ye?" John tried not to sound impatient.

"Whit if I canna dae it?"

"Dae whit?"

"Whit's suggested."

John sighed and stared at the ceiling. This man was impossible. Never a straight answer. Never in touch with reality. Never able to look after himself. That was the crux of it all. Lucas needed protecting, if only from himself. John took a deep breath and tried again. "Dae ye ken whit ye're lukin for?"

"No. But the word will be my direction forward. When I open my Bible whitivver I read will show me the way."

"If ye believe that." John lost patience.

Lucas continued to stare at the black covers. Silence returned. John hunched his shoulders and was preparing for another wait when his wife Marion burst into the kitchen. "Ah hear hooves comin up the farm track. Ower mony fur onythin less than a platoon."

John jumped from his chair, ran to the other side of the table, grabbed hold of Lucas and propelled him into the little hall.

Marion pulled all the jackets from the row of pegs, ran her fingers along the wood panelled wall, gave a quick twist, and a little door swung out to reveal a deep recess.

"No a word." John pushed Lucas inside and joined him.

Marion closed the door, re-hung the jackets then went into the kitchen. She looked out the tiny window to see the red-jacketed troopers clatter into the cobbled yard and dismount.

Captain Dominic McCann, captain of the Earl of Airlie's main platoon, knocked on the farmhouse door then pushed it open. Three steps more took him along the hall and into the kitchen where Marion was waiting. "Maam." He nodded. "Yer man wis seen in Douglas yesterday, alang wi the meenister ousted frae this parish. I'm here tae ask ye if he's here on this farm?"

Marion shook her head. "Why wud he be?"

McCann frowned. "In that case."

"Ye need tae mak a search," Marion snapped. "He's no here. But on ye go. Satisfy yersel."

McCann turned, marched out to the yard and barked orders to his men. Within minutes the farm was over-run as the troopers searched inside and out before admitting there was no sign of the two fugitives.

"Re-mount and wait." McCann went back into the farmhouse to find Marion still standing in the same spot. He nodded again. "It wud appear ye're tellin the truth."

Marion looked away and said nothing.

McCann hesitated then surprised himself by saying words best kept to himself. "Maam, I dinna approve o my maister's methods nor whit he's dain tae ye. I wis at Bothwell, at the battle, and saw whit happened. The earl came at yer man's horse, wavin his sword like somethin demented, demandin surrender. Yer man jist waited till the earl wis close enough then stretched oot tae cut the horse's traces. The auld man's saddle slipped tae the side an he fell aff wi a thump. Insteid o runnin him thru yer man wheeled roond an made aff."

"Ah see." Marion stared at the captain. "Ye're tellin me that ma John has tae suffer for sparin a life instead o endin it?"

McCann flushed. "It's a maitter o pride, Mistress Steel."

"Pride." Marion's voice sharpened.

"When the earl hit the ground and rolled aboot a young lieutenant laughed. Airlie heard him and flew intae a rage."

"An that's whit set aw this aff? A laugh. God's sake." Marion shook her head. "A great man lik that behavin lik a spoilt bairn. Ma John's become a wanted felon wi a thoosand merks on his heid while ah wis flung oot ma richtfu hame an hounded frae pillar tae post. An whit aboot ma pair weans? Whit hae they done?"

"Ye're safe here. This farm belangs tae yer faither-in-law." McCann hesitated. "Airlie canna touch ye as lang as ye dinna harbour yer man on this farm. If ye dae and the earl finds oot ye'll be back whaur ye started. That's why he sent me. If I'd found yer man he wis for the Tolbooth an ye'd be flung oot on the moor again."

Marion bowed her head. "Ah hear ye."

"Jist be carefu Maam. These are dangerous times and the earl o Airlie is a dangerous man." McCann clicked his heels and left, surprised that he'd said so much.

When John and Lucas stumbled out from their hiding place Lucas went straight to his Bible, still lying on the kitchen table.

He took a deep breath, opened his precious book and read a particular line from John 21 verse 15 – 'lovest thou me more than these?' He read it again, seemed to think for a moment then flicked the pages once more. This time he was confronted with Mark 3 verse 29, 'But he that shall blaspheme against the Holy Ghost hath never forgiveness, but is by danger of eternal damnation.'

His face tightened. "My God. Whit hae I done?"

John gaped at him. "Whit dae ye mean?"

"My honesty."

John grasped Lucas's arm. "Luk here sir. Enough's enough. It's time ye came intae the world wi the rest o us. Aw they fancy ideas are dain ye nae guid. Thur turnin ye intae a liability tae yersel an onybody ye meet. Tae be honest ah can haurly cope wi ma ain problems withoot addin the weight o yer precious conscience tae the load. Whae are ye kiddin? Tak a luk at yersel. Ye're certainly no kiddin me. No ony mair." John wheeled round and stamped out the kitchen, down the hall, then banged the outside door behind him.

When Marion looked out the window she saw him cut through the close, onto the path which lead to the moor. She turned to Lucas. "Ay sir. Whit hae ye done?" With that she hurried from the kitchen.

Confused and hurt Lucas looked down at the open pages still staring up at him. He read the words again. So that was it. Eternal damnation. God was telling him that he knew, had seen through the pretence and was now pronouncing judgement.

He thought about it, how his refusal to acknowledge a far away king as his spiritual master had triggered off every event that followed. His wife Bett had warned him what would happen, the law had carried it out, and still he'd imagined he could remain above it all. As for the words he'd spouted that last day in the pulpit, were they part of his pretence, his declaration as a principled man, prepared to pay any consequence for his words and actions? In another time he might have been an actor. He was good at it. On that occasion he'd stunned his listening congregation. But what about his own belief?

He shivered, remembering how poor Bett had been the one to

pay when the law sent a platoon to turf him out of his church and send him beyond his parish forever. The soldier in charge had turned the event into a tragedy when he'd whipped the horse, made it race down the narrow alleyway to crash against the house wall on the corner and leave Bett dying in the gutter. That day he'd lost her forever and yet he could still see her lovely face staring at him as if asking, "Whit hae ye done?"

If the truth be told he'd gone on making mistakes, the last one only days ago when he walked away from the man who'd trusted him, appreciated his support, believed he was at one with his determination to change the course of the country and bring it back to the true word. The true word. He shivered again, could see Richard Cameron's awful head swinging below that soldier's hand. The same one who'd caused Bett's death. Cameron's staring eyes weren't asking what he'd done, they were denouncing him.

And then he thought about John Steel. A man he barely knew who'd stepped forward to protect him, help him, support him, been with him yesterday in that crowd, who'd followed him when he'd turned and run, then guided him back across the moor, back to the safety of Westermains farm.

What a mess.

Head against his Bible he wept.

John sat on a drystane dyke which separated the top field of Westermains from rough moorland. From here he could just see the roof of his own farm. He hadn't been near the place in months. He missed it, the regular routine of the farming year, normal family life, happiness. It all seemed part of another lifetime.

Now he spent half his time dodging troopers, the other half pretending to lead some sort of family life as a lodger in his father's farm.

John was sure his father had been killed at Bothwell, a victim of the battle's aftermath when revenge had reigned unchecked. If this was true Westermains was now his. But how to claim it? As a wanted felon with a price on his head he'd forfeit the property.So long as death was unproven Marion and the boys were safe in that house, not struggling to survive on the open moor. As far as the law was concerned she was living with her

5

father-in-law. Whether he was there or not made no difference.

What had happened at Douglas was the stuff of nightmares. The law had proved its power against any dissenter. The threat was all too clear. It was a moment he'd never forget, when Richard Cameron's head had appeared from a sack to swing in front of the whole village, held by Crichton of all people. That captain seemed to dog John at every turn.

And then there was Lucas Brotherstone like some millstone round his neck. He had to be dealt with before he sucked John further into trouble.

Decision made he jumped from his perch and hurried back to the farmhouse to find Marion in the kitchen baking bannocks on the griddle. He tiptoed up behind her, grasped her waist and kissed the nape of her neck. "Ah'm sorry."

She stiffened, didn't turn. "Sorry isna enough."

"Ay. An ah need tae stert sortin it oot." He walked down the hall to the spare room where Lucas had retreated to stare out the window.

John coughed.

Lucas ignored him.

John crossed the room and spun Lucas round to face him. "Ah huv tae say this, sir. Ah ken ye're no pleased wi me but this time ye need tae listen. Ye've gone ower far wi this pretendin tae be somethin ye're no."

Lucas flinched.

John kept going. "It's like hain a stick tae beat yersel. An this last happenin in Douglas, seein whit's happened tae Cameron has warned me tae stop ye afore it's too late. Ye huv tae stop playin the humble, sufferin servant. Peace o mind is whit maitters, bein able tae sleep at nicht, no tossin an turnin wi self guilt."

Lucas flushed and turned back to the window. Finally he said, "Ye dinna understand."

"Is that so." John's voice hardened. "Frae whaur ah'm staundin ah'm unnerstaundin ye raither weel. An ken whit, ah dinna like it. Ye tak the words in the Bible an turn them intae aw kinds o fancy theories. Ah'll admit ye're guid at it. But ye're no a leader, nor even a true rebel. Accept it. Gang back tae Holland. Back tae yon college. Back tae yer students. They'll like yer clever twists an turns wi words. If ye bide here ye'll end up wi yer heid in a bag lik Richard Cameron. Is that whit ye want?"

"Ye want rid o me. Is that it?"

This time John flushed. "Can ye no see ah've plenty tae deal wi
withoot keepin a watch oot for a lame duck."

"And whit dae ye propose this duck shud dae?"

"Go intae toun, find Maister Middleton. He saw ye richt afore
an gied ye passage tae Holland. Ah'm shair he'll dae it again."

"So that's hoo it is?" Lucas's voice was icy.

"Ay. Come mornin ye're on yer way an nae arguin."

John woke to the sound of drumming rain on the farmhouse
roof. He listened for a while, the constant beat almost persuading
him to fall asleep again. And then he remembered what he'd said
to Lucas Brotherstone.

He sat up and rubbed his eyes. He'd meant every word. No
matter the weather he was for the city, to find Maister Middleton.

Lucas was too much of a liability to stay where the law was
about to take revenge against Richard Cameron's challenge. Few
would escape the consequences.

Now wide awake he left his warm bed to open the bedroom
shutters and peer out at the faint light of dawn with the rain
driving down from the moor and across his fields.

The click of the shutters woke Marion. "Whit's up?" she
whispered. "Huv ye heard somethin ootside?"

"Only the rain," John replied. "It'll be a dreich journey intae
the toon wi the meenister."

"Can ye no wait?"

"An gie him the chance tae tak aff on his ain? Naw. Ah want
him safe on a boat, on his way back tae Holland, an oot ma hair.
He's best awa frae here afore somethin bad happens tae him or
even oorsels."

"Ye'll need tae be carefu in case the troopers are aboot."

"No sae likely in this rain. Onyway, we're heidin for the toon.
It's the open spaces they patrol."

"Ah best see tae breakfast then." Marion quickly dressed and
hurried through to the kitchen.

Within an hour John and Lucas were in Waterside farm saddling
their horses which John had hidden in his mother-in-law's stable.

Even when they reached the Glasgow road neither said a word, both hunched against the wet, keeping their thoughts to themselves, no sign of the companionship they'd shared on their way back from that terrible happening at Douglas.

Beyond Hamilton John left the road and edged Juno under the shelter of a spreading beech tree. Lucas followed. They both dismounted and allowed the horses to rest and crop the grass. Nothing was said while they ate some of the food Marion had packed for the journey.

Just as they were about to remount a single figure on horseback appeared on the road.

"Bide whaur ye are till this yin passes," John warned. "An keep yer bunnet pued doon."

The rider drew level, turned to stare at the two figures under the tree then trotted on. John sighed. "Ah ken that yin. Ah hope he hasna guessed it's me."

"I doubt it," Lucas said. "He only glanced in passing."

"That's aw it taks an he's the vera ane tae tell tales for siller."

"I didna recognise him," Lucas said.

"He's no frae the village. Bides in Kirkfieldbank. Name's Sam Pate. Ah've come across him a time or twa at Lanark market. He works in the sale ring an is no weel liked for the way he haundles the beasts. Folk say he's aye hingin aboot, listenin an then whisperin in the sheriff's ear. We best hing back an let him git weel aheid. Nae use in askin for trouble."

"But surely – " Lucas began.

"Jist dae as ye're tellt," John snapped. "Ah want ye delivered safe an soond tae Maister Middleton. Aifter that ye can please yersel."

Sam Pate rode along the road without looking back. He didn't need to. One glance had been enough to recognise John Steel. A second glance at the beautiful, black Juno confirmed it. A horse like that was well known and admired. He grinned. If ye're aimin tae bide secret ye're goin aboot it the wrang way. Wi a bit luck ah'll be claimin the thoosand merks on yer heid Maister Steel. As for the ither yin. He's likely on the wanted list an worth a bit siller as weel. Ay. An it luks lik thur heidin fur the toon. Weel, ah'll be waitin when they arrive, waitin tae be thur shadow. An when the richt meenit comes tae caw in the law – " He rubbed his hands together. "A thoosand merks will be mine. Ay, John Steel. Weel met indeed." He slowed his horse to a walk and began to whistle.

As they joined the city crowds John's thoughts winged back a few months to his last visit. He trotted on remembering it all, forgetting the need to be careful, not noticing the figure watching their progress down the High Street.

He was thinking about his meeting with the goldsmith James McAvoy, whose name appeared on the official-looking document he'd found in his father's house. He'd made the journey to the city to find this man. And what a surprise it brought. McAvoy had been a good friend to Robert Steel, had invested an unexpected windfall and then gone on managing the income, re-investing and taking great care of all the profits. Robert Steel had never drawn anything from his account. John had inherited a tidy sum. Better still, the old goldsmith was willing to go on caring for his interests.

John had been waiting in McAvoy's dining room while a fresh bond was prepared when he'd seen a well-dressed visitor arrive and walk down the marble hall. When the visitor spoke he'd given himself away as Sam Galbraith the tinker who'd already caused so much trouble to John and his family.

John had stepped forward to challenge him.

"Ye're mistaken sir," Gaby insisted. "We've never met. My name is Davie Shaw."

Gaby's fur collar and fine clothes meant nothing. His voice was a giveaway. As for his choice of name, John had known the real Davie Shaw, a lonely old farmer who'd been found dead in his kitchen some months back. He'd been an old skinflint, thought to be wealthy although no money was ever found. Now John knew why. But before he could act Gaby had stepped sidewards, a slim blade flashing out from the fancy sleeve before he whirled round to race for the front door while John slumped to the marble floor with a knife between his ribs.

James McAvoy's family had nursed John, saved his life. The old goldsmith had even sent two armed men to deal with the so-called Davie Shaw. The trail went as far as Edinburgh then nothing.

"We'd best mak for the Coffee Hoose." Lucas cut into John's

thoughts. "It's jist ahint the Trongate. Maister Middleton seems tae be there there maist days wi ither merchants. It's whaur I met him afore he gave me passage tae Holland that first time."

"Jist hope he'll dae it again." John nodded and began to pay attention again as the crowd grew tighter around them.

The smell of bodies and the stench of rubbish hummed in the warm, damp air as they stopped in front of the impressive building which housed Glasgow's first coffee house. Behind them a shadowy figure also stopped and watched as they tethered their horses beside the fluted pillars then disappeared inside.

The fug from oil lamps and pipe smokers swirled round the gossip, mixed with the smell of hot food, and added to the almost overpowering heat in the coffee house.

John and Lucas waited till their eyes adjusted to the gloom then began to edge past food-laden trestles and rows of gossiping men.

They were almost halfway across the vast room when Lucas nodded towards one of the longest tables where at least twelve expensively dressed men of varying ages seemed engrossed in eating and talking, both at the same time. "That's Middleton facin us. Twa frae the end."

"Try tae catch his ee," John suggested.

As if in response the man looked up and stared across the crowd. Lucas smiled and raised his hand. The man stiffened then looked away and whispered to a serving girl placing a mug of ale beside his heaped plate.

She worked her way along the table, giving each man a fresh mug before walking towards the kitchen. She disappeared then came out again with a tray of food. This time she came close by Lucas and John. As she passed them she whispered, "The maister will meet ye in hawf an hoor. Go tae the back room o the Black Bull Inn an wait. Dinna speak tae him here." She swayed on with her heavy tray and returned to the long table to dish out more food.

"Nivver heard o the place." John looked at Lucas as if he should know.

Lucas shrugged.

"Richt." John frowned. "Oot o here."

Once in the busy street they could find no sign of the Black Bull tavern. They walked as far as the next square; nothing. Did the same in the opposite direction. Still nothing. John stopped, looked round for the most likely person to ask. An old woman was sitting on a doorstep alongside a fine looking collie dog. He went over to her and bent down to ruffle the dog's feathery ears. "Ye're a fine lukin beast." The dog's muzzle followed his hand and a long, pink tongue licked his fingers.

The old woman glanced up. "He's no for sale mister."

John smiled. "Ah'm jist admirin him."

"So whit ur ye aifter?"

"Jist some directions." He slipped a bawbee into the filthy hand. "Am ah onywhaur near the Black Bull tavern?"

The coin vanished and she pointed to a low archway opposite. "Ye're nearly there. Thru yon arch. It taks ye intae a wee yard. Turn left. Ye'll see it in the far corner. Richt tidy place, an clean. Ale's guid. The landlady's richt strict. Nae nonsense. Dependin on whit ye're aifter ye micht prefer somewhaur else."

"It'll dae fine." John laughed and signalled to Lucas.

They waited almost an hour in the back room of the tiny tavern, with time enough to eat a mutton pie with barley before Maister Middleton bustled in to join them. He seemed anxious, almost embarrassed to see Lucas again.

John leant forward, shook the old man's hand. "John Steel. Ye dinna ken me. Ah'm jist here tae see Maister Brotherstone on his way tae a place o safety. He's in need o a quick getaway but whit ah saw back in yon coffee hoose maks me think it's ower risky tae ask ye."

"Ay weel." Middleton glanced at Lucas. "Things hae chainged for the worse since we last met. Ye canna be too carefu these days."

"In that case I'm sorry tae bother ye a second time." Lucas cut in. "I shud nivver hae come." He stood up.

John pulled him back into his seat. "Let the man feenish."

Middleton flushed. "Aifter the news aboot Richard Cameron I'm thinkin the government's aboot tae come doon heavy on onybody no followin the official line." He peered at Lucas. "Ye were involved in that awfy happenin, were ye no? I heard ye'd come back tae support him."

Lucas didn't dare answer.

"A fine man," Middleton went on. "And a sad loss. Ye've been lucky tae escape wi yer heid on yer shooders. Ay. Men lik yersel are needed tae keep the cause alive."

Lucas still didn't answer.

"He'd be safe in Holland," John said. "Safe to continue the work."

"Jist so." Middleton nodded. "But it's no that easy. I've a guid business. It's taen years tae build it up and I dinna want tae lose it. Much as I want tae support ma Presbyterian freends I need tae keep ma back covered and no attract ony suspicion. Twa o the justiciary hae stertit eatin at oor table in the coffee hoose. Thur ears are aye flappin, an thur een are awhaur, watchin. They seem pleasant enough but I suspect it's aw a front. They're jist waitin for the wrang word or some slip up and I'd be locked up or worse. Still." He hesitated then shook his head. "Risk or no ye're a Cameron man and deserve tae be helped. Itherwise. And I dinna want that on my conscience. Richt, Maister Brotherstone, if ye can wait till the end o this week I can gie ye passage oot o here. Say Friday. My warehouse at the Broomielaw, afore midnicht. I'll hae my ferryman ready. He'll tak ye doon river and oot tae the tail o the bank, same as the last time. But mind times huv chainged." Middleton lowered his voice and leant forward. "These days it's haurly safe tae mak plans in yer heid let alane speak them for ithers tae hear. If the wrang ears wur tae git haud o ma offer, weel."

He took out a large handkerchief and wiped his brow. "Whit I'm saying is – "

"Ye're takin a chance on ma freend," John said. "Ye're even takin a chance speakin tae us here mair or less in the open. We baith unnerstaund that an baith gratefu fur yer continued support o the cause. Rest assured nae a word will be shared. An ony instructions will be followed tae the letter. We'll be as carefu as possible. An dinna worry, ah'll mak sure ma freend is there on time."

Chapter 2

"I'll leave ye tae it." Middleton pushed his chair back to leave as two burly men burst into the tiny room. He turned to protest. One of the men grabbed his jacket lapels, pulled him aside, then leant across the wooden table towards John. "Move yersel if ye value yer freedom."

Middleton and Lucas gaped as John jumped up and made for the door. The strangers called after him, "Doon that passageway, oot the kitchen door, intae the wee lane. Thur's a high wa tae climb, then skirt roond an mak for the maister's hoose. He's expectin ye. The back door's aff the latch."

The two men now turned to Middleton and Lucas. "Ye best mak yersels scarce. The law's comin, lukin fur Maister Steel."

Middleton asked no questions and hurried out of the room.

Lucas didn't move.

"C'mon. Move yer sticks afore it's too late." The strangers lifted him from his seat and almost carried him down the same passageway John had taken. He didn't argue and once outside obeyed the whispered instructions to climb the high wall. After that he was led across a small garden, past a heaped midden, through a narrow close and down a flight of steps to come out in the shadows of the busy street, just beyond the little archway.

"Bide still," the men warned and pulled him further into the darkest corner. "We need tae mak sure."

Just then three armed troopers appeared, forcing their way through the crowd. A stout man in a flapping coat ran behind. He was shouting instructions as they headed for the archway, passed through then disappeared into the yard beyond.

Shouts and sounds of arguing were heard before they came out again to march through the archway. The man in the coat looked annoyed. He pointed back at the cobbled yard as if insisting on something. One trooper seemed to lose his temper and turned to take a swipe at the angry face.

The man staggered back, fell against the wall. He stayed there, swearing as one of the troopers gave him a final kick before all three hurried out of the archway and ploughed back into the crowd as if making for the High Street.

Lucas's new companions nodded. Something seemed to be confirmed.

They waited in the shadows and watched till the man struggled up and walked away. They nodded again. One loosed his grip on Lucas's arm and ducked into the crowd to follow the angry back. The other pushed Lucas forward and began to steer him in the opposite direction.

Sam Pate didn't know if he should laugh, or cry, or grind his teeth. He'd watched John Steel and his companion go into the tavern, he'd even ventured inside to see them settle in a back room. When they ordered food and ale, well, the garrison was only at the top of the High Street. Easy to hurry there, pick up the support needed for an arrest, and be back before they'd finished eating.

Except the garrison commander had taken some persuading before he allowed three troopers to accompany Sam to the tavern. And when they got there no John Steel. The troopers had made a fool of him then attacked him. He rubbed his cheek and swore again.

His horse was still tethered outside the coffee house. He'd best retrieve the beast and get on his way to visit his sister. This had been the real reason for coming to town. At least he'd get a decent supper. "Ay," he groaned, "an a pair substitute fur the purse o money ah wis aifter."

As he turned into the narrow vennel that led to the coffee house a strong arm slid round his neck and jerked his head back. A soft voice whispered, "No a word if ye want tae keep yer heid on yer shooders."

He tried to resist. It made no difference. He was dragged sidewards into a close mouth, flung against the wall then made to wheel round and face a pair of calm eyes. Terrifyingly calm eyes. "Ah'm a pair man," he stuttered.

"Indeed ye are." The eyes dared him to look away. "It's a pair man as tries tae tak advantage o anither's misfortune."

"Ah dinna ken whit ye mean."

"Steel. Dis that name mean onythin ma freend?"

"Why shud it?"

"Whae else wis tailin the man wi that name, meanin tae git him arrested?"

"So whit?" Sam dared. "He hus a price on his heid."

"Is that so?"

The grip tightened. Sam was pulled so close the peaty smell of a single malt filled his nostrils.

"Ye shud be ashamed o yersel. Spyin aifter an upricht man lik that. But ah'm here tae help ye mend yer ways, an mind yer ain business. Frae noo on ye'll bide awa frae Maister Steel, or else – "

Sam tried to nod.

The eyes stared for a few seconds then blinked as a hard fist connected with Sam's brow at high speed. Everything went black. Legs buckling he hit the flagstones. His head rolled sideways, his body twitched twice then stiffened and lay still. His attacker waited a moment to be sure then stepped over the prone body and left the close.

Lucas was pushed in the back door of an enormous town house half way up the High Street. He was surprised to find John Steel sitting by a glowing range, in a well appointed kitchen, talking to an old man in a red dressing gown.

John looked up. "Sorry for leavin ye lik that."

"I'm at a loss tae understand whit's happening." Lucas peered through the candlelight at rows of shining copper pots neatly arranged on a long shelf beside a huge dresser bulging with fine china. In the middle of the room stood an enormous table with a pure white, scrubbed top. Many servants must work here for someone of great wealth and importance. "My," he whispered, "this is a fine hoose."

John turned to the old man. "And this is a fine man. Alloo me tae introduce Maister James McAvoy, goldsmith an freend."

Lucas looked more surprised.

"Maister McAvoy luks aifter ma investments. Last time ah wis here he even saved ma life."

"Whit?"

John nodded. "Ye mind Gaby the tinker back hame?"

"Indeed I do. He was forivver at the door aifter something. Bett aye fell for his sorrowful tales but his antics made me suspicious."

"Ye wur richt. He's an auld deil. Ah'll no tell ye the hale story except say he wis here in this hoose, an tried tae kill me. Nearly managed. If it hadna been for the maister an his grandson."

"I think the man's even mair confused, John." McAvoy waved Lucas to a seat beside them. "Sit doon sir. Let me explain." He waited till Lucas was settled. "When ye and John arrived in the toon twa o my men jist happened tae catch sicht o ye. They ken John and were aboot tae come ower and speak when they noticed yer shadow. Tailing somebody lik that is no a guid sign so they followed the man tae see whit he wis up tae. When they saw him gang intae the garrison they guessed it wis John he wis aifter, reporting him for a reward."

"And they came tae warn him?"

McAvoy nodded. "They tellt John tae come here whaur he'd be safe. And noo ye're here as weel. The man that brocht ye is Alex Jamieson. A man ye can trust. His brother Pete is nae doubt dealing wi yer shadow as we speak."

There was a light tap at the outside door and the other Jamieson came in to stand beside his brother. He looked across the room to McAvoy and gave a quick nod. "Is that aw sir?"

"Indeed. Much thanks." McAvoy smiled at the two rough looking men.

"We'll awa then." The brothers turned to leave.

"Haud on a meenit." John stood up. "Ye went tae an awfy bother back there."

Pete grinned. "When yon so cawed tinker stabbed ye in the maister's hoose we didna manage tae catch the auld deil. We dinna often fail so this time we made sure."

"Thank God ye did." John went over to the two brothers and shook their hands.

Both men looked embarrassed then Pete added, "By the way. Yer horse is in the maister's stable. Ye dinna want tae lose a fine beast lik that."

"Ye've thocht o everythin."

"We dae oor best." Pete grinned and signalled to McAvoy. "Nicht maister." The two brothers were out the door and away.

That night John and Lucas lay in comfortable beds but neither slept.

John was worrying over what might have happened. Lucas was worrying about returning to Holland.

At breakfast he dared to mention this.

John glared at him. "Ye're goin. Maister Middleton's expectin' ye. Nae ifs or buts."

They sat in silence then Lucas tried again. "I'm no a guid traveller on the sea. I wis richt ill yon first time, even worse on the way back. I'm no keen on the experience again."

"We can get ye something for that." McAvoy appeared in the doorway. There's a guid apothecary nearby. He'll sort ye oot. He sees folk private like in the morning, runs his shop in the aifternoon. I'll send a maid roond tae mak an appointment. Name's Spreul. John Spreul."

"Oh." Lucas looked surprised. "I ken that name. If it's the same man he's a cousin o my wife's. I havena seen him in years."

McAvoy smiled. "Nae doubt ye'll get special treatment."

Half an hour later a serving girl came back with an appointment for that morning.

Lucas put on his coat and prepared to go.

"Haud on." John stood up. "Mibbe ah shud come wi ye."

"Nae need John. Bide seated. The shop's only meenits awa." McAvoy began to steer Lucas into the hall. "Oot the front door, a few steps further and ye're at the crossroads. Turn left intae the Gallowgate, past the entrance tae Spoutmooth Vennel on yer left. The next ane's whit ye want, Dovehill Street. John Spreul's shop is richt at the top near the corner wi the Auld Vennel. Ye'll see a swingin sign wi his name on it. Ye canna go wrang."

The sign above the single-fronted shop said J. Spreul Apothecary. In the centre of the window was a handwritten announcement. *Elixirs, Tonics, Remedies. Private consultations 9-12 daily by appointment.* The two storey building was well maintained, the woodwork freshly painted, giving the impression of a well run, successful business.

Lucas turned the handle of the half-glass door and stepped inside. A little bell jangled and he stood a moment, nostrils twitching at the rush of smells from tobacco, sugar, spices, wines, herbs all mixed together, all trying to dominate. It felt exciting, strange, even more so when he saw the shelves tightly packed with glass jars, each with a white label, handwritten with strange letters, and filled with coloured powders and dried leaves. He wondered how anyone understood all this let alone know what to use for any ailment.

Behind a well-polished mahogany counter was a huge dresser with rows and rows of drawers. The topmost row was tiny, the second a little larger, then growing in size row by row to the bottom which was deep and wide. Again each one had a white label with handwritten words in some sort of strange code.

There was no sign of Spreul but he could hear low voices drifting through a half open door at the back of the shop. Too polite to call out Lucas waited as the murmured conversation continued. Finally a tall, thin man in a thick, woollen coat appeared. His face was chalk white and he sneezed several time as he passed Lucas on his way out of the shop.

John Spreul appeared. A sprightly looking, youngish man wearing a spotless white apron. Intelligent, sharp eyes stared at Lucas then the mouth smiled. "My, my, this is a surprise. Lucas Brotherstone. Guid tae see ye. It's been a lang time."

Lucas nodded. "Ay. My wedding day."

John Spreul's expression changed. "I wis sorry tae hear aboot Bett's death. And yer ither troubles. Her brither Andrew taen the news hard."

"He blamed me completely." Lucas flushed. "Mibbe he wis richt."

"Andrew's aye had an ee for his ane business. At the time the Presbyterians were causin problems. He didna see it wise tae side that way." Spreul frowned. "I had words wi him aboot it, tellt him his conscience wis mair important than a wheen extra siller. I even spoke aboot the cause for the Kirk, but he wisna listenin. I've hardly seen him since. But this is neither the time nor the place. We can talk richt aifter. Whit can I dae for ye?"

Lucas nodded. "I'm aboot tae mak a sea journey. I need somethin tae help wi sea sickness."

"An awfy affliction. But ten drops o the richt tincture three times a day will keep ye richt. Blessed thistle, wi some elderflower, peppermint and ginger usually does the trick."

Before Lucas could answer the shop door burst open and armed troopers filled the space. The leading soldier, a captain by his uniform barked out, "John Spreul?"

"Ay. Whit is it?" Spreul stiffened but appeared calm.

"Ye're under arrest. Ye're for Edinburgh afore General Dalyell."

"Whitivver for?" Spreul's voice sharpened. "I've done naethin against ony law. My business is registered. Everythin's legal."

"The general thinks different." The captain turned to Lucas. "Whit are ye here for?"

"I'm a relative. Here tae buy some medicine."

"Whit's yer name. Whaur are ye frae?"

"Brotherstone. Late o Lesmahagow. I wis the minister there."

The captain glared at Lucas. "Ane o they renegade meenisters ah'll warrant. And a relative o this man. No a guid sign." He turned to the trooper beside him. "Tie this yin up as weel."

Lucas began to protest but his arms were thrust up his back and tied tightly with rough twine.

John Spreul still stood behind his counter. He looked furious. "Hoo dare ye mak sic outrageous accusations. Ye've nae richt."

"I hae ivvery richt. I hae a warrant." The captain waved a piece of crumpled paper. "Since Cameron wis stopped in his tracks we're busy cleanin up the hingers on, makin sure the law is upheld."

"Whit has that tae dae wi me?" Spreul shouted. "I'm an apothecary, a law abiding citizen. I've done nothin tae merit this intrusion. I had nae connection wi this Cameron ye mention."

"Whitivver." The captain signalled to the second trooper. "Tie this yin extra ticht. He luks lik trouble. Tak them baith oot tae the cairt."

Lucas and John Spreul were half carried into the street and hoisted into a waiting cart to be driven away under tight, military escort.

Alex and Pete Jamieson watched all this from a close opposite then hurried back to James McAvoy with the news.

"The eedjit's no safe oot himsel. Ah shud hae gone wi him," John groaned.

"And end up arrested as weel?" James McAvoy spoke gently. "Yer freend's been sucked intae something beyond us. We'll jist hae tae wait and see whit happens."

The loaded cart rolled into the garrison yard. Spreul and Lucas were pulled off and made to stand against the stable wall. Two fresh horses were led out and both men were hoisted into the saddles then lashed to the traces.

"Sit there. Nae nonsense, or ye'll end up wi a bullet in yer heid afore ye reach Edinburgh. General Dalyell's expectin ye." The captain gave a signal. Mounted troopers lined up on either side and the small procession wheeled round to trot back into the street.

By the time the captives were led up Edinburgh's High Street they were slumped forward, more asleep than awake, so bone weary that what happened next seemed hardly to matter.

Soldiers with flaming torches came out of a tall, fortress like building and stood to attention as the escort stopped in front of the main door. "The Tolbooth governor kens aboot these twa. They're tae go afore General Dalyell," the captain announced. "He'll want tae see them the morn."

The prisoners were untied, lifted down, their wrists freed, then the captain handed them over. With a derisive salute he turned and led his platoon back down the High Street.

Strong arms forced Spreul and Lucas inside the building, pushed them up the narrowest, circular stone staircase, and into a tiny room with neither bed, nor table nor chair.

"Sleep weel," one of their gaolers laughed.

Neither man answered. They slumped exhausted to the floor and lay there unmindful of the filth or the faint scuttling noises nearby.

High behind them a sliver of a moon slid gently through the barred window to settle on their faces as they slept.

Lucas felt as if he was coming up from the depth of some murky pool. Every limb ached, his head thumped. What an effort it was to try and surface. Maybe it was a nightmare. Maybe he'd wake up and it would be over. Or maybe not. He opened an eye. It was true. None of it was wild imagining. He really was here, helpless to do anything other than lie very still and try to ignore the stench.

He closed his eyes again, forced himself to think through yesterday. Nothing made any sense. Finally he gave up and took another look at the mashed up straw that seemed to cover the floor in filthy heaps and waves. Among the nearest pile a pair of round eyes, small and bright, winked at him, disappeared for a moment, then seemed to edge a little closer. This time he could see a long, grey tail and the shadow of a fat body. He jerked back. The straw twitched. The eyes retreated a little but still watched. Suddenly afraid he sat up and flapped his hands.

"Mornin," a voice said. "I'll no say guid for it's no."

Lucas peered in the direction of the voice and saw John Spreul standing at the tiny, barred window. "Indeed it's no. But whit's tae be done?"

"We get oot o here for a start." Spreul sounded angry. "Somewhaur awa frae this stinkin, rat infested hole whaur we're expected tae sleep and shit on the same flair. I want a clean room, a table, a chair, and a proper bed. And I mean tae hae it." He strode through the filthy straw and hammered on the cell door.

A few minutes later the door creaked open and a burly shape filled the space.

"Whit's up?"

Spreul held out his right hand. A single gold coin glinted in his palm.

The burly shape seemed to understand. "Wud ye be lukin fur better accommodation, sir?"

Spreul nodded.

The shape stepped into the cell, became an overweight man in an ill-fitting, greasy uniform. He made to lift the coin.

"First things first." Spreul closed his hand.

"As ye wish." The man grunted. "Come awa an ah'll show ye. Twa flairs up the air's sweeter than here. Ah ken the vera room. The last occupant hud nae complaints. He'll no be back so if it suits jist say."

"Whit if he does come back?" Lucas asked.

The man laughed. "Nae chance. He's swingin frae the main gibbet above the front door."

Lucas gasped.

Spreul shook his head. "Leave it be. Jist follow the man."

The man led them up the twisted stairs, along a dark corridor to a door at the end. He pushed it open. "There ye are. A guid bed, a chair, a table, a wee windae that opens an inch or twa, a bucket in the corner fur the needfu, even a clean swept flair. It's oor vera best. Whit mair can ye want? Mind ye ah'll be needin anither coin tae the same value if ye want tae bide in sic luxury

21

wi somethin decent tae eat."

Spreul handed over the coin. "Ye'll get anither in a day or twa, provided we're weel luked aifter."

The man nodded and turned to leave.

"Haud on." Spreul stopped him. "I need ye tae bring me paper and pen. I must write an important letter. I want it delivered withoot delay tae John Grieg, my lawyer." Spreul opened his hand again. Two silver merks now sat there. "Ye'll get this aifter I hae a reply frae my lawyer."

"Ye're a hard task maister." The man grinned. "An nae fool either. Vera weel. Ah'll dae as ye ask."

Lucas watched the gaoler leave then turned to John Spreul. "Hoo did ye manage this?"

"Siller. The answer tae jist aboot onythin. I've heard tales aboot this place and kent whit tae dae."

"But ye gied yon man a lot o money. I cudna dae onythin lik that."

"I'm a business man, aye wear a money belt. Thank God I dae, and thank God the troopers didna think tae search me itherwise—"

"We'd still be doonstairs." Lucas shuddered.

"But we're no." Spreul stopped him. "And aince I pen a letter tae my lawyer he'll sort this oot. This has got tae be some kind o terrible mistake."

Lucas's opinion of John Spreul had been transformed since yesterday. He no longer saw an apothecary, a little known relative of his wife; here was someone who knew how to take care of himself, and at the same time make Lucas feel safe. In a strange way this reminded him of John Steel. John had looked after him, especially during his recent involvement with Richard Cameron. That had been a narrow escape, most of it thanks to John. What an effort John made to help him and yet he'd kept on behaving like a fool. No wonder the man had become so impatient. And now it was too late. "Thank ye," he muttered into the air. "I'm grateful."

"Nae need." Spreul seemed to assume these words were for him. He flapped a hand. "Onyway, if ye hadna come intae my shop at that moment mibbe ye'd be as free as a bird and no shut up in here. Mind ye," his voice took on a softer tone, "and dinna

22

be offended. But I need tae say this for yer ain guid. When yon captain asked whae ye were yer answer shud jist hae been a customer. There wis nae need tae tell him ye were a relative let alane a meenister. Whit ye said wis like buyin a stick tae hit yersel."

"I didna think," Lucas admitted. "It jist came oot."

"Frae noo on ye best be mair careful afore opening yer mooth. When we go afore Dalyell he'll try tae catch ye oot. And if he does…Dae I need tae spell it oot?"

"Are ye suggesting I lie?"

"Not at aw." Spreul shook his head. "I'm only saying there's mair than ain way tae tell the truth. I suspect ye've ane or twa things best no mentioned tae the likes o Dalyell. Noo sit doon while I call for some watter tae freshen oorsels afore we're marched in front o the great man."

Chapter 3

Ritchie Wilson stood outside the front door of Craighead Mill and blinked in the early morning sunshine as he enjoyed a quiet moment. Carts would soon arrive with sack after sack of fresh cut oats. He was expecting them, the fire below the kiln was already lit and warm air was beginning to filter through the perforated iron floor above. The metal was heating up nicely, the room was almost ready to start drying the new grain before the grinding could begin.

During the next two days Ritchie would use his wide-mouthed wooden shovel to turn and spread a thick layer of grain across the warm floor. Sometimes he even stretched the process a little longer to give his oatmeal a distinctive roasted flavour. The ladies liked this and were prepared to pay a little extra for Ritchie's special pin meal oats.

Today he'd need to grind the last few sacks from last year's harvest and be ready to move on. This year's crop seemed a good one and would keep him busy over the coming weeks.

The routine of the work, the need to pay attention, the responsibility, the trust to turn his customers' efforts into good grain and flour would be a blessing and help him cope with what was happening around him.

Rachael Weir's husband had been killed at Drumclog. She was Ritchie's sister. Her son Gavin was Ritchie's assistant. Yesterday the boy had told Ritchie he must turn to his mother, give all his attention to their farm. Ritchie had intended to hand over the mill to his nephew one day; now he could see years of training go for nothing. As for the thought of starting again with a greenhorn. He groaned then felt guilty. His problems were nothing compared to his niece Marion with her husband John on the run and constantly harried herself, even a baby born on the open moor. Then there was John's father disappearing near Bothwell at the time of the battle. No one knew the truth, could only guess.

Many of the villagers had been part of the so-called rebellion. Now they were trying to remain invisible, hoping the law would never know who'd been involved and come after them. Ritchie had fought at Bothwell. He certainly didn't want that secret to get out. This was bothering him as he walked up to the pond behind the mill to open the sluice gate and allow the water to run down the wooden trough and force the mill wheel round.

Behind him a voice said, "Guid mornin."

He spun round. "Gawd's sake. Whaur did ye come frae? Sneakin up lik that?"

John Steel grinned. "Needs must Ritchie. These days ye canna be too carefu, even in yer ain village."

Ritchie grasped John's arm. "Guid tae see ye. Marion tellt me aboot the meenister. Did ye git him safely delivered?"

"Naw. He wis on his ain fur a few meenits an somehoo managed tae git himsel arrested. He's been taen tae Edinburgh. God kens whit next."

"Whit aboot yersel?"

"Nae problem. Ah'm here safe and soond but blame masel fur no keepin a closer ee on the daft eedjit."

"Ye're nae his keeper."

"Mibbe so." John scuffed his boots on the dewy grass. "Onway, ah'm no here aboot the meenister, ah've come aboot oor oat harvest. The troopers seemed tae be patrollin elsewhaur the last few days an we managed tae git it aw cut withoot ony interruptions. Marion's bringin the cairt in later the day. We want some fur animal feed, some fur porridge, an some jist pin meal. Legally the crop's ma faither's. Naethin tae dae wi me. Ah'm jist sayin in case the law enforcers stert askin whae the oats belang tae."

"If they dae ah'll pit them richt. But ah canna see ony bother ower a pickle grain."

"Ah'm nae sae sure." John shook his head. "Since Cameron hud his heid aff the government's intae ivverythin. Folk that dinna even ken the man are sufferin. As fur this new oath o allegiance tae the king ony refusal gits ye locked up or worse. Claverhoose is oot an aboot wi his platoon askin that vera question. It's only a maitter o time afore he lands here so ye best be ready. If ah wis ye ah'd jist nod an agree, an keep yer heid on yer shooders."

Ritchie's face went white. "Hoo dae ye ken aw this?"

"Ah heard talk in the toun. Ay, an aboot Kirk attendance as

weel. It's noo a requirement no a choice. If ye step oot o line yer name's in a black book an nae doubt it'll be held against ye. Some pair craturs huv been strung up fur admittin they'd been at a field meetin. An if they've been near Cameron or ony ither big preachin name thur maist likely shot wi nae questions asked, nae trial, nae justice. Maks ye wunner whit's richt or whit's wrang."

"Surely no?"

"Think aboot it." John's tone sharpened. "Ah met Cameron, heard him preach aboot the way furrit, aboot resistance, rebellion an God kens whit else. It wis scary stuff but gie the man his due he spoke weel, richt convincin. Folk listened and seemed impressed, luked as if they believed ivvery word. That's whit worried me fur ah cudna help askin masel hoo he kent this wis the only way. No that it wis wise tae ask. As fur tryin tae suggest he micht be wrang or darin tae criticise, weel that wud hae brocht the wrath o God doon on ma heid. Determined an obsessed disna come near. An luk whaur it got him. Heid aff an stuck in a bag. That disna seem much lik the way furrit tae me.

The king's ivvery bit as bad. Believin he's above us aw an insistin on the divine richt o kings. Ah ask ye. Whit's that aw aboot? An hoo dis he ken he's that special? Cameron or King. Ane's as bad as the ither, an they baith hae followers, an the rest o us are left tae suffer the consequences."

"Ye best no say that ower loud in case the wrang ears git tae hear."

John grinned. "Ay weel, it needs sayin."

Before Ritchie could answer he caught sight of a flash of red o the bottom road. "Dear God," he spluttered, "thur here."

"An ah'm awa." John ran along the edge of the pond, up a grassy bank, then dived over a low wall to disappear among the trees behind the graveyard. Ritchie was left to his work, hoping that flash of red didn't mean a government platoon was about to arrive at his mill.

By ten o'clock Ritchie had almost forgotten about any visit from the law. He was well into a busy morning with several carts arriving together.

The drivers knew the routine. Each cart was reversed against the front wall of the mill then the farm-hands carried the heavy sacks of threshed grain through the open door opposite the grinding stone. Ritchie was waiting to count each sack, issue a docket and supervise the stacking of the sacks.

Once the carts were emptied Ritchie began to haul the sacks up three floors to the loft where they'd be stored in an orderly queue till the drying began.

Moving the sacks was slow and tedious but no longer the back-breaking work it had been. As a young man Ritchie hated having to struggle up steep, narrow stairs with a heavy sack on his back. Apart from the effort any slip could be disastrous. There had to be an easier, safer way and Ritchie had managed to work one out. Now he had a rope and pulley connected to the central gear shaft. At ground level he could hook a sack onto a strong chain then start the pulley to hoist the sack all the way up with no effort at all. Someone needed to be at the top, ready to unhook and stack the sacks but that was nothing compared to the effort needed before Ritchie's invention.

Today Gavin was up top, Ritchie at the bottom. They made a good team. It was all going smoothly when the captain of a government platoon strode into the mill.

Ritchie was looking up, watching the sack's progress, unaware of the soldier till a gloved hand landed on his shoulder.

He froze then turned to face a uniformed and helmeted figure who pointed at the clanging, clattering machinery and signalled stop.

Ritchie nodded and hurried to obey.

The noise ceased. The sack jerked to a halt and hovered half-way up on its journey.

Gavin peered through the open trap door at the shiny helmet below. The helmet turned. Gavin ducked back in case the man in the helmet looked up.

He lay tight against the gaps in the floor and tried to hear what was being said below.

It sounded serious, the tone accusing, as if Ritchie were being arrested. He strained, listened harder. Lanark was mentioned. Maybe even the Tolbooth.

That did it. His hand crept across the uneven floor to reach the pulley rope. His fingers closed round the thick, rough woven threads. He hesitated then squeezed hard and jerked the rope sidewards to release the chain.

The weight of the sack did the rest. Down it went to land on the shiny helmet. The soldier gasped, his knees gave way as he crumpled under the heavy sack which tilted to the side allowing a river of freshly threshed grain to spill out and almost bury him.

Ritchie gaped. "Whit the – " Terrified he looked up at the white face above, was about to shout when three troopers appeared in the doorway. They took one look at their half-buried captain and jumped on Ritchie, punching him senseless, then trailing him outside.

Up above a silent Gavin stayed perfectly still.

Ritchie came to with his face rubbing against the rough flank of a fast-trotting horse. He'd no idea where he was or what was happening. His head pounded, each breath was painful and a strong sweaty smell filled his nostrils and made him retch.

The mounted trooper holding him steady sensed this and whacked the dangling head. Ritchie vomited down the brown flank then knew no more as the platoon hurried on towards their Lanark garrison.

Captain Dominic McCann had also been senseless throughout the ten mile journey. Now his men carried him to his tiny room beside the back stairs to the stable, undressed him, wiped his face, laid him on his pallet, and hurried away to make their report.

It was the next day before McCann opened his eyes and wondered where he was. Something warned him to stay still. In spite of this the room swam. Even flat on his back he felt dizzy. Closing his eyes helped. He kept them closed and gradually drifted into sleep, a more natural one this time.

Ritchie eventually came to with a sound like many feet pounding on cobbles, except they seemed to be above his head. Was he under the street?

Dark as a cave, wherever he was stank worse than a midden. The smell waved over him, sticking to his clothes, covering his skin, squeezing inside his mouth to coat his tongue, filling his nostrils and making him retch again and again. Breathing slowly helped. Gradually he managed to control the vomiting. His fingers began to reach out, to touch what felt like limp, damp straw. That's when he heard snuffling and scratching beginning to circle his body. "Gawd's sake." He flapped at the straw. "Clear aff."

The noise stopped. He listened and waited. Nothing for a moment then it came again. Further back this time but still there. He peered into the gloom. Several pairs of tiny, bright, little eyes were fixed on him, unblinking and waiting. This scared him enough to crawl towards the outer wall and try to stand, but his legs shook too much.

Closing his eyes he thought about his mill, how well he ran it, how much it mattered to him. The picture grew clearer. He could see the carts lined up. The grinding floor with lines of sacks waiting to be hauled up and dried. He went over it all again. Everything seemed normal till he looked up, followed the line of the pulley, all the way to the trap door to see the bottom of a sack hurtling towards him, making him jump to the side before he heard a dull thud. And then he saw a pile of loose grain, a huge pile in the middle of his usually clean-swept floor. Except it wasn't just a pile of grain waiting to be brushed up, a pair of legs encased in fine riding boots was sticking out beyond. When he looked up again there was Gavin's face peering down at him, very white, very scared.

Gradually the sound of feet above quietened. The scuffling seemed to grow louder but didn't come any closer. The little eyes were still watching so he forced himself against the wall for support and stayed sitting up as best he could rather than have his face near that foul smelling straw which held those constant watchers.

Why was he here? What next? Helpless in every sense of the word Ritchie closed his eyes and tried to control his rising terror. He sat like that for a long time before the cell door opened a fraction. A metal bowl was pushed in then the door clanged shut again.

Jamie Ogilvie, earl of Airlie from Strathmore, marched into the Lanark garrison and heard the news about his captain.

He went straight to the sheriff's apartment and demanded the use of Meiklejon's best room to interview the injured man.

"He's still a kennin weak." Meiklejon explained. "Mibbe ye shud gie him a day or twa."

"Time is o the essence," Airlie snapped. "I've jist come frae the Privy Council in Edinburgh. Their lordships are much disturbed by the state o this country aifter Cameron's wee stramash. They want ony chance o an uprising stopped. And whit happens? I come back tae discover my ain captain is near killed by a rebel. I need tae hear the details frae the captain himsel and then we'll see aboot a hanging."

"As ye wish." Meiklejon shrugged. "I'll send somebody tae fetch yer man."

"Weel McCann, hoo are ye aifter that dunt on yer heid?" Airlie leant across the sheriff's oak table and studied his captain's pale face.

"Felt better sir." McCann tried to stand to attention.

Airlie flapped a hand. "Sit doon afore ye fa doon." He glanced at the sheriff.

The sheriff signalled to one of his men by the door who grabbed a chair and pushed it forward.

McCann nodded his thanks and sat down with a thump.

"Richt then, tell me whit happened."

"The problem wis – "

Airlie stopped him. "Ye let a rebel git the better o ye."

"In aw fairness," Meiklejon intervened, "yer man hud nae chance tae see onythin. A sack o grain cam straight doon frae above an near flattened him. When his men arrived he wis deid tae the world an hawf buried wi spilt grain."

"Hmm." Airlie frowned. "So hoo did this come aboot?"

McCann shrugged. "Ah'd jist sterted tae question the miller aboot takin the loyalty oath. We wur staundin by the big grindin stanes. Ane meenit he wis speakin tae me next meenit awthin went black."

"He must hae signalled. Warned somebody tae act against ye."

"He didna move, sir. He wis richt in front o me."

Airlie's brows almost met. "Gawd's sake McCann, a mere finger can mak a signal. I've done it masel mony a time."

"The miller seemed tae be on his ane, sir. We've nae proof he did onythin."

"Ye're the proof," Airlie roared. "Lying there wi yer heid staved in."

McCann didn't answer.

"So." Airlie started again. "That's aw ye can tell me?"

"Ay sir."

"Which means we need tae complete the picture oorsels. Ane thing's clear. The man attacked a representative o the law. Needs hanging."

"But," McCann dared.

Airlie glared at him. "The folk in yon village need a wee reminder whae's in charge."

Meiklejon leant towards Airlie and whispered, "The miller's a brither o ane o Maister Steel's relatives."

"Is he noo? In that case he must be a rebel and needs tae be dealt wi."

The door opened and a well dressed figure came into the room.

Airlie glowered at the thick, black riding cloak, the fine leather gloves, the hat with that famous white feather. "Whitivver ye're here for Clavers this maitter disna concern ye so let me get on and dinna interfere."

"As if I wud." John Graham of Claverhouse signalled for a chair, dusted it with his hat then slapped it down on the table. "Guid day gentlemen. Lik yersel Airlie I'm on my way back frae Edinburgh, on my way tae my new billet at Moffat. It seemed a guid chance tae drap in and see hoo weel the district's being patrolled." He sat down with a smile then turned to McCann. "My captain, ye're no luking vera weel."

"Neither wud ye if ye'd hud a fu sack o grain fa on yer heid frae a great height," Meiklejon said.

"Indeed?"

"He wis attacked going aboot his lawfu duty." Airlie still looked annoyed.

"Whaur aboots?"

"The mill at Lesmahagow. The miller is a relative o yon rebel Steel. He attacked my captain fur nae reason."

"Steel ye say. Ye mean John Steel?"

Airlie nodded.

"And of course ony mention o John Steel seems tae pit yersel in a richt temper. I tak it ye havena caught up wi him yet?"

Airlie scowled.

Clavers leant back in his chair. "I think I'm beginning tae see whaur this micht be going."

"Whaur it shud. Tae a hanging."

"Whit does McCann's report say on the maitter?" Clavers persisted.

"He canna mind onything ither than speaking tae the miller afore the bag fell on his heid." Airlie began to sound unsure.

Clavers leant towards McCann. "Ony chance it wis an unfortunate accident?

"Naw, naw," Airlie snapped. "Dinna stert that. The man's a rebel, grabbed his chance tae inflict injury on the law's representative."

McCann looked at his master, back to Clavers then gave a tiny nod.

"See." Clavers grinned at Airlie. "There appears tae be a smidgin o doubt. And being a relative o a rebel is haurly a crime in itsel. My ain fiancée's family support the Covenanters and naebody's mair loyal tae his majesty than my dearest Anne."

"Whit's that got tae dae wi it?"

"I'm jist stating a fact. A wee reminder. Onyway ye wurna at the mill." Clavers' grin widened.

Airlie guessed what Clavers was up to and struggled to keep his temper "The maitter needs tae be resolved."

"Indeed." Clavers leant forward and twirled the end of the long, white feather on his hat.

No one spoke for several minutes then Meiklejon suggested, "Since ye twa are no exactly o a mind hoo aboot sendin the man on? Somewhaur the maitter can be luked at mair objectively so tae speak. Somewhaur lik Edinburgh."

Airlie sniffed as if sensing an unpleasant smell under his nose.

"Ah'm jist sayin." The sheriff's tone softened. "It micht mak sense tae conseeder it."

Airlie's expression began to change. His eyes glittered. "Mibbe ye're richt. The Privy Council ken hoo tae be objective. The Lord Advocate sees tae that." He pushed back his chair and stood up. "McCann, gang back tae yer bed while I arrange for the prisoner's transport onwards."

"But," McCann tried to protest.

"Bed sir," Airlie snapped. "Awa and lie doon. Hae a guid sleep and mibbe waken up seeing things as they really are."

"Ay sir." McCann struggled off the chair and left the room.

Airlie smiled triumphantly at Clavers. He was taken aback when Clavers simply nodded and smiled back.

The garrison gaoler opened Ritchie's cell door. "Dae ye want the guid news or the bad news?"

Ritchie peered through the gloom at the voice in the passageway. "Gie me them baith."

The gaoler laughed. "The guid news is ye'll no hing the morn. The maister's sendin ye tae Edinburgh. Ye're tae go afore the Privy Cooncil nae less. Bad news is they'll hing ye in the Grassmarket wi thoosands howlin at ye."

"Bit ah huvna done onythin," Ritchie wailed.

"So ye say." The door clanged shut and the gaoler turned the key.

Chapter 4

Lucas Brotherstone jumped as the cell door swung open. There stood two Lyon Heralds and two Messengers at Arms, in their official robes.

A trumpet sounded. Lucas jumped again. "Whit's aw this?"

John Spreul smiled. "Their Lordships seem tae conseeder us important enough tae require an official escort."

"But we're no."

"We ken that but there's something aboot us they're aifter. Trust me this is political and politics is nivver straight furrit."

"Weel I've naething. Nae money. Nae parish."

"Ah, but ye kent Richard Cameron. The man whae frichted the wits oot their Lordships. Whae else did ye ken?"

Lucas looked confused.

John Spreul stepped close and whispered, "Ivvery scrap o information the Privy Council gits their haunds on helps against the opposition. Mind hoo ye go. Keep yer mooth ticht shut and gie naething awa."

"Whit aboot yersel?"

Spreul smiled again and stepped even closer. "I've been amang some o they councilors a guid few times. I've even treated ane or twa. Close contact and private conversations gie awa raither a lot if ye ken hoo tae listen. As they say, forewarned is forearmed."

"Enough. Whit's aw this whisperin aboot?" One of the Messenger at Arms stepped forward and handed Spreul a rolled up parchment. "This is yer indictment for treason and rebellion against his Gracious Majesty at Bothwell Brig."

"Is that so." Spreul took the parchment, read it, then threw it to the floor. "As a law abiding, loyal citizen and honest merchant I refute ivvery word on this paper."

"Tell that tae General Dalyell." The Messenger turned on his heel, swished his robe behind him. "On ye come." He nodded towards Lucas. "Ye as weel."

The Privy Council watched as John Spreul and Lucas Brotherstone were marched in to stand in front of them. Sir George Mackenzie of Rosehaugh, the heavily wigged Lord Advocate, stood behind a wide, polished mahogany table, shuffled a pile of papers, coughed and adjusted his black, silk robe. His smooth-skinned plump face, resting above a fine lace cravat, showed a man of excellent health and wealth, as did his dark eyes glowing with confidence. An almost smiling mouth also suggested he might be a pleasant companion. "Guid day gentlemen. I tak it ye unnerstaund whit ye're here for?"

Neither answered.

Mackenzie turned his attention on Lucas and waved a sheet of paper. "Whit I huv here says ye're a renegade meenister, ousted frae yer parish for treasonous words against His Majesty. No content wi that ye defied court orders and returned tae that very parish, as weel as consorting wi the infamous rebel Richard Cameron."

Lucas opened his mouth then remembered Spreul's warning and said nothing.

Behind Mackenzie Lucas could see an elderly, grizzled looking man. His thin, stern face framed with a thatch of white hair was startling, along with cold, piercing eyes, a long, beak like nose and slit of a mouth finishing off what seemed like a bird of prey waiting to pounce.

Spreul nudged Lucas. "Yon's Dalyell. He's kent as Bluidy Tam. Weel deserved by aw accoonts."

Lucas stiffened.

The old man leant forward. There was a creaking sound as the armour on his waistcoat complained. "Git on wi it Mackenzie. His Grace and masel are anxious tae see justice underway afore dinner time."

Mackenzie smiled indulgently. "Indeed." He pointed at Lucas. "Maister Brotherstone. Hoo dae ye plead?"

"Tae whit?" Lucas dared.

"Tae the accusation made against ye."

Lucas hung his head. "Ye're richt I wis ousted frae ma parish. But I wis desperate tae come back and pay ma respects at ma wife's grave. Surely ye wudna deny me that? She had her life cut short on the day I lost ma charge at Lesmahagow."

"So far so guid." Mackenzie nodded. "And whit aboot Cameron?"

"I knew the man. But I didna agree wi whit he proposed."

"And whit wis that?"

"Open rebellion, sir. I hae nae sympathy for that. Nane at aw."

"Is that so." Mackenzie's head shook as if in disbelief. "And hoo aboot witnesses confirming ye've been seen in that man's company at some o they forbidden open air meetings aboot the countryside?"

Spreul poked Lucas's back.

Lucas shrugged.

"Is that an ay or a no?" Mackenzie began to look annoyed.

Lucas shrugged again.

"Leave aff Mackenzie." Dalyell leant forward and banged the edge of the table. "Whit he says is neither here nor there. We ken the truth." He pointed a long finger at Lucas. "Sit doon man. We'll deal wi ye in a meenit."

Lucas obeyed and sat down.

Mackenzie nodded as if agreeing with the general. He waited while the old man leant back in his seat and whispered something to the ornately dressed younger man sitting beside him. An enormous, dark, curly wig framed an owl like expression as if this gentleman was a mere observer.

"Whae's that?" Lucas whispered.

"Duke o York nae less," Spreul muttered. "The king's brither. God kens whit he's here for ither than checking on the Privy Council. He'll be keen tae see hoo his Majesty's commands are being enforced. But I canna see whit interest he has in us twa."

Mackenzie adjusted his heavy robe again and puffed out his chest. "Noo for yersel Maister Spreul. We'll tak a luk at Bothwell Brig first."

John Spreul said nothing.

"We hae proof o yer involvement in that unfortunate happening."

"I doubt it." Spreul shook his head. "At the time I wis at sea, on my ain ship the *Josephine*, coming frae Rotterdam wi supplies o herbs for my apothecary work as weel as barrels for my business curing herring at Cartsdyke by Glasgow."

"So ye say," Mackenzie turned to a Messenger at Arms. "Bring in the witness."

A bedraggled figure, hardly able to walk, was almost lifted across the floor and pushed into a chair alongside Mackenzie's table. The man looked dazed, his clothes torn and covered in filth. He'd probably just come from the lower regions of the Tolbooth. He certainly smelt like it.

Mackenzie sniffed and held a piece of lavender-soaked muslin to his nose. "Richt Major Learmond, ye were captured at Bothwell?"

There was a slight nod.

"And ye saw a man by the name o John Spreul on Bothwell Moor, part o yon renegade army?"

Before Mackenzie could ask any more Spreul said, "A John Spreul is no this John Spreul."

Mackenzie waved the sweet-smelling piece of muslin at Spreul and smiled.

Spreul stepped forward. "May I ask yer witness a question?"

Mackenzie gave a mock bow and waved again.

"Thank ye." Spreul turned to the seated figure. "Major Learmond can ye tell me when ye saw this John Spreul?"

"The nicht afore the battle. Quite late. In fact it wis hawf dark."

"Dark." John Spreul smiled broadly. "Hoo cud ye tell whae the man wis?"

"Somebody said whae it wis. Ah'd nae reason tae disbelieve them."

"Word o mooth." John Spreul turned to Mackenzie. "I think the law wud agree this man is an unreliable witness. Onyway, like I said, I wis oot the country at that time. Further mair I hae twa cousins, baith cawed John Spreul. But I'm sure ye ken that aready. And I'm sure ye also ken they baith hanker aifter Presbyterian ways. Ane's a lawyer. The ither's a merchant. I ken for a fact they wur baith at Bothwell alang wi my brither James. My lawyer can easily provide the proof for ye. But lik I said, ye mibbe ken that aready."

Mackenzie's glanced back at Dalyell.

The old man's face darkened. "Ask aboot Archbishop Sharpe and his murder at St Andrews."

"I ken naething aboot the man or onything aboot his murder. I dinna even ken when or whaur it happened."

"3rd May on Magus Muir. No lang afore the battle at Bothwell Brig."

"I wis in Dublin then, on business. I go there twa or three times a year."

"So ye say." Mackenzie signalled to a leather clad figure hovering by the door. "Mibbe the hangman can persuade anither answer oot ye."

Spreul didn't answer.

"Come furrit." Mackenzie's voice sharpened. "Put the prisoner tae the test."

A large wooden boot-like contraption was carried in and laid in front of John Spreul. The hangman leant over Spreul. "Sit doon till ah pit yer leg intae the boot."

"Wait." A voice rang out from the back of the room.

Everyone turned to stare at the speaker who slowly rose to his feet.

Lucas gasped. "It's my brither-in-law Andrew." Everything was becoming surreal. Suddenly he could see himself sitting in Andrew's vast kitchen, telling him about Bett, hearing him shout who was to blame for her death. Why was he here, speaking out, especially after threatening Lucas and throwing him out of the house?

Andrew soon put him right. "Yer Lordships may I speak on behalf o yer prisoner John Spreul. There must be some mistake. He's my cousin. A Spreul same as masel. It's a weel respected name in the toon. He's a grand apothecary and merchant. I'm sure he'll hae treated and helped ane or twa o yer Lordships. Ye must ken thur's naething extreme or rebellious aboot this man. Nane at aw. Indeed, I'm prepared tae vouch for his honesty and loyalty tae the king."

"Are ye noo." Mackenzie's voice was silky smooth. "And whit gies anither Spreul the right tae come in here and interrupt important court proceedings?"

"I'm only trying tae prevent a possible miscarriage o justice." Andrew Spreul pointed at Lucas. "That yin's a different maitter. An eedjit whae cost ma dear sister her precious life wi his rebellious nonsense. He's guilty as charged. Dae whit ye like wi him."

Mackenzie spun round towards Lucas. "Is this richt?"

"Ay. Aboot being my brither in law."

Mackenzie's smile broadened. "Nae much love lost atween ye.

Or mibbe a wee grudge, enough for yer wife's brither tae want a noose roond yer neck while he persuades us tae let yer companion go free?" He turned back to Andrew Spreul and wagged a finger at him. "The law disna work this way my man. A wee word o advice. Ye've had yer say. We've heard ye. Noo sit doon and say nae mair. This court will decide whit's tae happen and doesna countenance ony unnecessary interference. Or mibbe ye'd care tae come oot here and join they twa prisoners?"

Red faced, Andrew Spreul sat down.

Mackenzie swung back round to the hangman. "Richt we've wasted enough time. Git on wi it."

Wedges were pushed into the contraption then the hangman hammered them further. John Spreul jerked back in his seat, his face contorted; he went deathly white and tears ran down his cheeks but he uttered no sound.

"Again."

More wedges were pushed in. As the hangman lifted his hammer to repeat the blow, Lucas Brotherstone slid off his chair and lay unconscious on the floor.

"Dae it richt." Dalyell stood up and shook his fist at the hangman. "Ye're useless."

"Ah'm dain it the way ah aye dae it." The hammer was flung down. "If ye're no pleased dae it yersel."

Dalyell looked as if he was about to jump from his seat and come at this minion who dared to defy him. The room went quiet while the hangman continued to glower at the great general.

"Enough." Mackenzie seemed to sense they were on the verge of a pantomime. He signalled to the hangman. "Remove the prisoner. We'll re-convene aifter dinner."

John Spreul's bloodied leg was pulled from the wooden boot and he was dragged away by two warders. Mackenzie pointed at Lucas's still figure. "Tak that waste o space awa and dump him wi his freend." He rubbed his hands as if he was neither disappointed nor angry by what had happened. He looked towards Dalyell and his important companion. "Gentlemen. Dinner time I think."

Lucas Brotherstone opened his eyes. He was back in the cell and there was John Spreul sitting on the only chair slowly pouring a bottle of red wine over his bruised and bloodied leg.

Lucas got up from the floor where he'd been dumped. "Can I help ye? Whit are ye dain that for? Ye paid a bonnie penny tae the gaoler for it."

"I need tae reduce the chance o infection and it's soothing some o the pain. If ye want tae help tear some strips aff the bedsheet and I'll bind masel up. The leg luks worse than it is. The hangman didna git far wi his torture."

Lucas quickly obeyed and handed thin strips of linen to Spreul. "Yon Mackenzie seems tae huv it in for ye."

"Ay." Spreul began to bandage his leg. "He's a richt deil. Mibbe he's aifter my property, businesses, money. Nae doubt he has some freend lined up tae benefit while he taks a cut. I suspect he'll declare me a rebel and put me tae the horn. That means awthing I hae can legally be confiscated."

"That's whit happened tae a man I ken." Lucas thought of John Steel. How he'd lost his farms and become a man on the run with a price on his head. By the sound of it John Spreul had even more to lose.

"Trust me" Spreul looked grim. "That's whaur it's going. As for us, it micht be the gibbet."

Lucas gasped and didn't dare answer.

Ritchie Wilson retched for the umpteenth time. Maybe it was the thought of what might happen when he reached Edinburgh. Maybe it was the rolling and juddering as the cart lurched in and out of so many deep pot-holes on the road.

He'd been lashed inside a covered cart and the flaps tied down leaving no way of seeing anything or guessing where he was. Already Lesmahagow and his beloved mill seemed like a faint dream, unlikely to be seen again.

He tried not to think ahead, forced himself to think through the platoon captain's visit to the mill, the way he'd marched in announcing he'd come to check on the loyalty oath, asking questions, demanding answers when a sudden whoosh brought a full sack of grain down on the unsuspecting soldier's head. And Gavin's white face staring through the open trap door three floors up. But who cared for the truth? The grand old earl at Lanark just wanted a hanging in the morning. The other fine gentleman had argued with the old earl, sounding almost supportive. But all the same, that smile, the glint in his eye seemed to suggest it was maybe just a game.

The captain, the one who'd nearly been killed under that grain sack, had been more forgiving. He'd actually said it seemed like a terrible accident. But how would the new judges at Edinburgh react?

The earl wouldn't be there, nor the captain, nor the fine gentleman, only the written report. Would it make any difference?

Mile after mile, hour after hour it kept going round in his head, tormenting him, scaring him more and more. By the time he was marched into the Tolbooth and flung into another stinking cell he was almost past caring what might happen.

Five days passed before John Spreul and Lucas Brotherstone were summoned back to the Privy Council, long enough for Jane Spreul to receive a message from her husband and act on it. She hurried back to the shop in Glasgow and emptied the cellar which was full of valuable items John had imported from the continent. Two carts then carried the precious loads to her sister's farm in faraway Peebles where they were well hidden.

"Why did the Privy Council no call us back like they said? Why noo?" Lucas looked worried when the gaoler arrived with their summons.

John Spreul frowned. "They're planning on catching us oot and need time tae mak some preparations. Noo mind, no a word unless ye huv tae."

"Whit'll happen?" Lucas persisted.

"Jist dae as I say."

Mackenzie, in his finery, was waiting for them, the table in front of him littered with books and important looking papers.

"As I thocht," Spreul whispered. "They're up tae something."

John Spreul's lawyer stepped forward and demanded his client's immediate release.

"Ye're a wee bit aheid o yersel." Mackenzie smiled a charming smile. "We hae anither maitter tae deal wi first." He turned to the nearest Messenger at Arms. "Fetch in the ither prisoner. The ane sent frae Lanark."

Ritchie Wilson was hustled in and made to stand before the

grand mahogany table. Scared and stinking after his stay in the Tolbooth he was further terrified at the sight of the Privy Council in all their finery.

Mackenzie's chubby finger pointed at one of the papers on the table. "I hae twa reports aboot ye. Ane frae the Earl o Airlie nae less citing ye as a rebel and wud-be murderer. Anither frae a dragoon captain disputing this and stating whit happened wis likely naething but an unfortunate accident."

"So it wis, sir," Ritchie stammered. "The captain wis askin me aboot the loyalty oath when a fu sack o grain fell on his heid an near killed him. It cam aw the way frae the loft at the tap o ma mill. Must hae slipped aff the hook haudin it. Neither o us saw it comin. It jist scuffed by me."

"And ye are?"

"Ritchie Wilson. Miller at the Craighead Mill in Lesmahagow. Ah dinna ken why the earl taen sae ill against me. Ah huvna done onythin wrang."

"Indeed." Mackenzie turned his back on Ritchie and addressed the Privy Council. "We appear tae hae a decision tae mak on behalf o oor esteemed colleague the Earl o Airlie."

Dalyell frowned. "Whit's Airlie daing sending this man aw the way frae Lanark ower sic an incident when he's perfectly capable o dealing wi the maitter himsel?"

Mackenzie nodded. "I suspect it wis a difference o opinion atween the earl and his captain."

"Easy resolved. Hing the man and that's an end o it."

"If it please yer lordships." John Graham of Claverhouse appeared in the doorway and smiled at the assembly. "I think I cud throw some light on this maitter."

"It's yersel Clavers." Dalyell's frown deepened.

"I happened tae be at Lanark when the miller wis brocht in and happened tae hear the evidence and the captain's plea for understanding the situation. It wis sincerely made. On this occasion I'm inclined tae ask yer lordships tae err on the side o clemency. Tae gie the prisoner the benefit o the doubt."

"Ye jist happened did ye?" Dalyell's brows nearly met.

"Please." The Duke of York waved Claverhouse forward. "Tell me more."

Clavers crossed the floor and space was made for him beside

his Grace. They spoke quietly. The Duke laughed then nodded towards Mackenzie. "Ask the prisoner if he's willing tae tak the oath o Allegiance?"

Mackenzie bowed then turned to Ritchie. "Weel?"

"Indeed sir."

"If he wis a Covenanter he'd refuse." The Duke smiled. "Tak him aside, gie him the Bible and hear him tak the oath. Aifter that let the man go aboot his business."

"Let him go?" Dalyell turned towards the Duke, seemed about to argue, hesitated, then shrugged.

Ten minutes later Ritchie Wilson was on his way out the courtroom.

As he passed John Spreul and Lucas Brotherstone he recognised his minister, almost spoke to him, then wisely looked away and walked on and out of the building.

As Ritchie made his way down the High Street a grand figure came after him. "A meenit."

He stopped, turned and saw the fine gentleman who'd spoken for him not once but twice. "Sir?"

The fine gentleman touched his shoulder. "Hoo aboot a horse for yer journey hame?"

Ritchie stared. "Ye've helped me enough sir."

"And mibbe ye cud help me tae."

"Ah dinna see hoo."

"A mill's an important place in ony village. Aw kinda folk come and go and staund aboot talking Ye must hear aw kinds o things."

Ritchie froze.

"Mibbe ye cud see yer way tae passing on a wee word here and there. Especially since ye've jist taen the oath o allegiance for his Gracious Majesty. And me being ane o his law enforcers it wud only be richt."

"Ye'd want it kept discreet sir?"

"Oh ay. My ear only. Naebody else needs tae ken."

Ritchie dared to nod.

"Richt. That's settled." Strong fingers squeezed Ritchie's arm. "Noo come wi me and we'll see aboot a horse tae get ye hame."

Claverhouse slapped the rump of the horse he'd hired for Ritchie. "On ye go. Safe journey. I'll be in touch."

"Thank ye." Ritchie didn't dare meet the eye of his new master as he turned away to edge the beast into the crowded High Street.

Claverhouse watched them disappear then smiled and strolled back to the court-house.

Ritchie's horse plodded out of Edinburgh. Ahead was a long journey back to Lesmahagow, long enough to try and work out how he'd handle Clavers' request. He considered his options. A wee word here and there tae the law while tippin the wink tae them as need tae ken micht dae the trick, keep yon devious gentleman sweet, an ma heid on ma shooders. Or mibbe no. One mistake and Clavers would have him. Glad to be alive he trotted on well aware of the dangerous road ahead.

When Claverhouse entered the court-room he found the place in an uproar with John Spreul's lawyer loudly disputing the evidence and statements from each witness lined up to accuse his client. He kept repeating, "Paid informers are illegal."

The Lord Advocate chose to ignore him. The noise increased. Finally Spreul himself intervened. He took a gold coin from his pocket, held it up for all to see then hurled it across the mahogany table. It rolled among the strewn papers and finally stopped beside Mackenzie. He glared at the coin then at Spreul.

Spreul glared back. "Ye ken whit this means. This coin pays for a legal instrument allooing me tae dispute whit's happening here. This is an illegal proceeding. I demand an instant acquittal and an apology for such ill treatment."

Mackenzie summoned the clerk to the council. Their heads came close as the Lord Advocate whispered, "Hoo does Spreul ken aboot this quirk in the law? Whae tellt him? Can we dae ocht aboot it?"

The clerk flushed. "I've nae idea hoo he kens or whae micht hae gied him sic information. I'm afraid he's richt sir, yon coin maks the prisoner's declaration a proper legal instrument. He's within his rights tae challenge the hale proceedings. Yer lordship hus nae choice but respond."

Mackenzie stared at the table, shuffled the papers. "Fetch oot the act we prepared yesterday. Thank guidness I persuaded thur Lordships that it micht be needed. I tak it ye've made sure it's aw signed and sealed?"

"Indeed sir. The document is here. Everything in order."

Mackenzie sighed, straightened his robe and his expression before facing Spreul. "The court accepts ye've made a richtfu and legal declaration against the present proceedings."

Spreul nodded.

Mackenzie also nodded. "Because of that we dismiss the previous charges and start again."

"But – " Spreul began.

"Nae buts sir," Mackenzie smiled. "Since ye seem sae weel acquainted wi the law ye'll ken the court has the richt tae dae this." He turned towards the assembled lords and clapped his hands. Dalyell started the debate and within minutes a long and tedious discussion and argument developed.

Spreul seemed to sense defeat and returned to his seat leaving his lawyer to argue as best he could. The possibility of witness coercion was mentioned. This brought howls of protest from their lordships. A louder howl greeted mention of torturing witnesses. The afternoon wore on. Whatever was said was refuted by either side. More important was the lack of firm evidence. Gradually the possibility of an acquittal began to appear.

Mackenzie now lifted the freshly signed document which would bring this unfortunate day to an almost satisfactory end. "This is an act specially prepared against current rebellion, signed and sealed by the fu Privy Council. John Spreul, apothecary frae Glasgow, by this act ye're charged wi attending conventicles which is entirely against the law o oor land. This court believes ye'll struggle tae disprove this accusation, especially when ye come frae a family wi strong Presbyterian leanings."

Spreul shook his head but said nothing.

This seemed to encourage Mackenzie. "Such activity merits a fine. For ye, sir, it's £500 sterling."

"Impossible," Spreul gasped.

"In that case ye'll be imprisoned tae sic times as the money micht be forthcoming." Mackenzie banged a small wooden gavel on the table-top three times then turned to Lucas. "Ye're similarly accused, as weel as aiding and abetting a notorious rebel. Since ye're a pair meenister the fine is waived. Five years imprisonment is yer punishment, tae be served on the Bass Rock. Ye'll be taken there in the morning." He banged the gavel again, announced the day's proceedings complete and stood there looking more exhausted than triumphant while Spreul and Lucas were marched away.

Back in the cell Spreul gave in to his frustration. "I kent fine they were up tae something. But tae stoop sae low." He turned to face the wall and said no more.

Lucas stared at the hunched shoulders and understood this was not a moment for question or comment. His companion had put up a brave fight, had dared to challenge the great and the good, even used their own law against them. And for what? Lucas felt even more helpless.

When the gaoler brought the evening meal he brought news that Spreul was also for the Bass Rock. "Ye'll no like it." He shook his head as if in sympathy. "Freezin cauld wi damp that seeps intae yer bones. Nae comfortable cell lik here, haurly enough room tae swing a cat. Little or nae daylicht. An dinna think aboot tryin tae escape. No when ye're twa miles oot tae sea."

"Whit?" Lucas sat down with a thump, his hands clenching and unclenching as he tried to fight against this terrible revelation.

The gaoler watched him for a minute. "As a meenister mibbe ye shud ask yer maister for some help. Ah wudna wish the Bass Rock on ma worst enemy." With that he stepped back into the dark corridor and slammed the cell door shut, leaving Lucas Brotherstone and John Spreul to their own thoughts.

Chapter 5

By the time Ritchie Wilson reached the town of Biggar his earlier resolve had almost vanished. Little wonder. He'd been cantering along with his head full of John Graham. One day soon that fine gentleman would be strolling into the mill expecting him to produce some worthwhile snippit to help him round up those still defying the king.

At least ah've only masel tae worry aboot. No lik oor Rachael, made a widow at Drumclog then her dochter in a richt pickle since her man wis declared a rebel aifter Bothwell Brig. If only yon daft minister in the village kirk hud kept his mooth shut insteid o shoutin frae the pulpit aboot the government an drawin attention tae oor village. Ah bet he wishes he hudna. Nae wunner. Lost his job, his hoose, flung oot the parish an then his pair wife deid.

An here ah am expected tae behave lik a turncoat an clype on the very folk ah care aboot.

Round and round it went like some jumbled nightmare.

He stopped at the village stable and allowed the horse time to rest and drink. A few passers-by stared at the unkempt, filthy creature sitting astride such a fine horse. He tried to ignore them and watched the animal satisfy its thirst with clean, sparkling water. All he'd had in that awful jail was a bowl of grey gruel and rank water in a rusty old tin. Bad as it was he'd been too desperate to refuse. At least that was past. Or was it? Feeling even more depressed he clicked the horse forward.

He was just turning onto the Lanark road, thinking about the long way still to go when something made him sit up straight. Eedjit so ah am. If ah turn aff here anither mile will tak me tae Greenhill Hoose whaur oor Sophie's housekeeper. Fancy forgettin that ma ain sister is nearby. Her maister's a miller lik masel. A guid man. He'll no mind Sophie giein her brither a bite tae eat, mibbe a bath. Ah cud certainly dae wi ane. Ay, Sophie'll see me richt. Mind settled he left the road and turned onto a narrow track.

Sophie Wilson heard horse's hooves clip across the little, stone bridge that led to Greenhill House. "Whit's this noo? As if ah huvna enough tae deal wi." She laid down a pile of freshly ironed sheets and went to the bedroom window. "Oh my. It's oor Ritchie. An luk at the state he's in." She turned, clattered downstairs and out the front door to stand in the tiny courtyard before Ritchie's horse had reached the end of the bridge. As he came through the close she grabbed hold of the horse's reins and stared up at him. "Ye're in an awfy mess. Whit happened tae ye?"

"Ah wis in the Tolbooth in Edinburgh."

"Whit for?"

"It's a lang story."

"Nae doubt. But first things first. Jump doon, tak yer beast roond the back tae the stable then come in till we git ye sortit. Talkin can wait."

An hour later Ritchie was scrubbed red, no longer smelling like a dung heap, beard removed, matted hair cut away, and every stitch of filthy clothes now adding to the flames in the big kitchen range.

"Here." Sophie fussed round him. "Up tae the table. It's rabbit stew wi barley dumplings."

He sat at the scrubbed table and ate the best tasting meal he could remember. After a second plateful of stew and a mug of ale the past few days seemed to fade a little. He began to feel as if he hadn't lost himself after all.

As the Greenhill workers came in for their meal one look from Sophie and they simply nodded and asked no questions. Small and quick as a sparrow, with a tongue to match, Sophie dominated the place. Everyone knew what was expected of them, took their responsibilities seriously and obeyed her every whim. In return they were well looked after, with a decent bed, good food, and proper wages. Whatever they thought of this unexpected visitor they kept to themselves, ate their meal then went back to work.

"Richt." Sophie sat down opposite Ritchie. "Tell me yer news."

As Ritchie's story unfolded his worries and fears came flooding back to almost choke him when he admitted the part John Graham had played in his survival.

Sophie listened in silence then said, "That's awfy but ye're no alane. We've hud oor ain ado. The maister wis lifted yesterday for gien Reverend Cargill a bed for the nicht."

"Cargill?" Ritchie looked surprised. "Ye mean yon meenister as wis connected wi Richard Cameron?"

"The very ane. Aifter Cameron wis killed at Airds Moss Maister Cargill taen ower. He went here an there preachin the word, persuadin onybody as wud listen tae join the resistance against the government. It came tae a heid at a meetin in Torwood near Stirling when he announced he wis excommunicatin maist o the great lords as the sons o Satan. He even had his words published an postit up for the world tae see. Thur lordships didna like that an offered thoosands o merks for his capture. No content wi a reward they sent mounted platoons tae scour the land but somehoo Maister Cargill managed tae keep oot o reach. At least he did till he arrived here at Covington twa nichts ago afore preachin in Thankerton. The maister met him, taen him tae the meetin place an wis fair impressed wi the sermon. When he saw hoo auld an tired the man luked he invited him back tae the hoose for a bite tae eat an a bed for the nicht.

It didna work oot for some deil tipped aff the law. A hale platoon arrived afore daylicht, tore the pair soul oot his bed, strapped him across a horse an rode aff. They say he's for the gibbet in Edinburgh." Sophie hesitated. "The maister's been taen as weel."

Ritchie shivered. "Ah hope he's no in the Tolbooth. Ah wudna wish yon place on ma worst enemy."

"That bad?"

"Ay."

Sophie's face went white. She looked away and the room grew quiet apart from the big wall clock tick-ticking away.

Finally Ritchie said, "Ah survived, so will he. Meantime, whit are ye dain aboot the mill?"

Sophie shrugged. "The maister's nephew Jonas can keep the mill workin. He's near feenished his apprenticeship. Mibbe the maister'll be back afore lang."

"Ah wudna bank on it." Ritchie shook his head. "Unless he has a John Graham lukin oot for him. Mind ye thur's a price tae pay for that. Ah need tae tell ye aboot it."

Red with embarrassment he began to explain his worst fear.

Sophie listened then said, "Yer fine gentleman soonds a richt deil."

Ritchie nodded. "A while back ah heard Cargill preach at an open-air meetin by Kypewatter. Ah mind him sayin that the deil comes in mony a disguise. Ah wunnered whit he wis on aboot but noo it's as clear as day." Ritchie stared up at the beamed ceiling as if searching for the answer.

Sophie watched for a moment then leant forward to grasp his arm. "Ye dinna huv tae dae it."

"Ah've nae choice."

"Thur's aye a choice."

Ritchie looked at her as if she was mad.

"Listen." Sophie took his face in both hands and leant close. "Ye canna dae it if ye're no there, an yer fine gentleman canna harass the folk ye care aboot."

"Whit aboot the mill? Folk depend on me."

"Ye're no the only miller at Abbey Mill. Ye've trained oor Gavin. Shairly he's capable?"

"Ay. But Gavin aready tellt me he needs ta gang back tae the farm an help his mither. She's been strugglin since his faither wis killed at Drumclog."

"Dis Gavin no owe ye aifter the way he drapped ye in it?" Sophie grinned at her joke. "Ah'm sure he'll want tae mak up for it. Think aboot it. If Gavin runs the mill whit's tae hinder ye dain the farm work for oor Rachael? She'll see the sense o it. So will Gavin. Is that no better than whit's waitin for ye?"

"But whit if ah'm seen? Rachael disna bide far frae the village."

"John Steel's still thereaboots an still free. He'll pit ye richt. Heavens, he's mairried tae yer ain niece. He'll help ye keep yer heid doon an bide oot o sicht."

Ritchie's face lit up. "My, ye've a guid heid on yer shooders."

"Of course ah huv." Sophie grinned. "Ah need it tae run this place." Her smile slipped. "An noo ah've the mill tae worry aboot till the maister comes back." She patted his hand. "But nivver mind. Ane thing's sortit."

Next morning Ritchie Wilson came into the kitchen at Greenhill expecting breakfast to be ready. Instead he found the fire unlit and his sister Sophie sitting at the table, her head in her hands.

"Whit's wrang?" Ritchie hurried over to her. "This isna like ye."

"Ah'm foonered." Eyes wet with tears Sophie peered at him through her fingers.

"Hoo come?" Ritchie sat down beside her and put his arm round her shoulders.

"The maister's nephew's awa."

"Awa whaur?"

"Awa hame. He's no comin back. His mither heard aboot the stramash here, her brither bein liftit an taen tae Edinburgh. The lad wis at Cargill's meetin alang wi the maister. She thinks somebody must hae seen him. She's worried in case word gits oot an he gits liftit as weel. Her man came late last nicht an taen the lad hame. Thur's naebody left tae work the mill. An the morn's delivery day fur eggs, ham, an meal tae the big hoose in Biggar as weel as the tavern an twa shops."

"Ah can dae it." Ritchie squeezed her hand. "Ah can work the mill nae bother, organise the delivery, an onythin else ye want."

"But ye're goin hame lik we spoke aboot. Tae help oor Rachael run her farm."

"She'll unnerstaund. Think aboot it. If Gavin runs ma mill lik we spoke aboot shairly ah can see tae yer maister's place till he comes back. Wud yer maister no want his mill tae keep goin?"

"But Rachael needs help wi the farm."

"She'll see the sense o it an be willin tae tak on some hired help for a wee while. Whit's wrang wi that?"

"D'ye think so?" Sophie wiped her eyes with the edge of her apron.

Ritchie nodded. "Tae be honest ah'd raither bide here a wee while. Ah'd feel safer wi a wheen miles atween me an yon John Graham. Rachael's farm's raither close tae the village."

"Ay, weel, mibbe." Sophie gave a half nod.

"Ah'll need a wee luk roond the mill, find oot whit corn or oats are waitin. Aifter that jist gie me the list fur the big hoose, a helper tae load the cart an wur sortit. Ah'm a guid miller Sophie. Ye can trust me tae dae a guid job."

"Ah ken." This time she gave a firm nod. "That's whit we'll dae but Rachael an Gavin need tae be tellt an we need tae ken if they agree. Ah dinna want ony bad feelin. Somethin lik that's best said face tae face. Mibbe ah cud go ower tae Lesmahagow an explain it tae her?"

"Ay. Best comin frae yersel. If ane o yer workers drives ye ower ye cud be back the morn wi it aw settled."

"Nae time tae lose then." Sophie stood up and yelled for the scullery maid to light the fire and prepare breakfast. As the girl scurried back and forward she added, "Ah'm goin on a visit but only till the morn. Ye'll tak chairge o the kitchen an see awbody's richt fed. Thur's plenty in the pantry so ye'll manage fine."

The girl looked alarmed but didn't argue.

Soon the kitchen range was hissing as usual and the room sprang to life with the girl stirring the porridge, heating hunks of bread in the side oven, slicing a pile of ham then setting the table, while Rachael bustled about packing a basket to take to her sister.

Within an hour one of the men brought a horse and trap into the yard, helped Sophie into the passenger seat and off they went on the long drive to Waterside farm.

Ritchie watched them rattle over the hump-back bridge. "Ay," he whispered to himself, "this parteeclar ill wind has blawn me some guid aifter aw."

Chapter 6

John Spreul and Lucas Brotherstone felt the cart stop. They sat up as the tarpaulin was pulled back a little.

Lucas crawled along the rough floor of the cart and peered out. His nostrils twitched. Fish. That smell could only be fish. Along with it came a quick slip-slapping sound which seemed to be coming from a line of girls nearby. Dressed in dull grey, hair covered by bright kerchiefs, fronts protected by sack aprons spattered with shiny fish scales they were expertly slicing and gutting tiny silver shapes then dropping them into open barrels lined up in front of them. As they worked they sang, their voices rising and falling in some strangely worded song, the rhythm dictating the speed of the cutting.

Behind them a four-storey sandstone building suggested a warehouse or some sort of marketplace with people coming and going through two wide arches at the far end of the building. Above this tiny windows peered down at the busy girls while men bustled back and forward dragging the full barrels of fish over to waiting carts. As soon as one cart was loaded it moved off and another took its place.

Piles of lobster creels, boxes, and fishing nets strung out like washing filled the space between the low harbour wall and a gaggle of untidy-looking thatched cottages.

Any other time Lucas would have been intrigued, eager to see, to ask questions; today it was only part of an alien world.

He turned to John Spreul. "Is this whaur we get the boat for the Bass Rock?"

"Likely. I hope the sea's calm."

Lucas nodded and thought about his trip on the *Marianne* to Rotterdam a year ago when he'd escaped from Scotland to teach in the Presbyterian College in Utrecht. That journey had been filled with days and nights of retching and constant dizziness. The return a few months later had been no better. "Ah'm no a guid sailor," he confessed.

"So ye said when ye came intae ma shop for a remedy. If ye hadna been in ma shop at that parteeclar meenit ye wudna hae gotten yersel arrested."

"Weel I wis. And it's ma ain fault for speaking up and annoying yon captain."

"The benefit o hindsicht's a wunnerfu thing." John Spreul was about to say more when a fat, bearded face peered over the cart rail. "Doon ye git an nae nonsense."

Legs stiff and numb after hours in such a cramped space made it difficult for them to move let alone try to swing over the tailboard. The bearded soldier lost patience and dragged them both over onto the cobbles. "Move yersels or else."

Neither answered.

The soldier grinned. "Yer new abode's waitin fur ye aifter a wee boat trip. But first ah've a wee job fur ye baith." A musket shaft poked Lucas's back. "Git ower tae that line o fish barrels an load four ontae this cart."

Lucas and John Spreul struggled with the barrels but finally managed to heave them on board.

"Richt. Ye've hud yer exercise. Noo up ye go an sit doon again."

"Whit aboot the boat?" John Spreul asked.

"We dinna board here at North Berwick. It's a shorter crossin frae Canty Bay alang the coast a bit. C'mon, git movin, we jist stoaped here tae pick up they fish barrels fur the garrison, tae gie them a wee chainge frae solan geese an mutton. Hurry up, we've the tide tae catch an deliver ye twa afore nicht."

Crammed under the shut tarpaulin alongside four herring barrels John Spreul and Lucas could hardly breathe during the next few miles. It was a relief when the back cover swung open again and they could gulp some fresh air.

Down from the cart they were forced to carry the barrels along a sandy beach and onto a narrow stone quay. An open boat with a single red sail was tied up at the far end.

"Keep goin," the soldier ordered. "The barrels need tae be loaded afore ye sit doon."

By the time the barrels were on board John and Lucas were puffed out, sore and shaking and gratefully slumped down at the back of the boat.

A soldier sat on either side, two others sat at the front, while a grisly-looking, broad-shouldered man stood at the helm. A boy on the quay loosened the tethering rope and threw it into the boat. The man caught it, waved his thanks then used an oar to gently push the boat away from the rough stone wall. Once clear he turned the wheel. The prow swung to the left and began to nose past several anchored fishing boats and into the open space of what looked like a calm sea.

Their destination beckoned and seemed no distance away.

Out from the shore the air freshened as the wind increased to fill out the sail. No longer limp and sluggish the boat responded and cut through the water. On their right they saw a dark castle on the edge of a high cliff. "Yon's Tantallon," John Spreul pointed at the damaged ramparts. "Seen better times by the luks o it."

"So have we," Lucas grunted.

An hour passed. The Bass Rock seemed to grow larger, to fill the sky. The waves began to spray over the thick sides of this mahogany boat, the *Sula*, named for the Solan geese who dominated the rock, their white plumage giving much of it the look of a recent snow fall.

The boat swung closer till it was almost under a rocky overhang where white topped fume covered the lower reaches of this vast hulk. Lucas and John Spreul gripped the handrail and stared horrified at clouds of wings swirling above, their harsh cries filling their ears like an ominous warning. Now they could see a fort-like line of rough, stone buildings, somehow managing to cling to the steep-sided rock. Tiny, black holes were set in these walls. Once or twice Lucas thought he saw a pale face in one of the dark spaces as if someone was watching their arrival.

"No the kindest place tae spend time." John Spreul's knuckles gleamed white against his dark coat. He stared at them and sighed. "No that I intend biding in this awfy place. I've aready instructed my lawyer tae work on oor behalf and get us baith cleared o this monstrous charge afore the winter sets in. Itherwise – "

"We micht be deid wi the cauld or starved tae death."

"It'll certainly be cauld but we'll no starve. I'll mak sure o extra rations, enough for us baith."

"That'll cost money." Lucas protested. "I hae nae way o paying ye back."

John Spreul shook his head. "Nae maitter. We've started this thegither. We'll see this thru thegither. Dinna worry, I hae the means tae mak oor stay a bit easier."

Instead of being pleased or relieved Lucas slumped down further in his seat. First John Steel had supported him, made decisions for him, cared for him. Now John Spreul was taking on the same role. He turned away to hide his frustration and watched the boat cautiously edge round the sheer wall of rock into a tiny, protected inlet where steep twisted steps were cut into the rock.

Four men in uniform waited on a lower step to grab a rope from the boat and haul it in as close to the rocky wall as possible. Once secured the boat bobbed gently while the soldiers lifted the barrels clear.

"Richt." One of the soldiers summoned John Spreul and Lucas. "Welcome tae the Bass Rock. We'll tak guid care o ye." This seemed to amuse the others who laughed as they pushed their two new prisoners up the steep steps towards the fortress.

"Ay," John Spreul whispered to Lucas, "welcome indeed."

The noise and smell from the solan geese grew worse as they climbed the ill cut, slippery steps to this strange fortress tacked onto the rock. The higher they went the more the wind whipped round their legs, almost tipping them over.

On the topmost step a man in a long overcoat and tight fitting cap was waiting as if to meet the new arrivals. "Guid day sirs. Welcome tae this special place. I'm the garrison commander, charged wi yer weel bein an safe keepin." He chuckled as if amused. "Richt. On tae yer new abode." He raised a gloved hand and two soldiers hustled Lucas and John Spreul through a low archway and along a narrow cobbled passageway cut directly into the side of the bare rock. On the other side rose rough-hewn stone walls broken only by a long row of solid, oak-studded doors. The screeching and flapping continued above. Lucas and John Spreul glared up at the offenders.

The guards grinned. "Ye'll git used tae it."

Half-way along this passageway two doors stood open. John Spreul was pushed into the first dark space, the door pulled shut then Lucas was catapulted into the second.

He wheeled round. The door was already shut. He heard the bolt slide into place. This was it. His stay on the Bass Rock had begun.

Lucas closed his eyes. This seemed to make the bird cries grow louder. They filled his head along with a constant thud, thud which had to be the waves breaking below. As for the damp and cold he could feel it seeping through his clothes, settling on his skin. Soon it would be within, gradually taking over to numb his mind and destroy whatever resolution he might still have.

He stood there a long time before daring to open his eyes and peer through the gloom, to study this tiny space, his space. The walls were rough-hewn stone; even in the half-dark they glistened with damp. High up on the nearest wall was a narrow, open slit which seemed to serve as a window. Opposite stood the stout, locked door. Below this slit was a long, narrow slab of stone, probably a bed. On it sat a neatly folded blanket, a tin mug, a plate and a spoon so eating seemed to be allowed. Beyond the narrow slab he found a small, round hole in the floor suggesting some sort of toilet provision. There was no sign of a wash-bowl, no towel, no soap.

Normally a fastidious man he was well-aware of how much he already stank. It looked as if that was about to get worse.

The door suddenly opened. A figure filled the space. Lucas turned to stare at the shape. It was the man in the overcoat, the governor. Lucas began to feel afraid but the governor made no attempt to come into the dark space, made no threat. When he spoke his tone was almost friendly. "Weel sir, ye best settle yersel. Ye'll be here for a while. But first ye need tae ken hoo we dae things aroond here."

Lucas said nothing.

"Maist o yer time's spent in here, on yer ain. But bein a meenister ye'll nae doubt welcome the opportunity tae convene wi yer heavenly maister an mibbe contemplate the earthly sins that brocht ye here. If the weather's guid ye'll git oot for a wee daunder up tap for a word wi ane or twa fella prisoners. Ye hae a lot in common." The commander chuckled. "Richt noo we hae mair than thirty meenisters so ye'll no miss oot on arguin an preachin. Ah've nivver met sic folk for disagreein wi ane anither.

Yer cell's aw clean an ready for ye. We've laid oot a new blanket, a mug, an a plate, an ye'll see thur's even a wee hole in the flair tae shite thru. Whit mair cud a man want?"

Lucas still said nothing.

"An of course we'll feed ye. Twa meals a day, gruel in the

mornin an somethin mair fillin at nicht. In atween times yer stomach's allooed tae rummel. C'mon man cheer up. Ye'll dae fine. Ye're ane o the lucky yins wi a freend oot there willin tae mak sure ye're aricht."

"Ye must be mistaken." Lucas spoke for the first time. "Naebody kens nor cares whaur I am let alane bein prepared tae luk oot for ma welfare."

"Oh but ay. Somebody wi a deep pooch has guaranteed tae pay fur extra meat an a warm jaiket afore the winter sets in. Whitivver happens ye'll neither starve nur freeze tae death. Ah wunner whae ye shud be thankin? Nae names wur mentioned but that kinda money suggests somebody important."

"My companion John Spreul said he'd help me."

The governor shook his head. "Naw, naw. The money's comin frae Glesca wi instructions hoo it's tae be spent. Ah need tae keep a record. No that ye'll git ony less or mair than is due. So there ye are. Lik ah said, cheer up. Things are no as bad as ye thocht." He raised his gloved hand. A guard leant in, grabbed the door handle and pulled at it. The door swung shut, the bolt clicked, the shadows deepened as Lucas sank to the floor and burst into tears.

Two days passed before he saw the proper light of day. Apart from meal times, with its brief human contact, he was left entirely on his own.

At first he tried to pass the time pacing the floor, back and forward, measuring his steps, trying to vary them, then he tried staring up at the slit of a window, counting each white wing flashing past the narrow space. Finally he sat down on the stone shelf and waited for his demons to come calling.

One by one he was reminded of each stupid action, all the way from that Sunday morning when he'd stood in his pulpit and opened his mouth to start off this nightmare. He travelled through each dreadful event, right to that crowded square in the centre of Douglas, watching Richard Cameron's severed head swing back and forward like the final condemnation. Me and my precious conscience, hauding oot against Ritchie's radical ideas and determination tae embrace treason at ony cost, even if it meant being a martyr for the cause. He shook his head, knew this was only an excuse when none was needed. This had him jumping up again to pace, then watch the birds, then back to those waiting demons.

By the time his cell door opened and he was invited to take a walk outside Lucas's reaction was to run into the daylight as if it alone might save him from himself.

John Spreul was standing in the passageway. He looked as calm as ever. This startled Lucas, warned him about the importance of appearance. He straightened up, pretended the past hours had been tedious, nothing more.

"Ay," John Spreul agreed. "I'm gled tae be oot in the air."

Together they walked towards the archway where a guard directed them onto the path for prisoners to exercise. As they climbed beyond the fortress wall Lucas said, " I seem tae hae a benefactor, willing tae pay for extra meat, even a warm winter jacket. The governor said he'd nae idea whae it is. Since ye'd aready offered I thocht it wis yersel but he said no. Dae ye ken ocht aboot it?"

John Spreul shook his head. "Whit aboot yon freend ye spoke aboot, that helped aifter ye lost yer kirk?"

"John Steel's a farmer. Noo he's a declared rebel, on the run himsel. Whaur wud he get that kinda money?"

"Whit aboot James McAvoy? He's a wealthy man as weel as a carin man?"

"But he haurly kens me. I wis only in his hoose because o John Steel."

"Weel jist be gled ye've got this anonymous freend. Time'll tell whae it is."

Lucas sighed and they both said no more till they reached a small, grassy plateau where a few sheep were quietly grazing alongside a group of dark figures who seemed deep in conversation till they spied Lucas and John Spreul.

An elderly man in a black cloak waved them forward. "Come ower and gie us yer news."

John Spreul strode over to shake the old man's outstretched hand. "John Spreul, apothecary frae Glasgow." He turned to Lucas. "My companion is Lucas Brotherstone, ousted meenister frae Lesmahagow."

The old man nodded. "John Blackadder. I lost my parish a few years back and ended up here wi a wheen ithers." He looked hopefully at Lucas. "Hoo goes the cause?"

Lucas stiffened. "The cause is feenished."

The old man gaped at him. "Shairly no. I ken it's been hard since yon terrible defeat at Bothwell but whit aboot Richard Cameron? Is he no staunding oot against the government? We heard he's back frae Holland, travelling the land, spreading the word. He's a fine preacher. Folk must see the sense in whit he's saying aboot keeping up the resistance against the anti-Christ."

"Ritchie's deid. Killed at Airds Moss on 22nd July by government troops. The only thing he's managed tae dae is become a martyr."

The old man turned and waved the others in his group to come forward. "Wud ye jist repeat that, sir?"

"Richard Cameron's deid." Lucas tried to shout above the screeching birds. "The government has killed the cause stane deid. We're aw prisoners here for nowt."

Shocked faces watched Lucas hurry away down the path and back through the archway.

John Spreul looked embarrassed. He held up his hands in apology. "He's no himsel. No aifter whit he saw wi Richard Cameron. He's – "

"A renegade frae the truth." Blackadder spat out the words. "I want naething tae dae wi him."

The others muttered and seemed to agree.

"Gie him a chance tae explain." John Spreul excused himself and went back down the path to find Lucas.

Lucas offered no apology. "The truth will oot. It needed saying. Why pretend?"

"Because we're stranded here, cheek by jowl wi ane anither. Whit dae ye think yer words will dae tae men lik that? Maist o them huv been here for years, suffering for their beliefs and ye come alang denying the worth o their sacrifice. God sakes man, dinna mak yer life ony mair difficult than it is."

As the days passed John Spreul's words echoed over and over. Lucas began to wish that he'd spoken rather differently to John Blackadder.

Chapter 7

After Lucas Brotherstone was carted off to Edinburgh under armed guard James McAvoy had warned John Steel, "There's naething ye can dae. Lik I said yer freend's been sucked intae something beyond us. Gang hame and wait for news o whit's happening."

"Cud ah no go tae Edinburgh?"

"Dinna be daft. Ye're a named rebel and need tae be carefu for yersel and family. They need ye mair than yer meenister. Try and be patient. I hae freends and folk I can trust tae find oot whit's become o Maister Brotherstane. At least he's in guid company. John Spreul's naebody's fool. Aince I hae some word I'll let ye ken."

John rode out of Glasgow with mixed feelings. Part of him was worried about Lucas's possible fate, another was admitting a sense of relief. James McAvoy's *something beyond us* kept repeating in his head. And yet he felt guilty. If only ah'd gone tae yon apothecary shop wi Lucas ah'd hae seen somethin wis up an pued the eedjit oot afore it wis too late. He shook his head. An noo ah'm mair or less aff the hook. Nae mair worryin ower a man as disna ken his ain mind. Not quite convinced he rode on with Lucas's horse trotting alongside.

John saw the tail of a familiar cart. He called out and hurried forward.

Gus McPhail turned and smiled. "Tether yer horses tae the back rail an come up on the cairt."

John nodded and joined the older man. "So whit's been happenin? Ony news ah shud ken?"

"This an that." Gus pointed at the two horses. "Whit's the ither horse for?"

"Ah wis tryin tae deliver the meenister intae safe haunds an git him awa back tae Holland but it didna work oot." He told Gus the whole story.

"Dinna blame yersel. That man's worse than a bairn. His ain worst enemy. If ye hudna luked aifter him sae weel he'd be deid by noo, killed on Airds Moss alang wi Richard Cameron. Aifter aw the bother he's pit ye thru yer conscience shud be clear. If ye dinna mind me sayin ye're ower saft herted. Stoap blamin yersel."

John grinned. "Ah've heard that afore."

"Weel tak note. When ye git back ye'll hae the troopers tae contend wi. They've upped the patrols, arrivin at aw times o the day an nicht at different farms, turnin the places inside oot an then comin back the next day tae sweep ower everythin again."

"Whit's brocht this on?"

"Ah cud be wrang but mind hoo Ritchie Wilson got cairted awa tae Edinburgh?"

"Ay. Ane o the platoon captain's wis in the mill an got knocked oot. Ritchie got the blame. But whit's that tae dae wi extra patrols?"

"Ah think it follows on frae that. Ye see Ritchie wis chairged wi attackin the captain but let aff aifter Claverhoose spoke up for him. Ah think thur's mair tae it. The commander's troopers huv been roond the village as weel askin if onybody's seen Ritchie. Ye see he husna come back frae Edinburgh. Ah suspect Claiverhoose is waitin fur him. That yin dis naethin withoot guid reason. Soonds lik he's got somethin special in mind for Ritchie."

"Lik a wee thank ye fur savin his skin?"

They travelled on in silence for a while then Gus said, "Yer brither-in-law Gavin's runnin the mill. Hud tae ah suppose itherwise whaur wud folk tak thur grain? Jist as weel he's mair or less feenished his trainin. Ritchie hus made him a guid miller so nae worries there."

John frowned. "Whit aboot his mither? He wis helpin her wi the farm as weel as workin wi Ritchie."

"She's hired auld Maguire frae the Neuk farm. Mind ye it's a funny business wi Claverhoose at the back o it or ah'll eat ma hat." Gus nodded. "Very suspeecious. He's hud yon captain Crichton an a fu platoon oot on the moor then up at yer ain farm as weel as harassin Marion at Westermains, demandin tae ken whaur ye micht be."

"As if she'd tell him onythin. But aw the same it's nae richt that she's tae pit up wi that. Ah've a lot tae answer for."

Gus poked him. "C'mon man. Whit's happened has happened. Yer challenge is tae bide free till aw this is by wi."

When they reached the track leading to Waterside Farm John jumped down from the cart and untethered the two horses.

"Gavin gied the meenister a horse. Ah best tak it back afore ah gang hame masel."

Gus nodded. "Tak care. If ye need onythin jist ask."

John reached up and grabbed Gus's arm. "If ye happen tae pass Maister McAvoy's hoose cud ye mibbe stop an ask if he's got ony news for me?"

"Nae problem."

Rachael Weir saw John come up the farm track and was waiting for him in the courtyard. "Gled ye're back safe. That wis an awfy business aboot the meenister."

John gaped at her. "Hoo dae ye ken?"

"Ma sister Sophie wis here. She tellt me. But come in till ah explain it richt."

"Ah'll stable Gavin's horse first then ye can tell me everythin."

In the kitchen John listened in silence to a complicated story about Rachael's brother then said, "Ah jist hope Claverhoose disna find oot whaur he is."

"That's whit ah said." Rachael nodded. "Mind ye, oor Sophie's takin ivvery precaution. She's made Ritchie dye his hair an grow a beard. She's even got him usin anither name as weel as tellin folk he's a relation frae Fife. Mind ye it's odd hoo Ritchie fetched up in the Edinburgh court at the same time as the meenister. Hoo did the pair man git arrested an taen there?"

John told her what happened then asked, "Did Ritchie hear whit happened tae Maister Brotherstane?"

"Naw. He wis oot yon court an awa lik a whippet."

"Ah see. An are ye managin withoot Gavin's help?"

"Ay. Auld Maguire's dain weel. Onyway, needs must. Ye see Gavin feels responsible for whit happened. He drapped the grain sack on yon captain's heid no Ritchie."

There was an awkward pause then John said, "Ah see."

Rachael shook her head. "Jist lik his faither. Act first an damn the consequences." There was another awkward pause as Rachael twisted the ends of her apron strings round her fingers. "Ah often think aboot yon day at Drumclog when ma Tom galloped oot tae dae battle by himsel. No his maist sensible moment an noo he's lyin in the graveyard. Ah'm sure ye ken whit ah mean."

"Only too weel." John sighed but said no more.

Chapter 8

John left Juno in the stable at Waterside and cut across the fields to Westermains. As he walked he thought about Rachael's brother. Something about his story didn't add up but right now he'd other things to worry about. The moment he arrived home Marion's reaction confirmed it when she threw herself at him and held on as if she'd never let go. "It's been terrible while ye wur awa wi the meenister. Crichton and his platoon's been here time aifter time threatenin me an the bairns, demandin tae ken whaur ye micht be. When ma mither tellt me aboot uncle Ritchie, hoo he'd seen Maister Brotherstane in the same Edinburgh court as himsel ah wis frantic wunnerin if Crichton kent somethin ah didna an wis jist stringin me alang tae torment me."

"Ah wisna wi the meenister when he got arrested. Ah've asked Maister McAvoy tae find oot whit's likely tae happen an let me ken."

"No John." Marion stepped back. "Let it go. Ye've a price on yer ain heid."

"Ay but – "

"But nuthin. Think aboot it. The government's set on revenge aifter yon stramash aboot Richard Cameron so ye're in even mair danger than afore. That's whit ah tellt Wull Gemmel when he arrived the ither day wunnerin if ye'd come tae some meetin at Logan Hoose nixt month. Somethin aboot plans tae cairry on the field preachin."

"Ay. Nae chance. Ah've enough on ma mind withoot ony ither plans."

"Ah hope that disna include the meenister."

John pursed his lips and looked away.

That night John spent hours staring into the dark. Sleep was impossible. Eventually he sat up and stared at the tiny lines of dawn beginning to shine through the cracks in the shutters. Whit am ah lyin here fur? Jist git up. Dae somethin usefu.

Slipping out of bed he gathered his clothes from a chair by the door, tiptoed through to the kitchen and dressed quickly. Minutes later he was in the back shed looking for his tool-bag. The fence along the bottom field was broken. More than once the boys had been sent to chase the sheep from the turnips. That needed doing before anymore were eaten.

He carried some wood along with his tool bag, inspected the damage then started to fix the gap in the fence. There was something satisfying about tearing off the broken planks and then breaking them into smaller pieces. He worked away steadily, gradually repairing the long jaggy space left by the determined sheep. Almost finished he straightened up and looked round. It was a grand morning, the dewy grass sparkling the way he loved, the air fresh with just a hint of a breeze, everything green and growing. This was more like it. And then he caught a glimpse of red, a flurry of it moving among the beeches on the Lesmahagow road above the next field. He stared. There it was again along with the sound of hooves drumming on hard shale.

He watched the lead horse turn off the road onto the Westermains track. Christ. No again. He ran to the far end of the field, jumped the fence then slid down the bank towards the Logan burn. From here he could watch the visitors and stay hidden.

As the platoon drew close he recognised the lead figure. Poor Marion was about to be harassed again.

Crichton jumped down from his horse and strode over to peer in the little farmhouse window. Marion Steel was ladling porridge into bowls, four bowls. He smiled to himself and turned to signal his men forward.

Marion jumped as the outside door burst open and several pairs of heavy boots stamped along her hall. She stood up straight and prepared to face the invaders.

"Whaur is he?" Crichton marched into the kitchen and pointed at the four steaming bowls on the table. "Twa bairns, twa adults. Ye're caught oot this time."

Marion tried to look less scared than she felt. "Ye forgot the baby. No that she's the age fur porridge. Ye're still wrang – thur's only me, twa weans an Fly. That maks four. Did ye no ken a collie likes porridge in the mornin same as us?" She took one bowl and placed it on the floor where Fly obligingly scoffed the lot.

Crichton scowled and turned way. "Search ivvery room. Mak sure Steel's no here."

Five minutes later, "Naethin sir."

He marched outside. "Check the byre, the sheds, ivvery corner. That rebel's here somewhaur." He stood in the middle of the courtyard snapping his whip against his long riding boots while the whole farm was thoroughly searched.

"Naethin sir."

Disappointed and angry he remounted his horse and led the platoon back down the track towards the road. Just before the little wooden bridge over the burn he stopped. "Somethin lyin against that fence stab ower ther." He pointed. "Sergeant, tak a luk."

After a couple of minutes the sergeant called back, "Twa fresh planks here an a tool-bag. Luks lik somebody – "

"Wis oot here mendin yon fence an saw us comin. Somebody whae disna want us tae see him. Dismount an search amang the trees then work yer way alang the riverbank. Oor freend micht be closer than we think."

"No if he's ony sense," the sergeant whispered as he tethered his horse and began to walk through the dewy grass towards the river.

Half an hour later the troopers gave up and returned to their horses. "Whaur noo sir?" The sergeant sounded less than pleased with his captain.

Crichton turned and pointed back to the moor above the farm. "We'll dae a sweep up there. Ye nivver ken whit we micht find."

As the platoon trotted past the farmyard and on towards the moorland track Marion watched and worried. She'd no idea where John might be.

The troopers were barely out of sight when John appeared by her side. "Eedjits," he muttered. "Daft eedjits."

Marion rounded on him. "Mibbe thur daft eedjits but jist mind thur dangerous eedjits as weel." She left the rest unsaid.

As the troopers climbed the track into the moor a gentle mist rose from the heather to creep after them. Within minutes they were trotting through cold, wet tendrils softly blanking out the world around. Each rider could just about make out the man next to him. Other than that everything was covered by a still grey curtain which even seemed to muffle the horses' breathing.

"Keep movin," Crichton ordered and cursed himself for giving in to his own bad temper. Steel was still free, had probably been laughing while he watched Crichton playing his role as official hunter. He'd been aware of this even as he ordered his men to search along the riverbank. If only, he wished and brushed misty droplets from his eyelashes.

"Sir?"

Crichton swung round in his saddle, peered towards his sergeant's faint shadow. "Whit is it?"

"Wud it no be better tae stoap an wait till this lifts?"

"We go on." Crichton clicked his horse forward but allowed the beast to use its own senses to pick a way through this grey world of nothing.

The horses plodded on, their riders slumped in their saddles resigned to seeing nothing, hearing little other than the occasional clip of a hoof against some unexpected hard stone. Time seemed to drag till it no longer mattered. And then a slight whisper of air moved among them like a hint of possible change. Horse and rider responded. Alertness returned as the watery wall began to lift, giving glimpses of heather and fern. Faint shadows became solid shapes. A hint of colour appeared behind the wispy trails. "It's liftin," Crichton called out. "A few mair meenits an wur clear."

He was right. A closed door swung open and the platoon stepped into the light of a clear day. Ahead was a small farm, beyond it a winding track. Close by two men were cutting peats.

The troopers blinked at the sudden change then trotted forward.

Crichton reined up by the men and their stack of fresh cut peat. "Whaur's this?"

The older man laid down his long-handled knife and pointed towards the farm building. "Priesthill Farm by Muirkirk."

"Hoo dae we git tae Lesmahagow withoot crossin the moor again?"

"If ye want tae bide clear o the mist jist follow the track aheid till ye hit the road then turn richt for Strathaven."

"Jeezus." The sergeant turned to Crichton. "Wur miles awa.

Hoo did we manage this?"

Crichton ignored him and asked, "Aifter Strathaven?"

"Richt again ontae the Lesmahagow road an keep goin. It'll tak a while though."

Crichton waved the platoon forward. Only the sergeant nodded his thanks.

The two peat-cutters watched the soldiers ride down the long hill to the road.

"They didna seem that bad," the young man said.

The older man smiled. "They wur lukin for help. Anither time micht be different."

It was almost dark before the platoon clattered into their barracks. Unfortunately Crichton's commander was waiting for him. "Lang day Crichton?"

The captain jumped down from his horse and saluted. "Scoutin across the moor, sir."

"And whit's the result?"

"Naethin tae report, sir."

"Wasted effort then?"

Crichton flushed. "We were searchin for John Steel."

"Ah." Claverhouse smiled. "The elusive rebel." He pulled a folded paper from his coat pocket. "It jist so happens that I hae a letter here frae my auld freend Airlie up at Strathmore asking aboot progress on that very maitter. Whit shud I tell him?"

Crichton's flush deepened. "We're makin ivvery effort an expect the richt result afore lang."

"Promises, promises." Claverhouse laughed at his captain's expression. He flapped the folded paper under Crichton's nose, turned on his heel and walked away.

Too tired to take off his uniform or boots Crichton flopped down on his straw pallet. Sleep beckoned but with it came a sense of unease, as if a pair of amused, brown eyes were watching him, reminding him of all the times the man behind those eyes had either bested him or escaped from right under his nose. Even with a thousand merks on his head John Steel was still free, still able to torment him, make him look a failure.

Having Crichton on his tail only added to John's frustration as he waited for news of what had happened to Lucas Brotherstone. Knowing nothing made him guess, then think the worst, then blame himself. And still no word came from James McAvoy.

Late one afternoon Gus McPhail stopped off at Waterside Farm and asked Rachael Weir to pass on a message for John. "It's frae a James McAvoy, an important man in the toun an guid freend tae John. He wants John tae pay him a visit urgent like. Ah shud gang up tae Westermains an tell him masel but ah'd raither no wi they troopers on the hunt."

Rachael nodded. "Nae worries, ah'll pass it on as an when ah can."

Gus had barely gone a mile from the farm when he met Crichton's platoon. He stopped to let them pass. Crichton drew alongside and stared at Gus "We saw ye comin alang the track frae Waterside."

Gus forced a smile. "Ah wis deliverin stuff for Mistress Weir. As ye can see ah'm a carrier."

"Wis her brither there?"

"Whit brither?"

"Ritchie Wilson. Ye must ken him."

Gus stiffened. "Ay. He's the village miller. Why wud he be there when he wis arrested an taen tae Edinburgh a while back?"

"Whit aboot John Steel?"

"Whit aboot him? Luk sir, ah drive ma cart in an oot the toun. Ah work lang hoors, cover a wheen miles an try tae gie a guid service. That means mindin ma ain business withoot indulgin in tittle tattle or nosyin intae corners as dinna concern me."

Crichton leant closer. "An whit if ye did see or hear somethin in ane o they corners, somethin the law shud ken aboot?"

"Ah'd pass it on, sir. Lik ony decent citizen."

"Ah'm shair ye wud." Crichton pulled his horse to the side.

Gus nodded his thanks and slowly edged past the line of troopers.

Crichton watched him go. "That yin's worth the watchin."

His sergeant frowned but made no comment.

James McAvoy's message was like a summons and John was keen to leave for Glasgow.

Marion glared at John. "Ah dinna like this. Nae doubt it'll be aboot the meenister. No that ah wish ony ill on him but yon man's brocht us nuthin but trouble."

"Ah canna help it. Ye've got tae unnerstaund he's an eedjit as needs watchin fur his ain sake."

"Ye're ivvery bit as bad fur dain it." Her hands flapped in John's face. "An much guid may it dae."

John pulled her angry face close and kissed the end of her nose. "Ah'll gang ower tae Priesthill in the mornin an ask fur a lift afore Gus leaves for the toun."

"Guid tae see ye." James McAvoy steered his visitor into the privacy of his upstairs sitting-room and closed the door. "Sit doon. Mak yersel comfortable afore the fire while I tell ye whit's happened tae yer freend." The old man sat down in his favourite chair and wrapped his fur-lined robe round his legs.

John waited till his host seemed comfortable then said, "Ah hope it's guid news."

"Tae be honest, no. Maister Brotherstone's been sent tae the Bass Rock prison alang wi John Spreul. They baith had a trumped up charge lodged against them. Naethin wis proved but it made nae difference tae the ootcome."

"Whit dis that mean?"

"They're baith captive tae the whims o the Privy Council, shut oot there in the Firth o Forth till their lordships decide itherwise. Cud tak years an no wi the best treatment. In my opinion the only option wis tae offer the prison governor a bit siller on the side and ask that yer freend gits mair tae eat and mibbe a warm coat afore the winter sets in. It disna soond much but it cud mak aw the difference tae a starvin man, shut up in yon hell hole. Life in a place lik that haurly bears thinkin aboot."

"That's fur me tae dae, no yersel sir. Mibbe ah cud use some o the money ye've invested fur me. Cud ye advise me?"

"Lik I said I've aready made contact wi the governor on the Bass Rock, suggesting some extra payment micht help mak yer freend's life a bit easier. But if ye're happy tae tak on the responsibility I'll mak the necessary arrangements on yer behalf withoot drawin ony attention."

"Ah'd be obleeged."

"It's easily done. That parteeclar governor's nae averse tae a bit extra money arriving discreet like an goin straight intae his ain pooch. John Spreul's wife has been making similar enquiries. When I heard this I got in touch wi the lady. She's worried aboot her man's health and desperate tae see hoo he is for hersel. The pair man wis tortured for shouting at the Lord Advocate during the court case."

"Wis he hurt bad?"

"He has difficulty walkin but itherwise weel enough. They put his richt foot in a wooden box shaped lik a boot and then drove in wooden staves each time he refused tae tak back his words."

"Did they dae onythin tae Maister Brotherstane?"

"It wis jist John Spreul as got the special treatment. That's why Mistress Spreul wis asking aboot makin a personal visit."

"Ye mean goin tae the Rock itsel?"

James McAvoy leant forward. "And if Spreul's lady wife maks sic a journey wud it no mak sense for her tae tak a manservant alang tae ensure her safety?"

John sat up straight. "Ye mean?"

"Indeed. But only if ye want tae. It wudna be the easiest undertakin an ye'd need tae be extra carefu wi a price on yer ain heid."

John thought for a moment then nodded.

"Richt. Mistress Spreul's visit is arranged for the 29th o this month. Cud ye be in North Berwick the day before?"

John nodded again.

"Perfect. I'm helping the lady wi her plans. She's allooing me tae sort oot the transport and a few ither details."

"Will Mistress Spreul be agreeable tae me goin as weel?"

James McAvoy grinned. "I taen the liberty o mentioning yer interest. Rest assured the mistress has aready said she's happy tae hae yer company."

Marion was furious with John and let him know it. To her surprise he didn't argue or defend his plan, simply stayed very still and quiet till she eventually ran out of breath.

In spite of the distance John decided against a coach journey and set out on faithful Juno several days before the arranged meeting. That way he could take his time, avoid well used roads and sleep rough each night rather than lay himself open to any unnecessary risks.

Once in North Berwick he searched out the best stable, paid for Juno's care over three days and walked to the Harbour Inn as per his instructions from James McAvoy.

The Jamieson brothers were waiting at the door of the inn. They smiled and shook hands with him. "Come in. The mistress is waitin thru the back." They led him along a narrow corridor to a private room, gave a gentle knock on the door before opening it and announcing, "Yer new man-servant, Maam."

Helen Spreul, a slim, pale-faced, anxious looking woman, elegantly dressed in dark travelling clothes was sitting on a bench by a frugal fire. She held out a gloved hand and smiled at John. "Gled tae meet ye." She didn't mention his name.

John took her hand, and gave it a firm squeeze. "Maister Brown at yer service, Maam."

Helen Spreul's smile broadened. "It'll be a new experience for us baith. But please sit doon, I'll ring for some food. Ye must be hungry aifter yer journey." She lowered her voice. "Mibbe we shud hae a wee talk and mak sure oor stories match. Jist in case." She turned to the Jamiesons standing by the open door. "Wud ye twa care tae eat as weel?"

The Jamiesons shook their heads. "Oor orders are tae keep an ee oot." They closed the door and clumped back down the corridor.

Helen Spreul pulled a bell rope on the wall behind her seat and a few minutes later a serving girl brought in a steaming ashet. John smelt the meat and potatoes and needed no persuasion to start eating.

Half an hour later the Jamiesons opened the door again. "The cairt's here Maam."

Helen Spreul nodded and bent to lift a bag at her feet. John leant forward and took hold of it. "We'll stert as we mean tae gang on. Whit else dae ye hae?"

"Twa hampers and a basket wi four live hens."

John gaped at her.

Helen laughed. "The prison governor has agreed tae them. It'll gie my John and yer freend fresh eggs. I've included seeds for the birds tae keep them healthy. The hampers hae some extra food as weel tae keep them going in the meantime but I've made arrangements for extra rations tae be delivered ivvery month. Maister McAvoy said ye're dain the same for yer freend. Between us we shud mak life a bit mair pleasant for them baith. Wi a bit o luck their imprisonment will no last long."

"Ye're weel organised," John complimented her as he carried out the luggage then conveyed his new mistress to her seat at the front of the cart. "Wi yer permission Maam ah'll join ye." He jumped up and sat beside her.

The driver climbed aboard and signalled for the Jamiesons to take the second line of seats. "Richt. Aff we go."

The cart rumbled along the harbour road then began the long climb out of the town. Soon they were passing open fields and prosperous looking farms. Life seemed good around here although neither John nor Helen Spreul paid much attention. They were too busy glancing at the strange shaped rock out there in the Firth of Forth.

The cart slowed up beside a sign saying Canty Bay. The driver pointed at it. "That's whaur supplies an prisoners gang oot tae the rock. But ah unnerstaund yer visit's tae be mair discreet."

"Jist mak sure it bides that way," the Jamiesons growled.

"Nae worries," the driver grinned. "Ah dae this aw the time. Thur's mony a comin an goin tae the rock that naebody ivver hears aboot. The governor oot ther is aye open tae certain requests."

"Fur a wee conseederation, nae doubt," the Jamiesons suggested.

The drive smiled but didn't answer.

No-one spoke after that.

A couple of miles further on the cart turned off the road to follow a dirt track which took them through a dark wood. On the far side the driver pulled up the cart beside a high brick wall with a strong, metal gate at one end. He jumped down, opened the gate and led the horses into a square, cobbled yard. He nodded to his passengers. "This is North Lodge. Ye'll be here a wheen hoors waitin fur the tide. Five o clock shud see ye crossin."

John helped Helen Spreul down and turned to see a stout man in a filthy overall by his side. "Welcome tae North Lodge. Ma maister's expectin ye. He has a meal ready an then ye can rest till the tide's richt." He pointed to the cart. "Leave yer baskets be. We'll see tae them an tak them tae the boat."

He led them into a grand looking sandstone house. Once inside they walked on thick carpets along a wood-panelled hall with dark portraits peering from the walls till they reached an ornately-carved double door.

He knocked loudly then swung the door open to reveal a large, elegantly furnished, candle-lit room. "Sir. Yer visitors are here."

In the middle of the room a table was spread with a selection of cut meats and a huge china dish piled with a selection of vegetables and roast potatoes. Wine and ale flagons were lined up at the far end of the table alongside a large fruit cake, a complete cheese, and a basket of sweet biscuits.

An old man in a dark velvet doublet and breeches, fine white stockings and silver-buckled, shiny shoes stood by a blazing fire. He bowed a bald head towards them. "Come awa in. Ony freend o James McAvoy is welcome here." His smile was welcoming although his eyes were warily checking them over. "Lik I said. Come awa." He stepped forward and conducted Helen Spreul to sit at the top of the table then turned to the others. "Richt gentlemen. I dare say ye huv an appetite aifter yer journey. Please, eat and enjoy."

John and the Jamiesons sat down and wolfed into the food then downed a tankard or two of ale.

Their host stood by the fire watching with an amused expression. Finally he said, "Noo mak yersels comfortable. Ye've a wheen hoors tae wait afore ye move on."

Helen Spreul moved to a chair by the fire and sat there quietly contemplating the flames. After a while she looked up and turned to her host. "Ye've been mair than kind sir."

"And still a bit mair tae dae Maam. I need tae see ye and yer servant safe across tae the prison and safe back afore the tide turns."

"And whae am I beholden tae?"

"A freend o James McAvoy is aw ye need tae ken."

Helen Spreul nodded and went back to watching the flames.

The old man turned to the others. "Noo that ye're fed and watered, I'll leave ye tae amuse yersels. I hae things needing attention. When it's time tae go my man will tak ye doon tae the boat." He pointed at the Jamiesons. "Noo mind, ye twa. Ye bide here till the mistress and her servant come back. The governor on the rock's only expecting twa visitors. He's only been paid for twa if ye unnerstaund my meaning."

The Jamiesons opened their mouths as if to argue.

John leant forward and whispered, "We'll be fine."

The old man laughed. "Rest easy. Did I no say that James McAvoy's a guid freend. We go back a lang way."

"In that case." The Jamiesons went over to the table and began eating again.

It was barely daylight when the man in the filthy overall appeared. "If ye please Maam. Time tae go."

John and Helen Spreul tiptoed past the Jamiesons, now snoring by the dying embers of the fire, and followed their guide out to the yard.

Without a word he opened a side gate and headed down a steep path which led back into the wood. The grass on either side grew tall and swished as they pushed their way through. In parts the path was almost overgrown with jaggy brambles which kept snagging Helen's long skirt, forcing her to stop and free herself from the sharp thorns.

Towards the edge of the trees their route grew steeper and they had fleeting glimpses of the sea below. Soon they were slipping and sliding and losing their balance.

"It's too steep, I canna manage." Helen Spreul sounded frustrated.

The guide half turned and laughed. "Sit doon. It's safer." He sat down and slid away.

John and Helen did the same and within seconds they reached the beach with sand so soft it swallowed their ankles. Even the guide was puffing. "We'll staund a meenit an git oor breath back aifter that excitement."

Helen Spreul dusted herself down and stared out towards the monstrous shape of the rock. "Nearly there." She turned to the guide and frowned. "Whaur's oor boat?"

"Aw in guid time, Maam." The guide pointed towards a long rocky outcrop on the left. "If ye're ready we need tae walk ower there."

They followed the stout, little man across the soft sand then scrambled up layers of rough rock. Halfway up he slipped behind a large boulder and disappeared. When John and Helen Spreul followed they found they were standing above a perfect little circle of an inlet cut out of the natural rock. A rowing boat loaded with two hampers and the hen basket sat in the still water. Above it hung a thick rope ladder.

The guide climbed down and signalled for the other two to follow.

Helen Spreul didn't hesitate. She hoisted up her skirt and half-slid half-clambered down to land safely in the boat.

John had never been in a boat let alone climbed down to one. He stared at the little circle of water and didn't move.

The guide looked up and seemed to lose patience. "C'mon man. We need tae go wi the tide."

John took a deep breath, edged onto the top of the ladder, gripped the rough fibres as tightly as he could and felt for the first rung, then the second, then the third. The next one down and his feet almost touched the wooden floor of the boat. A strong hand grabbed his sleeve and pulled him into the centre of the boat. "Sit doon beside yer mistress an dinna move."

Red with embarrassment John obeyed.

The guide untied the rope from a thick metal ring fastened into the rocky wall then a gentle push sent the boat out a little way to begin sliding towards a narrow passageway. Arms outstretched, palms flat against each side the guide eased the boat along, round a corner and into the open sea.

John looked back. The entrance was gone.

"Dinna worry," the man grinned at his anxious face. "Ah cud find the way in ma sleep." He sat down, picked up the oars and began to row steadily towards the massive shape in the distance. John watched the man's steady pull on the oars, the way the boat responded, cutting through the water, and yet the rock ahead seemed to be defying all this effort by drifting further away.

Further out from the shore the boat began to dip and rock.

John looked more anxious.

"Stoap worryin." The guide frowned at him. "This is an easy crossin. The sea's calm enough. Ah'll hae ye on the rock in nae time."

John said nothing and kept his eyes fixed on their destination.

As they drew closer he gulped at the sight of so many birds circling above, constantly calling, filling the air with their sharp cries. Below the white curtain of flapping wings he could see a long fortress-like building with tiny holes in the wall. He wondered if they could be windows or holes for a cannon's muzzle. The way the building clung to the side of the rock seemed impossible, as if it was about to drop down into the sea below.

The guide seemed confident enough to row close in beside the sheer cliff face of the lower rock then nudge his way along till he reached a short outcrop. Somehow he managed to force the boat round this projection to find what he was after, a tiny piece of shelter from the main surge of the sea. This had to be the landing spot for right in front was a narrow, irregular stair cut into the rock itself, twisting and turning its way to the fortress above.

Two uniformed men came down the steps and stood while the guide threw a rope towards them. They caught it and pulled the boat towards the steps.

The sea surged, a wave broke over the rocky outcrop, drenched the men and made the boat swing out.

Both men pulled harder. The boat steadied.

"Richt," one of the men shouted, "Ye need tae jump across. We'll catch ye."

Helen Spreul stood up, edged along the side of the boat, steadied herself then leapt towards the outstretched hands.

John had no alternative but to follow.

Chapter 9

After his outburst with the ministers Lucas Brotherstone became a lonely man. First he tried apologising to Blackadder then he tried to explain the truth of the matter but the old man refused to listen, only turned his back and walked away. The others saw this and simply followed his lead. Lucas would not be tolerated. John Spreul remained friendly, walking with him as before, discussing their possible appeal, describing how his wife was briefing his lawyer and even planning a visit to the Rock. Sometimes he'd look at Lucas's haunted expression and try to reassure him. "Jist gie the meenisters time, they'll come roond."

Lucas would nod and appear to agree but the time alone in his cell was having its effect, distancing him from the reality of his situation as well as allowing an over active imagination to flourish with no distraction.

Each day he'd turn to his Bible, searching for some explanation, some reason for all this. Each day he'd read John 21 verse 18 'thou shalt stretch forth thy hands and another shall gird thee, and carry thee whether thou wouldest not.' This particular verse seemed to be telling him something but try as he might he couldn't work it out. This had him on his knees for hours trying to pray, trying to bargain with his master. "If only I kent Lord, I cud thole this place and aw its deprivation."

No answer came so maybe the all-seeing didn't know either, or worse, didn't care.

Each night seemed endless with only faint scuttling in the corners of his cell for company until daybreak when the birds woke and their screeching cries would fill his ears again.

Sometimes Bett would arrive in the night, appearing from the dark, her lovely face so vivid and real he'd reach out to touch only to realise the truth and be left hugging himself, rocking back and forth, pretending it was nothing but a stupid dream.

One of the guards took note of this lonely man who'd been cast aside by the other prisoners. Ay, he smiled to himself, that yin's strugglin. He'll dae.

Next morning when delivering the breakfast gruel he broke the normal routine and spoke to Lucas. It was only, "Guid mornin," but it was a start.

The next morning Lucas was close by the door, waiting. This time he said, "Guid mornin," and smiled as he bent to lift his meager breakfast bowl.

Days passed, more words were exchanged and Lucas began to look forward to those few moments of conversation.

This was just what the guard wanted but he took his time and played the young man like a hungry trout.

After a few more mornings the burly figure stepped into the cell and handed the food bowl into Lucas's hand instead of laying it by the door. "Is somethin wrang?" he asked. "Ye luk a bit doon."

"Nae mair than usual." Lucas nodded and took the bowl.

"If ye dinna mind me sayin ye seem awfy alane." The guard tried to look sympathetic. "Yer freends seem raither unfreendly when ye're supposed tae be walkin thegither an talkin tae ane anither."

"They dinna like hearin the truth aboot oor cause against the government. When I tellt them hoo things really are they turned against me. Aw except ma freend John Spreul."

"Ay, it's guid tae be gratefu. Even fur sma mercies." With that the guard withdrew and closed the door.

Next morning the guard began to reel in his fish. "They say writin's guid if ye're on yer ain."

"Indeed. But in here I hae naethin tae write wi."

"An if ye hud?"

"I'd be richt grateful."

"Wud ye noo." The guard pursed his lips then smiled.

Several days passed with the usual small talk then Lucas was handed a small, rough sheet of blank paper along with his bowl of gruel.

That afternoon he told John Spreul what had happened.

"I'd be careful if I wis ye," John Spreul frowned. "Yon guard's worth the watching. Onyway, I've got pen and paper. I bocht it frae the governor last week. Ye're welcome tae a share. I'll gie ye whit ye need aifter oor walk."

John Spreul was generous, he even offered a candle and a tinder box. Lucas almost skipped back to his cell to write and write till it was too dark to see his words. After that he lit his candle and continued till it burnt out. He covered his paper with questions about the whys and the wherefores, attempts at explanations and answers then arguments. After that he slept soundly for the first time in weeks and only woke when the cell door opened.

"Mornin." The guard held out a second sheet of paper.

"Thank ye but there's nae need." Lucas pointed to a tiny shelf piled with papers. "See. I hae paper and ink. I've aready been writin."

The guard glared at him. "So ye'll no be wantin this?" He crumpled the paper and threw it on the floor. "An here wis ah thinkin – "

"Thinkin whit?" Lucas was shocked by the sudden change of attitude.

The guard didn't answer. He stepped closer and peered into Lucas's face. The blast of stale breath reeked of strong ale, and the near sight of bristly cheeks and blackened gums alarmed him enough to back off. The guard followed, grabbed Lucas's arms and propelled him across the floor to the wall opposite. "Ah wis thinkin we cud hae somethin goin. Somethin special."

"Whitivver dae ye mean?" Lucas tried to push the moon-like face away but rough fingers gripped his neck, forced him round to stare into a pair of dark eyes with an excited, hungry gleam.

"Ye're a fine lukin young man so ye are." A rough hand moved slowly down Lucas's chest, circled his stomach then reached between his legs to give a firm squeeze. At the same time the other hand took hold of his breeches and gave a sudden yank. "Ah wis hopin ye'd be gratefu an willin. But nae maitter. Sometimes it's mair excitin this way." A round belly bounced and rubbed against Lucas. Further down there was no doubt about the hard rod poking forward.

Terrified Lucas tried to speak, to protest, to plead. Only a choking sound came. He tried to wriggle free but those searching hands now gripped like a vice while the fat body almost pushed all the air from his body.

"Come on. Ye ken ye want tae." The gravelly voice changed, almost purred with persuasion but there was no gentleness in the way Lucas was whirled round to face the wall. Another push had his teeth rattling against the damp stones Again he tried to speak or even scream for help. No sound came. He could do nothing as strong arms snaked round his waist, pulling him closer than seemed possible while podgy fingers probed and tormented. Hot breath skimmed his neck and a sticky tongue licked round his ears before a set of gums gnawed along his shoulders and down his arms. Finally there was a loud grunt and the hands changed position to lift Lucas clear of the floor. For a moment his attacker held him there in blissful anticipation while the tip of his penis tickled that exact spot on Lucas's quivering behind. One last check, another tickle to make sure. "Got ya." He was rammed down to meet a powerful upward surge as what felt like a rod burst through, thrusting till it was all the way in and the real business could begin. Legs now locked round Lucas the guard's heavy body forced him to tip over, his face scraping the stone floor while the burning-hot rod continued to push in and out, demanding more, increasing the rhythm to the sound of loud gasps.

"In the name o God whit are ye at Gumsy?" The garrison captain appeared at the open door and gaped at the writhing contortion inside the cell. "Stoap it this meenit." He ran forward to try and pull Gumsy clear of his victim.

Gumsy clung on, continued thrusting.

The captain swore and resorted to slapping the bare, bucking behind. Finally he kicked hard between the open legs.

Gumsy and Lucas yelled in pain then Gumsy released Lucas and slumped to the side. "Whit did ye dae that fur? Ah'm only hain a wee fuck."

"No in here ye're no. Least o aw wi a helpless meenister." The captain grabbed Gumsy's ankles and dragged him towards the door.

"Let go," Gumsy wailed, "ah'm no feenished."

"Ay ye are." The captain bent over to punch Gumsy in the mouth. "Ye're on a charge for this. Buggerin a defenceless prisoner when ye're supposed tae be lukin aifter him. God kens whit the governor'll say."

Gumsy's answer was to stumble to his feet and lurch towards Lucas.

"Enough." The captain dived at the ankles again. Gumsy lashed out and the two men rolled back and forward in a desperate struggle with Gumsy now hindered by his breeches sliding further down his legs.

Lucas jumped up to barge past them and out the open door.

"Christ." The captain let go of Gumsy and chased after Lucas who was now through the archway, heading for the steps to the landing stage. "Stoap man. Stoap!"

Lucas kept going.

When the captain reached the top step he saw a dark figure, hair on end against the wind, arms outstretched as if about to fly. Mesmerised he watched the inevitable as Lucas launched himself high in the air to hang still for a terrible moment then drop towards the waiting waves.

Lucas flew through the air while the white sea flume lifted towards him in welcome. He tried to respond, to cry out, "Lord cleanse me," but the salty water filled his mouth, the waves holding his body, freezing his limbs and mind while he watched his own life's bubbles rise to the surface.

Somewhere deep within came, "Whither thou goest." He knew that voice and it brought no reassurance. Richard Cameron was condemning him yet again, taking him back to that busy square in Douglas where he'd watched a severed head swing back and forward. He'd run then. Not this time. There would be no escape as the light dimmed and darkness beckoned.

Pulling a boat hook from the wall the captain dashed down the slippery steps to lean out as far as he dared and peer into the murky water. The waves moved back and forward. There was nothing else. The boat hook would not be required.

"Guid day. I tak it ye're Mistress Spreul. Is this yer manservant?" A tall man with a wary expression waited at the top of the long flight of twisted steps from the landing stage as the two visitors climbed towards him.

Helen Spreul signalled yes and stopped as if to regain her breath. She used the moment to whisper, "Mind John, tak care."

"Dinna worry, ah'm fine." John nodded and tried not to look as anxious as he felt.

They resumed their climb.

The Bass Rock governor in immaculate uniform seemed a picture of authority even if his expression seemed somewhat uneasy. He stepped forward and spoke to Helen Spreul, "I'm the governor here, Walkinshaw's the name. Yer husband kens ye're coming. He's waiting in his cell. My garrison captain will tak ye there." He snapped his fingers and a guard appeared by his side.

Helen turned and looked back down to the landing stage. "Whit aboot ma hampers, and the hens?"

"On ye go and see yer man. The guide that brocht ye here and my men will fetch them up." He nodded towards John, "Yer servant can wait in the guardroom alang wi the guide and bide oot the wind."

"I wis hoping ye'd alloo my servant tae visit my husband's fellow prisoner Lucas Brotherstone?"

"Whit for?" The governor frowned.

"Maister Brotherstone wis his meenister some time ago. It wud pass the time better than waiting in the guardroom. Yer prisoner micht benefit frae a talk wi a freendly face."

The governor's face tightened. "I gied permission for a visit tae yer man naething else."

"Whit if I paid a wee bit extra?"

The governor shook his head and turned to his captain. "Tak Mistress Spreul thru and wait in the passageway till she's ready."

Helen followed the captain while the governor glared at John. "Ye can wait in the guard room." He pointed to a small hut-like building behind him. "Yer guide will join ye in a meenit or twa. And mind bide there. Nae wanderin aboot. This prison has strict rules aboot whit's allooed."

John nodded and went into the building and sat on a bench by the window. He wished he'd been able to argue, to insist on seeing Lucas but how could he as a mere servant? Onyway, he micht hae gied me awa. He shrugged. Mibbe it's jist as weel yon governor wisna on wi it.

The guardroom door banged open and Helen Spreul appeared.

John jumped up and stared at her white face. "Whit's wrang?"

"It's yer freend the meenister. He's deid. My John's jist tellt me."

A pale, thin faced man in worn clothes stood beside her. The governor was with them looking extremely displeased.

John stared at the three figures. "Hoo come?"

No one answered.

"But he's a young man an healthy."

John Spreul stepped forward. "Ay he wis when we got here but a place lik this has a terrible effect on folk, some worse than ithers. Lucas didna dae weel. I blame masel for no making mair effort tae help. If I had he micht still be here. He jist seemed lik ane o they folk as needed – "

"Lukin aifter." John couldn't stop himself.

The governor coughed. "The prisoners on this rock are luked aifter as best we can under difficult circimstances. Whit happened wis maist unfortunate."

John Spreul rounded on him. "That sir, is an understatement."

"This kinda thing has nivver happened on this rock afore. And nivver will again. Believe me the incident is bein thoroughly investigated."

John looked completely confused. "Whit happened? Wis he ill? Did he huv an accident?"

The governor went white. "He…Ane o the guards taen advantage."

"In whit way?" John persisted.

The governor didn't answer.

John Spreul glared at him.

The governor still said nothing.

John Spreul glared at him again then glanced at his wife. "It's no something I care tae say." He flushed bright red. "A guard interfered wi him. I think the richt word is buggery."

John closed his eyes and heard the governor say, "My captain saw whit happened. He intervened and stopped the attack. He wis aboot tae help the prisoner when the man dived oot the cell and ran awa screaming lik a banshee. The captain chased aifter him but he wis ower fast and ran doon the steps tae the landing stage afore he cud be caught. Next thing the eedjit flings himself intae the sea and gits swept awa."

"Is this true?" John opened his eyes and stared at John Spreul.

John Spreul nodded. "I didna see whit happened but I heard him scream. The captain came back aifter Lucas had disappeared and confirmed it aw."

"Whit aboot the attacker?"

"Safely locked up," the governor replied. "He'll be aff tae

Edinburgh on the next supply boat alang wi my report."

"An then?" John persisted.

"He'll get his just desserts. I hae a guid reputation as governor on this rock and I intend keeping it. Men stuck oot here thegither for months on end need strict discipline."

"So whit went wrang?" John Spreul sounded sarcastic.

"It taks ane rogue that's aw. But rest assured I'm dealing wi it."

"So ye say." John Spreul handed his wife a small packet. "I've written a fu account o the incident. I even had the captain sign whit I wrote. Tak it tae oor lawyer. Mibbe pair Lucas will get some justice that way."

"I dinna think so." The governor held out his hand. "That packet's going naewhaur. Ye're my prisoner and I decide whit gangs oot o here and whit disna."

"If I canna tak the packet I can still tell the story, ivvery terrible word," Helen snapped. "For God's sake governor, hae some peety? Surely ye can see there's nae excuse for whit that man did. It needs tae be tellt and tellt completely."

The governor flinched and studied his polished boots for a moment. "I shud hae sent him awa frae the start. I cud see he wis trouble. No a man ye cud tak tae. Face lik a turnip, piggy een, and nae ears. Said they were cut aff by rebels at yon battle at Bothwell. Ah'm no sae shair though. Didna seem much o a sodjer, mair a skiver. Been here three months and haurly done a hand's turn. The sergeant had him on a charge umpteen times for ignoring orders and gien lip tae the meenisters. He wis aye swearing at them or making a fool."

"Why ae ye telling us aw this?" Helen Spreul demanded.

"I'm jist tryin tae explain that Gumsy is raither unusual."

John suddenly realised what he'd just heard. "Did ye say Gumsy?"

The governor nodded. "Ay. Nivver kent his richt name. He aye answered tae Gumsy. Why? Dae ye ken him?"

"Naw," John lied. "It's jist sic a queer name."

The governor gave John a hard look.

John quickly asked, "Whaur is a body likely tae wash up?"

It seemed to work. The governor shrugged. "Depends on the tide and the weather." He frowned at Helen Spreul. "If ye want a wee while, private like wi yer man, weel, time is passing and the tide winna wait. I suggest ye go back tae yer man's cell and no waste ony mair time."

"It wis far frae a waste o time." Helen squeezed her husband's hand and looked as if she'd burst into tears. "Under the circumstances I think we hae something mair important than oorsels tae attend tae. I best git back and see if justice can be done for yon pair young man."

As they walked down the steps to the landing stage John was thinking about a morning before the Battle at Bothwell when a renegade by the name of Gumsy was caught stealing from the ministers' baggage. The fuss that followed had ended with the man's ears being cut off as a punishment. It was a horrible memory. And that name. And no ears. It was too much of a coincidence. It had to be the same man.

The governor and John Spreul accompanied the two visitors right to their boat and waited while they boarded it. "Richt." He signalled to the guide to cast off then turned to John Spreul. "No the best o visits?"

"No," John Spreul admitted. "But there will be ither times."

"Only if I say so." The governor spoke slowly. "Did ye really expect me tae alloo yer ain accoont tae go onywhaur withoot me reading it and approving? Ye micht hae important freends oot there willing tae pick up whit ye say and run wi it. Jist mind they're oot there. Ye're here and likely tae bide that way."

John Spreul didn't answer but stood watching his wife sail away.

The governor and John Spreul remained silent while they made the difficult climb back up to the garrison. At the top the governor shouted for a guard to take John Spreul back to his cell. "And whaur's Melville?"

"Here sir." His captain appeared.

The governor pointed to the door of his order room. "I need a word in private."

The captain marched into the sparsely-furnished room and stood by the well-scratched table that the governor used as his desk. It was piled with papers, books, files, all in neat order for Governor Walkinshaw for a meticulous man with all his paperwork up to date. Now his expression showed worry and confusion.

He stood staring at his overloaded table then at his captain. "Hoo did I miss oot on that scumbag?"

The captain looked puzzled. "I cud hae tellt ye frae the stert."

"Cud ye noo?"

"Onybody lukin at Gumsy can see he's evil. It's written aw ower him plain as day."

"And somehoo I didna see it."

"So it seems sir. Raither unfortunate as it turned oot."

Walkinshaw glared at his captain. "I certainly didna like the luk o the man but classing him as evil aifter yin glance is a bit strong. I read the reports aboot him. No guid. But I've seen worse, and when he arrived we were a few men short wi nae mair likely tae appear in the near future."

"Ye'd nae option sir. Ye'd the runnin o the garrison tae conseeder. Ah'm no blamin ye, ah'm jist sayin. Ah thocht Gumsy wis worth the watchin an ah've been keepin an ee oot. Jist as weel ah did. He micht hae killed yon pair young man."

"As guid as." The governor shook his head slowly. "And noo I've the garrison's reputation tae conseeder as weel as seeing that renegade gits his just deserts." He stared at one particular pile of papers, shuffled them then laid John Spreul's packet on top before turning to his captain. "Why did ye sign Maister Spreul's accoont o whit happened tae the meenister? Did ye no think aboot the damage it cud dae siding wi a prisoner? That kinda going on maks us luk lik prize eedjits. Christ man, I'll be lucky tae remain in service, nivver mind still be the governor aifter this gits oot."

"It'll come oot onyway, sir. The hale rock's buzzin wi it. The ither meenisters talk aboot naethin else. Somebody's sure tae slip word tae the first boat as comes in. Is it no better for it tae be the richt story, carefully written by a prisoner wi naethin tae hide? As far as ah can mak oot Maister Spreul's a weel respectit man. Thur's naethin in his words that blames ye or us. He jist described whit happened."

"And he wis only able tae dae that aifter ye gied him ivvery detail."

"An it's aw true. Ah only tellt it as it wis. Ah've seen mony a thing in ma time but that taen ma breath awa. Ah near spewed at the sicht o Gumsy astride yon young man, pumpin awa as if his life depended on it. Ah didna enjoy describin it tae Maister Spreul an ah dinna think he enjoyed hearin, nivver mind writin it doon. If yer report says the same it'll staund ye in guid stead."

"Hoo come?"

"Weel sir, when ithers git haud o the story they'll add thur ane bit an mair. Afore ye ken whit's happenin the hale thing micht be oot o haund. Wud that no be worse? Thur's nae disrespect intended tae yersel, sir. Ye've aye been fair wi me. The men think the same. If ah wis ye ah'd alloo Maister Spreul's letter tae go tae yer maisters alang wi yer ain on the maitter."

The governor frowned and sat down.

"Luk sir, hoo can yer maisters blame ye for whit happened when they expect ye tae run this place wi hauf the troops ye need? Bein picky aboot whae ye tak on as a guard disna come intae it. Ye shud remind thur lordships hoo difficult it is. As fur an animal lik that. Hoo wur ye tae ken whit he'd dae? "

The governor frowned again. "He needs tae hing, naething surer."

The captain nodded. "If yon pair laddie hudna flung himself intae the watter richt noo he'd be aff his heid an a jibberin eedjit fur the rest o his life. Ye didna see his face, his een. Ah did. It's an awfy business but play it straight sir an ye'll be seen for the man ye are." The captain ran out of breath and a long silence grew between the two men.

Eventually Walkinshaw sighed. "Richt then Melville, ye've said yer piece and I've listened."

"Ah meant ivvery word, sir."

"Richt then, on ye go and mak sure there's nae slip up in guarding Gumsy. He's tae bide locked up, chained tae the wall nicht and day. Nae exercising, nae fresh air, nae nuthing. Mak sure naebody speaks tae him. No a word. We'll need tae feed the bugger but nae mair than basic rations. And see that ony food's slipped roond the door and jist left near him. We tak nae risks till he's on the next supply boat and awa tae the Tolbooth in Edinburgh."

"Ay sir." The captain saluted.

John remained silent as they set out on the boat journey back to the shore, his expression warning Helen Spreul and the guide to leave him be. Not that she knew what to say.

She was also worried about her husband. He didn't look well and his damaged foot would need extra strong salves and clean bandages if it was ever to heal. She'd have to make up what he needed and have it sent out as soon as possible. Then there was the business to protect before the law claimed everything as would surely happen. Thank guidness John's ships are baith based in Holland, that should save them frae they greedy lords whae see a prisoner's property as fair picking. First I need to visit oor lawyer Henry Vance, see if he can progress some justice for Lucas Brotherstone. Aifter that anything moveable and valuable must disappear.

She was so engrossed in her thoughts that she barely heard John say, "He didna deserve that."

The guide paused in his rowing. The brief change in the oar movement alerted Helen that John was speaking to her.

She leant forward. "Forgive me. I'm being selfish and thinking aboot my ain problems. I'm sorry but I dinna ken whit tae say aboot yer freend's death ither than I canna think o onything worse."

John sighed. "Ay. But there's mair. Ah ken yon Gumsy. Ah've met him afore."

"Whit?"

John nodded and told her the story of Gumsy's thieving at Bothwell and how his ears were cut off.

Helen listened then said, "Whit ye've tellt me cud nail the deil. Bad as his crime is he'll only serve a few years and be oot again. This evidence micht change everything."

"Hoo?"

"Think aboot it. Fighting as a rebel is a crime in itsel but chainging sides and kidding on he's something else, tae tak on guarding the kind o men he'd been fighting alangside, weel that soonds lik treason."

"But hoo can ah dae onythin aboot it?"

"By using the law."

"But ah'm on the wrang side o it masel."

"If I tak yer evidence tae oor lawyer Henry Vance he'll mak sure it reaches the richt ears. If ye write it doon as best ye can and sign it and I counter sign it micht be enough for yer freend tae git a chance o proper justice."

"Ah'd like that."

"Richt. When we git back tae North Lodge I'll ask oor host for pen and paper. It shudna be a problem. He seems mair than willing tae accommodate us."

"An he said he's a freend o James McAvoy. If need be ah'll remind him." John lapsed into silence again, this time thinking about the words he should use against Gumsy. It felt like he was doing very little and too late. But at least it was something.

The Privy Council was due to meet in an hour. Mackenzie, the Lord Advocate, had time to read his letter from Governor Walkinshaw on the Bass Rock prison asking for advice on an unpleasant and pressing matter. Along with the request came the governor's report and one from a prisoner by the name of John Spreul. Mackenzie well remembered this man with his absolute refusal to accept the charge against him or be cowed by the great lords on the bench.

However, the reports reassured him. Unpleasant as they were the problem could be easily solved with a quick hanging. Mackenzie even wondered why Governor Walkinshaw had seen fit to bother him. A simple hearing before a magistrate would do.

As he was reading a messenger arrived with a packet from the lawyer Henry Vance. The covering letter indicated he was forwarding further, relevant evidence pertaining to a recent incident on the Bass Rock. In his role as guardian of the law the Lord Advocate might find the contents of interest. Since Vance was also John Spreul's lawyer the packet's arrival seemed more than coincidental and had Mackenzie spreading out the papers on a table to compare them.

The lawyer's evidence made him smile. It stated that the man, named as Gumsy, a serving guard on the Bass Rock, who'd been charged with assault, buggery and dereliction of duty, was also guilty of treason.

Vance was presenting this statement signed by a witness who believed he had proof of this treason. The witness had been a captain in the rebel army before the battle at Bothwell where he'd caught a man named Gumsy stealing from the ministers' baggage. The thief had been unrepentant and the witness then requested a whipping as punishment. The leader had gone further, ordering the man's ears to be sliced off as a permanent reminder of his crime.

Recently this witness had visited the Bass Rock prison with Mistress Spreul, and heard a full account of the guard Gumsy's attack on a young minister, Lucas Brotherstone. He'd further discovered that this guard had lost his ears. The name and the missing ears pointed to this being the same man as he'd encountered at Bothwell. The governor's description of the man confirmed his belief that the man had pretended to change sides, to masquerade as a loyal subject of his majesty. As such he must be guilty of treason.

The statement was signed by the witness *John Steel* and countersigned by *Helen Spreul*.

John Graham of Claverhouse and Jamie Ogilvie the earl of Airlie came into the room and found the Lord Advocate studying the papers spread across a large table.

"Is this for oor meeting?" Claverhouse asked.

Mackenzie glanced up and shook his head. "It's an unfortunate business waiting tae be dealt wi." He explained what it was then added, "I wis jist wondering if I cud use it as an opportunity. The Covenanters aye present themsels as holier than thou. If this traitor whae's ane o them can be presented as the very opposite it micht serve oor cause. Whit if he turns oot tae be the deil's acolyte, indulging in witchcraft as weel as aw this fornicating he's charged wi?"

Claverhouse's eyebrows rose.

Mackenzie nodded. "Sic talk micht fricht oor guid citizens and put them in mind o Major Weir. His case caused an awfy stramash a while back. It's still talked aboot. His goings on had folk luking askance at their so cawed betters. Ye see this Thomas Weir appeared tae be a paragon o rectitude till he wis uncovered as having his way wi his ain sister, ither women, even a variety o animals. Word got oot that sic an upricht, Bible quoting citizen wis also a warlock. Aifter that naething wud dae but he'd tae be dragged ootwith the city walls for a public burning. A wooden stake wis hammered intae whit wis left o his heart. The toon council even made sure that his ashes were scattered beyond the city limits then sprinkled wi quicklime."

"Whit dae ye propose?" Claverhouse seemed puzzled.

Mackenzie smiled. "Tae turn this treason on its heid and use the charge o witchcraft tae suggest whit micht lie below aw this covenanting piousness and Bible thumping."

"Soonds raither far fetched tae me." Claverhouse laughed. "Dae ye really think yer citizens are that gullible? Whit dae the reports say aboot this felon?"

Mackenzie seemed put out at this reaction and pointed at the papers. "See for yersel."

Claverhouse came over to the table and began to read. When he reached the witness signature he smiled, read the name again then called to Airlie who was waiting impatiently by the open door. "Jamie. I think ye shud tak a luk at this."

Airlie shook his head. "Coont me oot. I want naething tae dae wi ony devilish nonsense."

Claverhouse grinned. "Please. Indulge me. Ye'll no be disappointed."

Airlie reluctantly joined him and began reading. When he saw the witness signature he stabbed at it. "Hoo come?" He glared at Claverhouse.

"Perfectly possible," Claverhouse suggested. "John Steel wis at Bothwell. Ye ken that tae yer cost."

"And he's still free," Airlie spluttered, "stravaiging the country making a fool o us, the law, this very government. It needs tae stop. Hae I no said so often enough? Christ's sake, hoo is it possible for the likes o Steel tae visit the Bass Rock as if he's entitled tae, and speak wi the governor nae less? And him a man on the run wi a thoosand merks on his heid." Airlie lifted the paper as if to tear it apart.

Claverhouse quickly removed it and handed it to a surprised Mackenzie. "Jamie's pride has jist taen anither dunt. He's got a special interest in this parteeclar witness, ye see."

Airlie's face was bright red. "When I git haud o him."

"So ye say." Claverhouse ducked an angry swipe. "Ye'll need tae catch him first. Or mibbe it's time tae gie up on yer obsession wi the man. Did I no warn ye that mibbe ye'd met yer match in John Steel?" Still chuckling he almost danced towards the door then wheeled round. "Time for oor meeting gentlemen. Come awa and no keep oor esteemed colleagues waiting."

A few days later the Lord Advocate did try to use Gumsy as his scapegoat. First he was drugged then half-hanged to make sure he was unconscious and wouldn't struggle while he was dragged beyond the city walls and tied to a stake.

The burning went well with a large audience watching and sniffing the roasting flesh while Mackenzie stood at a distance and felt rather pleased with his idea.

As soon as the event was over Gumsy's fame took off. Many a howf and tavern resounded to his so-called exploits with man and beast. Many a joke was made and many a song sung but somehow few if any citizens ever made any covenanting connection. The Lord Advocate would be disappointed. Everyone seemed too busy fancifying ever darker and more heinous deeds, enjoying the fun of it all as Gumsy's wandering cock became a legend.

Chapter 10

John was glad to be going home. The past few days had been more difficult than he could ever have imagined. As for Lucas, he could neither think about what had happened nor let it go.

Helen Spreul was now on her way to Edinburgh with John's signed statement that Gumsy had been a rebel at the time of Bothwell Bridge. She'd promised to take the document to her lawyer and seemed convinced he'd make good use of it to gain some justice for Lucas.

The brief stay in North Lodge had been an experience, with its strange host who seemed to be a friend of such an important, upright citizen as James McAvoy. John nodded to himself. Ay, yon's a man tae be reckoned wi.

As for the Jamiesons, when he told them about Gumsy they'd hinted at ways and means of dealing with him. All this kept John going for many a mile. With no Lucas to irritate him or worry over he should have felt some relief instead of a growing sense of regret. But he couldn't get rid of it.

After a few, miserable hours huddled behind a thick beech hedge, John rose before daylight and pressed on towards the coming dawn and the little town of Biggar.

When he arrived, the stable was just opening. Juno deserved a decent feed and a rub down. He left her there enjoying a sweet-smelling nosebag and asked the lad about the best place for breakfast.

"Crown Inn, sir. Bottom o the High Street."

"Richt. Ah'll no be lang."

He'd almost reached the inn when a delivery cart drew up by the main door and the driver began to unload baskets of eggs, butter and two big ham joints. He stared. "Ritchie. Ritchie Wilson."

The driver whirled round and saw John. "Keep yer voice doon. Aboot here ma name's Archie Simpson. Onyway, whit are ye dain here at this time in the mornin?"

"On ma way hame frae a wearisome journey. It's taen a while

tae git this far. Ah'm tired, hungry an fair scunnered."

Ritchie nodded. "Weel met then. Ah can mibbe help. If ye dinna mind waitin till ah mak this delivery ye can come wi me tae Greenhill Hoose. Ah'm bidin there wi ma sister Sophie. She's hoosekeeper tae the miller at Thankerton. He's been locked up in Edinburgh fur giein Reverend Cargill a bed fur the nicht. Oor Sophie asked me tae help wi runnin the mill fur a wee while. Aifter whit happened tae me in Edinburgh ah'm in nae hurry tae gang back hame. Greenhill's no far oot yer way an ye'll git a decent breakfast."

"Soonds guid tae me. Ma horse is at the stable. Ah'll fetch her while ye're sortin things oot here."

Ritchie was waiting when John returned. "Tie yer beast tae the back o ma cairt an up ye git."

Minutes later they were at the bottom of the High Street, turning onto the Thankerton Road and heading for open country. During the three-mile drive to the farm Ritchie prattled on about the mill at Thankerton, how different it was to his own Abbey Mill, how he'd become a delivery man, how he was enjoying this new experience.

At first John nodded and listened. Finally he said, "Ma mither-in-law tellt me aboot Claverhoose speakin up fur ye in court an then suggestin ye owe him a wee favour, lik spyin fur him. She's richt worried aboot ye."

Ritchie flushed. "Oor Sophie must hae passed on the word. Ye ken whit sisters are like. Ah wish she'd kept her mooth shut fur the less as ken the better. Ah hope ye'll keep it tae yersel fur ah'm nae prood o it."

Ritchie's sister appeared when the cart clattered into the farmyard. "Ye've been quick this mornin." She stopped and gaped at John. "Whit are ye dain here?"

"It's a lang story." John smiled at her anxious face.

"Ay weel. In ye come an we'll see whit's whit."

Words bounced back and forth across the table while both men ate a huge breakfast. One seemed as embarrassed as the other as they shared their awkward stories, offered opinions and sympathised with each other over what might have been.

Eventually Sophie stopped them. "Ye cudna mak up whit's happened tae ye twa. Ane's as bad as the ither. Mind ye, ah feel for yon pair meenister." She shook her head. "But frae noo on ye baith need tae luk oot for yersels an think lang and hard aboot whit nixt. Ritchie has only himsel tae think aboot, but John, ye've a wife an family. Hoo is yer pair wife managin tae cope wi aw this?"

"No as weel as ah'd like," John admitted. "Ah feel fur her an wish aw this trouble wis by wi."

Sophie frowned. "It'll no be ony time soon. Thur's talk in the toon aboot the government tightenin thur grip on us aw. Apart frae nae mair backslidin in kirk attendance we've tae gie the curates proper respect as weel as takin an oath o allegiance tae the king. If we dinna dae as wur tellt it's the jail or worse."

Ritchie raised his tankard. "That's why ah'm happy tae bide here a while. Oot o a certain gentleman's clutches."

John raised his own tankard. "Jist mak sure that gentleman disna sniff ye oot. He'll no be best pleased at ye scupperin his wee scheme."

"We'll dae oor best," Sophie cut in. "Ritchie's got a new name an a story tae go wi it. Ah've tellt the folk hereaboots he's ma maister's cousin come doon frae Perth tae help run the mill till the auld man's oot the Tolbooth."

"Aw the same, watch oot fur Claverhoose. Ah hud a run in wi him a while back an ended up wi a heavy fine an a week in Lanark tollbooth. It wisna pleasant but ah think ah got aff lightly."

Ritchie's face went white.

"Ach, ye'll be fine." John pushed back his empty plate, drank the last of his ale then stood up. "That wis grand Sophie. Thank ye. Noo if ye'll baith excuse me ah'll heid fur Lesmahagow. God kens whit's been happenin while ah've been awa."

John came over the brow of the hill above Westermains and immediately pulled Juno into the shelter of the birchwood. Below he could see red jackets scurrying about the farmyard, driving his cows from their byre, opening the hen coops, even chasing the sheep from their pen to run onto the moor. All he could do was grit his teeth and stay hidden till the mayhem died down and the troopers left.

Even from a distance he recognised Crichton astride his chestnut horse, supervising the whole performance. He glared at the proud figure. Nae doubt Airlie's shoutin at Claverhoose aboot the need tae catch me. The grand commander will growl at Crichton, an then he'll tak his temper oot on ma pair Marion.

Eventually Crichton signalled for his men to give up their search and re-mount before galloping off in a great flurry leaving a cloud of dust on the farm track as the platoon headed for the Lesmahagow road.

Juno seemed to sense it was safe to walk on and began to pick her way through the ferns and onto the little farm path.

Marion must have seen the horse and rider approach. She came racing round the end of the farmhouse to grab Juno's bridle and pull John from his saddle. "Thank God." She hugged him and buried her face in his jacket. "See yon Crichton." She began to cry. "He enjoys tormentin folk an causin havoc."

"Ay weel." John held her tight. "Ane o they days it'll be the ither way roond."

She looked up at him. "It canna come quick enough."

He smiled down at her wet face. "It micht no be the morn but trust me it'll happen. An ken whit, he'll no like it."

"Ay weel." She refused to move.

After a few minutes he managed to ease back and lift the corner of her apron to wipe some of the tears. "Noo, wi madam's permission ah'll try an catch oor beasts afore they aw disappear."

Together they began to round up their scattered cows, then summoned Fly to deal with the sheep before they strayed too far.

John waited till supper was over and the children in bed before telling Marion about his journey to the Bass Rock. He spoke slowly, choosing his words carefully, missing nothing but not exaggerating. Marion sat very still, her face growing ever more white, although she neither interrupted nor asked him to stop.

Once he'd finished, she grasped his hand and simply shook her head. After that they sat in silence by the fading embers of the fire, watching how the gradually decreasing circle of light continued to keep the deepening shadows at bay, much like the real darkness that threatened their own lives.

That night he couldn't sleep for thinking about Crichton. Twice before he'd managed to make that cruel idiot look the fool he was. Both times he'd paid a price. A price worth paying. He began to think about possibilities, began to understand how dangerous it might be this time. And then he thought about the Jamiesons again. Ay. Yon twa brithers micht be the anes tae sort him oot.

Mibbe ah shud hae a wee word.

He began to relax, to slowly drift off. A plan could wait. Ay. And then he remembered Juno.

He sat up abruptly.

"Whit's up?" Marion woke with a start. "Did ye hear somethin?"

"Naw. It's Juno. Ken hoo ah've been keepin her at Waterside, weel awa frae they troopers' spyin een. Richt noo she's in oor stable. Aifter gaitherin in the beasts, an hain a guid meal, an playin wi the bairns, an then tellin ye aboot ma journey an pair Lucas."

"Ye forgot." Marion sighed. "So did ah."

"Whit if the troopers arrive again in the early mornin? Ye said thur back an furrit aw the time tryin tae catch ye oot. Crichton kens ma Juno an if he sees her?"

Marion's lip trembled.

"Nae worries. Juno's fur Waterside richt noo." John was out of bed grabbing his clothes from a chair. "Her an me ken the way fine in the dark. Done it often enough."

"Whit aboot ma mither? Ye'll fricht the wits oot her arrivin in the middle o the nicht."

"She'll unnerstaund when ah tell her."

"On the way back mind tae climb a bit higher an come thru the birchwood. Ye can hide amang the trees if onythin's happenin."

"Ah ken, Ah ken. Dinna worry."

Two hours later John was walking through the breaking dawn, enjoying the sweet smell of dewy grass that brought a cleansing to the day, while the dawn chorus of bird after bird added its own welcome. As he entered the birchwood a fat blackbird dived past almost screeching in his face. He grinned at the angry bird as it flapped among the branches then perched there watching him with its head on one side.

He nodded to the yellow-rimmed eye. "Apologies Maam. Ah didna mean tae disturb ye."

The bird ruffled her feathers, jumped into the undergrowth and disappeared. He listened and heard the sharp claws scuttle among the dead leaves. Wish ah cud hide as easy as that. Ay. An a pair o wings wud help as weel. He walked on feeling strangely happy.

A minute later his mood changed as he heard the familiar sound of drumming hooves in the distance. He hurried to the edge of the little wood and peered out to glimpse a flurry of red as a mounted platoon turned onto the Westermains track.

Once again he'd have to watch the farm being turned upside down.

John Graham and Jamie Airlie were travelling back together from a Privy Council meeting. It had been a stormy one with much arguing and debate over growing rumours of Covenanting support on the rise again.

The journey was proving equally difficult for Claverhouse with Airlie continually moaning about the lack of arrests in the south-west of the country.

"Cameron's deid," Clavers growled, "so's Cargill, alang wi a wheen ithers hanged at the Grassmarket. Ye saw them yersel. Withoot ony leaders the rebels are at a loss. It's taking time but we're getting there."

"That's no hoo I see it," Airlie disagreed. "We need tae move faster. No gie them the chance tae gaither again or find some ither preacher tae fire up their resolve. And whit aboot Steel? Ony progress in finding him?"

"I hear whit ye're saying and I'm surprised. Aifter aw yer years locked up in yon Tower in London as Cromwell's guest I'd hae thocht ye'd learnt the meaning o patience."

"Whit's that got tae dae wi onything?"

"I'm jist saying."

"Is that so. Weel let me remind ye I had aw the patience I needed and mair. I dinna deny I had ma ain difficulties aifter oor defeat back at Worcester. It wisna easy aifter ma capture but I didna gie up aince I kent the king had managed tae escape. That kept me goin, even though I wis locked up for ten years till his majesty returned in triumph, so dinna tell me aboot the need for patience."

"Weel done." Clavers sounded almost sincere.

"And it aw got better when yon so-cawed Lord Protector Cromwell got his comeuppance wi an execution and his heid stuck up on a pole."

"I doubt the great man wis much bothered since he'd been deid for three years and needed digging up for the event."

Airlie glared at him. "Justice wis seen tae be done."

"Is that whit's bothering ye aboot Steel?"

"Steel is aw aboot – "

"Yer dignity," Clavers grabbed his chance. "Or mibbe mair aboot the loss o it."

After that they rode on in silence, resentment humming between them till they reached the little town of Biggar.

Clavers signalled for their escort to stop then turned to his companion who was still scowling. "Hoo aboot some dinner? Wud that put a smile back on yer face?"

"Whitivver." Airlie refused to be drawn.

Behind Airlie his captain spoke up, "The men wud appreciate a wee break, sir."

"Richt." Clavers looked over his shoulder and winked at the captain.

"I seem tae mind ane at the bottom o the High Street. Will I check it oot, sir?"

"We'll aw go," Clavers replied. "Nae point in wasting time."

A few minutes later the mounted group stopped in front of the Crown tavern and drew a fair amount of attention.

The men dismounted as a delivery cart pulled up behind then veered into the road and took off again. Clavers caught sight of the driver, then turned to Airlie's captain. "Git a man tae follow yon cart. See whaur it goes then come back and report tae me, only me."

Instead of issuing this order, Dominic McCann took on the task himself.

The loaded cart had already pulled into the yard of Thankerton Mill. McCann stopped at the entrance and saw how the driver still sat in the driving seat. He edged his horse forward. The driver heard him approach and turned.

"Weel I nivver. Whit are ye dain here?"

Ritchie Wilson jumped as if stung. He turned and gasped at the sight of McCann. His face was ashen. "I'm jist helpin oot here. Dain a favour for a freend."

"When ye shud be at yer ain mill in Lesmahagow. Dae ye no

ken me, man? Dae ye no mind me speakin up for ye?"

Ritchie's shoulders slumped. "Ay sir. Ah wis gratefu that ye believed ah hudna drapped yon sack on yer heid. No that onybody else said a word in ma defence."

"So why is my commander interested in ye? He saw ye back there in the toon and sent me tae find oot whaur ye were goin."

Ritchie began to tremble. "Claverhoose spoke up fur me at the court in Edinburgh an then wantit some pay back. He's expectin me tae spy for him."

McCann stared at the pathetic looking figure. "Is that so?"

"Are ye here tae tak me back tae face him?"

"No, no. Jist find oot whaur ye are and report back."

Ritchie gaped at the soldier.

"When I gang back and mak ma report the commander's likely tae heid oot here on a wee visit. I suspect he's no best pleased wi ye so mibbe ye shud mak sure ye're no here. In fact I'd suggest ye bide oot o sicht for a while."

"An whit wud be in it fur yersel, sir?"

"Naething." McCann smiled at the astounded expression then trotted away whistling to himself.

When Claverhouse heard McCann's report he took two men with him and rode out in high spirits to Thankerton Mill to find the place deserted and no sign of the miller. Very annoyed, he galloped back to town.

McCann was sitting by the inn window finishing his meal when the commander strode into the inn. A minute later an angry figure was looming over McCann's table. "Whae did ye send aifter yon cart?"

The captain looked up, his face respectful. "I went masel, sir. Did I no say? Ye sounded as if it wis important. Is onythin wrang?"

"There's nae sign o the miller or his cart. The place wis deserted."

"I'm sorry sir. He wis there."

Clavers gave McCann a long, hard stare." I ken ye're Airlie's man."

McCann nodded. "As his captain I obey orders and respect ma superior officers. That includes yersel, sir. Lik ye said, I followed the driver, saw him pu intae the yard. Aifter that I came back."

"Naething mair?" The commander's eyes scanned the captain's face. "Mibbe ye mentioned ma wee request tae Airlie?"

"Why wud I?" McCann held the commander's gaze.

"Ken whit?" Claverhouse almost smiled although his eyes were icy cold. "I'd like tae believe ye."

"Sir?"

Claverhouse didn't answer and turned on his heel.

McCann watched him go then took a long drink of his ale.

A few days later John Graham made a special visit to Craighead Mill in Lesmahagow. Gavin Weir was busy weighing the last of the week's grain when the commander strode in and banged the main door shut behind him.

Gavin jumped, then turned and almost froze at the sight of his important visitor. "Mornin sir. Whit can ah dae fur ye?"

"That depends." Claverhouse smiled. "I'm luking for Ritchie Wilson."

"He's no here, sir. Troopers liftit him aifter a wee accident a few weeks back in this mill. We huvna seen him since. They say he's been taen tae the tolbooth in Edinburgh."

"Is that so. And whit are ye daing here?"

"Ah'm his nephew, Gavin Weir. Ah've jist feenished ma apprenticeship an able tae keep the mill goin till ma uncle comes back."

Claverhouse stepped forward. "And when is that likely tae be?"

"Ah've nae idea, sir. We've hud nae word since he wis taen awa."

A gloved hand lifted Gavin's face and tilted it towards a pair of unblinking, grey eyes. They studied the young man's expression for a moment then the hand withdrew. "In that case I'll leave a wee message for Maister Wilson."

"But ah've jist tellt ye, sir."

"I ken fine whit ye said but I'll leave the message onyway. If ye happen to hear frae yer uncle or mibbe even see him jist say that John Graham wis here asking aifter him." Clavers patted Gavin's red cheek. "That's aw. I'll leave ye tae yer work. Guid day, Maister Weir." The commander walked out leaving a worried Gavin behind.

Rachael Weir gasped when she heard about Claverhouse's visit to the mill. "We best let Ritchie ken."

"An then whit?" Gavin asked.

"He gits awa as far as possible. Mibbe leave the country for a while. Plenty ithers huv done it."

"An if he disna?"

"He'll need tae think aboot playin the commander's game or becomin a rebel lik pair John."

"Uncle Ritchie canna go on the moor lik John. He's nivver done onythin lik that. As fur jookin aboot an hidin, he cudna survive."

"He still needs tae ken whit he's up against."

Gavin nodded. "If ah leave the noo ah cud be back in the mornin afore onybody notices ah'm awa."

"Whit's up?" John appeared in the kitchen door. "Ah wis jist ower seein tae Juno an heard yer voices. Apart frae soundin anxious ye baith luk as if the cat's deid."

"As guid as." Rachael turned to Gavin. "Tell him whit's happened."

John didn't seem surprised. "Claverhoose disna mak a guid enemy."

"That's whit ah thocht," Gavin said. "Ah'm aff tae gie uncle Ritchie the guid news."

"Let me go. Noo that Clavers kens whae ye are he's likely got a man keepin an ee on ye. Likely he kens ye're here."

"But ah bide here." Gavin frowned.

"Ay, that's expected. But whit aboot goin oot ontae the road an turnin the wrang way?"

"Ye'd be seen jist as easy an ye're a named rebel."

"Naebody will ken onythin if ah gang alang the burn then cut across the fields."

"Ah cud dae that."

"Ay." John admitted. "Whit ah'm sayin is ah'd like tae go. Git awa fur a wee while. The troopers are dementin us wi constant visits at Westermains, searchin ivvery corner ower an ower. Ah've been on the moor the last few days in case they arrive unexpected like."

"They seem determined tae catch ye," Rachael said.

"No as determined as me tae bide free. A ride ower tae Thankerton wud pit me elsewhaur fur a wee while. Marion wudna huv tae worry aboot me bein caught unawares an ah'd be dain Ritchie a guid turn. Whit's wrang wi that?"

Rachael nodded.

Gavin frowned. "Hoo is it ye aye git yer ain way?"

John grinned. "As if. C'mon, jist indulge me."

John went back to Westermains and told Marion his plan. Instead of arguing she surprised him with another suggestion. "Whit aboot the news ye're waitin on frae Maister McAvoy? He's mibbe hud word frae the lawyer whae's tryin tae sort oot some justice fur pair Maister Brotherstane. Mibbe ye shud travel on tae Glesca aifterwards?"

"Are ye wantin rid o me?"

"Quite the opposite. But ye ken yersel hoo Crichton's nose is itchin tae catch ye. The thocht o it's tormentin him somethin terrible. He's aboot that often ah'm feart he micht catch ye unawares."

"Richt then. Mibbe ah cud bide a nicht at Greenhill then ride on tae the toun." The familiar sound of hooves stopped him from saying any more. With a quick kiss he was out the door, across the yard, past the byre, up the path to the birchwood and heading for Waterside to collect Juno.

"Whit shud ah dae?" Ritchie wailed when he heard the commander's message.

"Sit ticht but be carefu, very carefu," John said. "Ye're a wheen miles frae Lesmahagow. Mibbe far enough fur Clavers tae gie up on ye."

"Whit if he disna an comes aifter me?"

"Forewarned is forearmed. Ye disappear at the least sign."

Ritchie glanced at his sister then John, but said nothing.

Chapter 11

John stayed overnight at Greenhill House then set out for Glasgow as planned.

If James McAvoy was surprised to see John he didn't show it as he gently steered him into his private sitting-room. "Richt." He pointed to a chair by the usual roaring fire. "First things first. Sit doon. Whit I have tae say can wait a few meenits." He rang the little silver bell balanced on the arm of his armchair and ordered food for his guest.

Ham and cheese, along with a tankard of ale, appeared like magic. McAvoy waved the tray of food over to John. "Eat up then we'll talk."

"Considerate as ivver. Thank ye." John quickly cleared the plates then looked up. "Noo if ye please?"

McAvoy nodded. "The word frae Edinburgh is no pleasant but mibbe ye'll see it as a kind o justice for yer pair freend's suffering."

John cringed at the description of Gumsy's end. "Hoo come? A burnin? Is that no fur witches? Ah ken he wis evil, but aw the same."

"Gumsy's death wis supposed tae show that Covenanting folk are no the holier-than-thou as they mak oot. A bit lik Major Weir a while back."

John looked puzzled.

"He wis an Edinburgh cooncillor, richt weel thocht o. Aye quoting frae the Bible. On the face o it he seemed as pure as the driven snow till he wis uncovered as a warlock in league wi the deil. It caused an awfy stramash and he ended up burned at the stake. The Lord Advocate must hae thocht it wis a guid idea tae put Gumsy's story aboot and suggest he wis in cahoots wi the Covenanters and him the deil incarnate instead o a pair madman. It tells ye a lot aboot a justiciary whae's nae averse tae scraping the gutter when it suits him, especially when he organised a burning at the stake same as Major Weir. On this occasion he raither misjudged. Instead o turning the Edinburgh citizens against the Covenanters they saw Gumsy for the desperate craitur he wis, ripe tae become a terrible joke. Ivvery howf and tavern rang wi stories. Sarcasm wis the least o it. I wudna dare repeat some o the songs penned aboot him. Whitivver pain yon guard inflicted on Maister Brotherstone he mair than paid for it." McAvoy hesitated. "So far we've heard nae word aboot a body being washed ashore."

John studied the brightly coloured carpet for a minute before looking up at the old man's concerned face. "Mibbe jist as weel. Whit aboot John Spreul?"

"Still on the Bass Rock. Still protesting his innocence, demanding an apology alang wi his immediate release. The Privy Council are laughing at him, telling him tae pay his £500 fine or bide whaur he is. And so it goes on." James McAvoy sighed. "At least Mistress Spreul managed tae spirit her man's possessions and siller awa afore their lordships got haud o it. She's a brave and clever woman. She'll need tae be for the Privy Council seem set against the pair man."

John nodded. "She wis helpful tae me an ah wish her weel. As fur payin Maister Spreul's fine. Ah did think aboot offerin then realised a man lik that wudna thank me. He hus plenty money, cud dae it an nae miss it. It's the principle an guid luck tae him wi that."

"Anither thing." James McAvoy's voice hardened. "The Privy Council hae made it clear that onybody representing the country's legal government hae their lordships authority tae deal wi ony perceived deviation frae the law. Suspicion aboot onybody attending a field-preaching meeting cud mean a long prison sentence, transportation tae the colonies, or even instant death. Refusing the oath o allegiance tae his majesty brings the same. There's neither rhyme nor reason in whit's happening. Can ye imagine hoo some o they so-cawed law enforcers micht behave?"

John nodded. "I git the picture."

"As a man wi a price on yer heid."

"Ah need tae be careful."

"Indeed ye dae. And whit aboot yer wife and family? Dae they no deserve a better life; ane withoot aw this worry?"

John studied the pattern on the carpet again. "Mibbe ah shud tak them somewhaur weel awa frae aw this hassle. It's jist – "

"Yer roots are deep. I understand that. Yer faither felt the same. But sometimes – "

John glanced up. "Ay, it needs mair thocht."

"And mind ye're no short o siller. Whit I hae invested for ye continues tae grow nicely. Ye cud dae mony a thing. Go onywhaur. If I can advise ye, jist ask."

"Thank ye." John leant forward to grasp the old man's hand.

James McAvoy looked relieved. "Ye did weel by yer unfortunate freend and hae naething tae feel guilty aboot. Whit's happened is by wi. The morn's anither day."

John rose as if to leave then stopped. "If ye dinna mind, sir, ah'd appreciate a word wi the Jamiesons. If thur aboot that is?"

James McAvoy stiffened. "As it so happens baith brithers are awa on some business for me. They'll no be back afore next week."

"Mibbe anither time then?"

"Indeed John. And nae offence meant, but the Jamiesons' world is a kennin different tae yours or mine. In my line o work I need sic folk. I appreciate whit they dae for me and value them highly, but dinna venture intae that world masel. Be careful, for these men cud lead ye intae places ye micht regret."

John left for home with the old goldsmith's words ringing in his ears. What was best seemed obvious. Or was it? Would it really be the right thing to do? Where would he go? What about his farms, his land, his beasts, never mind the problem of finding a way to deal with Crichton? Emotion and logic kept up a fierce battle throughout the thirty miles home. Confusion was still to the fore as he approached the familiar fields and his beloved moor.

It was early evening, the air quiet and still except for the gentle rise of moisture from the grass with its hint of mist or even frost to come. Hardly a bird to be heard. Everything so peaceful it was hard to imagine the threat this place now faced. An me as weel, he admitted and turned onto the old drovers' road to try and avoid meeting anyone.

As John rode into the Waterside farmyard, he saw a trap sitting close by the house door. A man sat holding the horse's reins like a servant waiting for his master. John was about to veer round by the hay shed, then stopped. The man's back seemed familiar.

He edged closer and recognised Jonathan Meek, Sophie's

handyman. "Jon. Whit are ye dain here?"

The man turned and pointed towards the house. "Mistress Sophie best tell ye."

John blinked but didn't press further. He jumped down from Juno and took her into the stable. "A meenit lass an ah'll be back tae sort ye." He hurried over to the farmhouse and into the kitchen.

Gavin, his wife Janet, Rachael and Sophie Weir sat at the kitchen table. The room was half dark. No lamp was lit. The fire was almost out. No one spoke. No one moved.

"Whit's wrang?" John broke the shadowy silence.

Sophie looked up and John saw a pair of eyes red-rimmed and wet with hours of tears. "Whit is it?" His voice dropped almost to a whisper.

"Ritchie's deid. Shot in ma kitchen, sittin at the table same as we're dain the noo. It happened a few hoors aifter ye left fur the toun. A platoon arrived an burst intae the hoose withoot a by yer leave. The yin leadin them, ah think he wis a captain, kent whae he wis aifter. Somebody must hae tellt an here ah wis thinkin the folk roond aboot believed ma story aboot Ritchie bein ma maister's cousin. This captain nivver said a word jist marches up tae Ritchie, yanks him aff his chair an presses the nose o his pistol hard against his heid. Before ony o us cud say a word or dae onythin the pistol went aff. The noise an smoke blasted roond the kitchen an near deafened us as pair Ritchie jerked up in the air then fell furrit wi his brains an blood spreadin in a puddle across ma clean-scrubbed table. Ah didna scream nur move. Ah cudna." Sophie gulped and closed her eyes. "Mind hoo ye said tae watch oot fur Claverhoose?"

"Claverhoose shot Ritchie?"

"Naw. But as guid as. Whae else sent yon captain? Worst o it wis he enjoyed whit he did; that fu o himsel."

John nodded and guessed who this must be.

"He tellt us he wis here tae let Ritchie Wilson ken hoo he'd let the great man doon. Aifter that the troopers jist walked oot again an galloped awa leavin us tae try an believe whit had happened."

John sat down beside Sophie and held her hand while she wept. After a while he turned to the others. "Ah've jist come frae the toun whaur ah learnt that frae noo on onybody conseedered suspect by the government is fair game fur ill treatment. Luks lik Ritchie wis ane o the first tae suffer frae this new rule."

"Whit's tae be done?" Gavin's voice trembled.

"Apart frae buryin yer uncle we need tae be mair vigilant oorsels an hope this kinda terror disna last."

"Ah wis mair thinkin aboot fightin back." Gavin sounded resentful.

"Wur ower far doon the line fur that." John rounded on him. "Us against as mony weel armed law enforcers. They jist keep comin. Mair an mair o them."

Gavin's lips clamped shut, but he looked defiant.

Sophie pushed back her chair and stood up. "Ah best git back. Greenhill's in an uproar. Ah'll no be surprised if ma workers huv run awa." She pulled her shawl tight round herself. "Jo will drive me back an help me see tae Ritchie. Ah'd like tae bring him here, see him buried at hame whaur he belangs."

Rachael gave her sister a hug. "Everythin will be ready fur him."

Sophie sniffed her thanks and bustled out to the waiting trap.

Minutes later the horse and trap was trotting down the track with three shocked faces staring after it.

Finally Rachael turned to John. "Can ah leave ye tae tell Marion?"

"Ay."

"Richt," Gavin said, "ah'll gang intae the village an see aboot gittin a hole dug in the graveyard an ask aboot somebody willin tae tak the funeral."

"Ah'll see tae Juno then git awa." John gently squeezed Rachael's hand. "Onythin ah can dae jist ask."

"Ay," she sighed. "Jist tak care yersel."

As John walked across the yard to the stable the cold evening air hit him like a punch, reminding him of James McAvoy's words.

Chapter 12

Marion's reaction to Ritchie's death was more anger than grief, the same fiery spark she'd shown way back at the time of Lucas Brotherstone's first declaration against the government. A moment later it was gone, replaced by an almost haunted look as she whispered, "Whit if ye're nixt?"

"Dinna even think it." John pulled her close. She struggled at first then the trembling began, then enough tears to soak the front of his shirt. He waited till the snuffling stopped and gently lifted her face towards him. "Wud ye like tae be awa frae here, somewhaur safe? Nae mair Crichton an his platoon tormentin ye when he disna git at me? If that's whit ye want we hae enough siller tae dae it."

She blinked at him. "Whit aboot yersel?"

This time John blinked but didn't answer.

Marion pulled away. "Ah thocht so. An if ye bide we aw bide."

John hugged her again. "Ye're a defiant wumman."

"An ye're an eedjit John Steel. Whit made ye think sic a thing let alane say it? We've come a lang way thegither. Why wud we gie up noo? Nae way. Nae fur Claverhoose, or Crichton, or the government, or even the king himsel."

Next morning no troopers appeared. No need for John to high-tail it onto the moor or crouch in his secret, airless hiding place in the hall with heavy boots tramping past inches away while the house was searched. Had word reached the authorities about Ritchie Wilson's funeral? Were they waiting for that?

"Whit if they try tae stoap it?" Marion asked.

"Mair like hingin aboot tae see whae's there."

"Lik yersel?"

"An a wheen ithers lik cousin Davie. He's been on the wantit list since Bothwell same as masel. Mibbe ah shud warn him."

"Wud it no be best fur ye baith tae bide awa an bide safe?"

"Claverhoose nivver dis whit's expected. Ah'll tak a walk ower tae Skellyhill an see whit Davie thinks."

"Ye're a pair o eedjits, that's whit ah think." Marion banged the

110

plates down on the table. "At least hae some breakfast afore ye go."

It was a frosty morning. John's boots crunched over sparkling slivers of grass as he crossed the fields to Skellyhill farm. The cold air caught his breath, made him slow down and enjoy glimpses of blue sky where the rising swirls of mist were parting to reveal a few shafts of sunlight.

He stopped on the brow of the hill and waited as the view expanded onwards and outwards, all the way to the distant Tinto hill.

Below him the grey stones of the farmhouse began to glisten in the sun. It was a fine looking place, everything in order and a credit to David's wife. After Bothwell, Mary and Marion Steel had taken on much of their husbands' work; they'd had to when their men were often forced to hide on the moor or be captured. Claverhouse and his troopers had much to answer for but right now it didn't matter, not on such a grand morning.

His good mood vanished when he saw a man's figure squeeze out of a downstairs window of the farmhouse, jump the garden wall and race across the field that sloped towards the burn.

It was Davie. John was about to run forward when the leading horse of a mounted platoon charged out behind the long byre and galloped after the fleeing figure.

John shaded his eyes for a better view.

Crichton was leading the pack, beginning to gain on David Steel before he dived over the bank and disappeared through the tall ferns.

The steep slope forced Crichton to rein back as the fugitive landed in the water and began to stumble downstream towards the wider Nethan with its borders of thick bushes.

The trooper rode along, only feet above the figure stumbling through freezing water, sometimes ankle deep, sometimes almost up to his waist, or forced to climb over boulders or slide on mossy stones. All this slowed him down and seemed to use up extra precious energy. He fell several times as his struggling grew worse.

Crichton called out, "Stop. Surrender. Ye'll be weel treated. Dinna be a fool man. Stop!"

David Steel ran on.

Crichton called again.

This time the fugitive hesitated, took a few steps then stopped. Crichton repeated his promise.

David's bedraggled head slowly turned to stare up at the soldier. A moment passed then he nodded and threw away his pistol.

Crichton grinned. "That's it. Up ye come."

David crawled up to the waiting rider and stood there dripping and shivering as other troopers arrived to surround him.

"Back tae the farm," Crichton ordered, "We'll deal wi him there."

His young lieutenant winced at this but said nothing.

John climbed in the open window and crept to the door. Everything seemed quiet. No voices. No feet moving about. He took a chance and tiptoed along the narrow hall to the kitchen where David's wife was staring out the window.

"Mary?"

She spun round and gasped at the sight of him. "It's nae use John. Ye best git oot o here afore they troopers come back. They near caught Davie. He only got oot the back bedroom windae as they cam in the front door. He wis in bed. Ye ken hoo his chest bothers him? Weel this time he's been richt poorly. When ah heard the horses ah warned him but he wis ower slow. He wisna able."

"Ah saw them gallopin alang the tap o the burn aifter him." Before he could say any more they heard a harsh voice outside. Heard the order, "Prepare tae fire."

"No!" Mary Steel rushed out the kitchen, out to the courtyard to find her husband kneeling in front of a row of troopers, each with a loaded musket. He looked so ill, so beyond caring that she stood there staring, unable to speak, to plead or even show any defiance.

Behind the troopers loomed Crichton on his chestnut horse. "I gave ye an order. Git on wi it."

Muskets were raised. The troopers took aim, then the young lieutenant shouted, "Stop."

The troopers held fire.

The young man turned towards his captain. "Ah heard ye, sir. Ye promised fair treatment."

The men lowered their muskets.

Crichton stood up in the stirrups. "Of course I did. Hoo else wud the craitur surrender?"

"But ye promised, sir."

Crichton leapt from his horse. "Git oot ma way." He pushed his men aside, grabbed David Steel's hair and lifted the head towards him. Without another word he rammed his pistol against the grazed cheek and pulled the trigger.

David's head jerked sideways with the force of the blast that filled the enclosed space, then bounced back off the walls while a cloud of acrid smoke momentarily hid the executioner and his victim.

"No!" Mary ran forward as Crichton released his grip and allowed the crumpled body to drop. By the time she reached her husband he lay still, the only movement from a thick oozing of dark blood as it spread in a circle around his shattered head

The young lieutenant stared at Crichton. Crichton stared back. Behind them the men held their muskets and shuffled their feet as the captain stepped forward to punch the young man in the chest. "Dae that again and ye're on a charge."

He spun round towards the others. "An order is an order. Jist mind that. Noo mount up. We're feenished here."

Captain Crichton ignored the woman weeping over the figure spread-eagled on the cobbles and trotted his fine horse through the close entrance with the air of a satisfied man.

"Come on, lass. Intae the hoose." John tried to prise Mary Steel from her husband.

"Jist a meenit." She untied her apron and gently lifted the shattered head clear of the blood-soaked cobbles to slip the cloth underneath and slowly wrap it round. "That's better." She fastened the apron ties in a neat bow then turned to look up at John. "He wisna weel, John. Itherise they'd nivver hae gotten haud o him."

John didn't answer. He concentrated on steering Mary into the house then sitting her down.

Her face was white, her hands folded in her lap. She appeared completely calm. This disturbed John even more. He wanted to rush outside, find someone, anyone to help lift that awful body from the middle of the yard. Instead he forced himself to wait, to give the stricken woman time.

She didn't move. Didn't speak.

He pulled a chair alongside and sat down beside her. Many minutes passed. Finally she turned to John and whispered, "Cud ye mibbe help me bring Davie intae the hoose?"

"Least ah can dae." John stood up and they went out to the yard together.

"Richt." John positioned himself by David's covered head. "Tak his feet. Ah'll haud his shooders an try tae balance his heid."

Mary bent to grasp her husband's ankles. John saw her hands tremble and was tempted to say stop, wait till ah fetch help, but he saw her expression and began to pull David into a sitting position. The wrapped head nodded like a broken doll before coming to rest against his chest. "Richt." They lifted and between them they managed to keep the body more or less level. Mary took a step back. John came forward. They repeated this till they reached the house, to lay David Steel's body on the kitchen floor.

"Bide there while ah fetch a bed sheet." Mary hurried into the bedroom and came back with one of her best sheets. She opened it out then placed one edge against David's side. "Noo slide him ontae the sheet. Pu the ither edge ower then keep goin till he's richt inside. The linen's thick an strong. It'll haud firm while we lift him ontae the table." Her voice remained calm.

Together they heaved the white bundle onto the kitchen table then stood back.

"Richt, John, ah dinna want Davie left here on his ain. Will ye bide here wi him while ah gang intae the village fur help?" She shook her head. "Ah ken whit ye're thinkin but ye canna go. Yon captain an his platoon micht still be aboot. We dinna want anither happenin."

Before John could argue she was down the hall and away.

The ghost-like shape on the table reminded him of that first battle at Drumclog, when Gavin and Janet Weir had been forced to wrap their father's body before they could carry it away. If only? If only it could have been different then? If only it could be different now? The silence in the room was unbroken, not even the ticking of a clock, as he stood there staring at the window trying to blot out that picture of Crichton doing his worst.

Mary appeared in the doorway with her two sisters. She signalled for them to wait then came over to John. "The platoon's still in the village. Ye best mak yersel scarce in case they come back."

"Ay weel." John looked embarrassed. "Let me ken aboot the arrangements." He squeezed her fingers, nodded to the two horrified women and left the kitchen. Once in the hall, he headed for the little bedroom and back through the open window.

Marion wanted to go over to Skellyhill to comfort Mary. John found it difficult to dissuade her. They were still at odds that evening when Gavin appeared looking flustered. "Ritchie's funeral's sortit. At least ah think it is. Ah jist hope the troopers dinna interfere." He turned to John. "Ah heard ye wur in the middle o that business wi pair Davie."

Marion glared at John. "Ye nivver said?"

"A meenit can mak a difference. Ah didna want tae – "

"Worry me." Her voice rose.

"Whit aboot pair Mary? She saw ivvery thin."

"Whit if ye'd been a meenit earlier?" Marion sat down with a thump.

"Ah'd hae been runnin doon the burn same as Davie but ah wudna hae stopped or listened tae the likes o Crichton. Davie wis ower trustin, aye wis."

The first of December was a cold day to be out and about but Lesmahagow kirkyard was lined from wall to wall for Ritchie Wilson's funeral. The entire village seemed to be there.

When sheriff Meiklejon's appointed curate vanished from their village with a full quarter's pay the villagers had said nothing. Once he found out, he'd punished them by closing the kirk and ordering them to walk three miles to the next village and listen to an indulged minister each Sunday. The Weirs wouldn't want a man like that for Ritchie's funeral. Who would they ask?

A slightly built, fair-haired young man, dressed in sombre black and carrying a large Bible appeared on the edge of the crowd. He was accompanied by a tall, well-dressed, older man.

"Whae's that?" One of the mourners nudged the village shopkeeper. "Ye'll ken if onybody does."

The shopkeeper nodded. "The auld yin's Wylie McVee. Comes intae ma shop noo an again. Bides in Logan Hoose, oot by Birkenheid, at the end o the road afore the moor. Drives a braw horse an trap. Seems weel aff."

"So why bide sae far oot?"

"The farther oot the better if ye want tae be left alane these days."

"Is he takin the service?"

"Mair lik the young man cairryin the Bible."

"Ye mean the boy?"

The young man left his elderly companion and walked through the crowd to stand beside the rough-hewn coffin waiting by a freshly dug grave. He paused, bowed his head in respect to the occasion then looked up and nodded towards the rows of solemn face. "Friends, I'm privileged tae be here amang ye as we prepare tae commit oor brither's mortal remains tae the earth, comforted in the knowledge that oor Sovereign Master and Lord has gathered him safely into his loving arms." The face might be young but the tone and words carried all the weight of the occasion.

The prayer and eulogy that followed gave Ritchie a kind and thoughtful send off with just the right amount of defiance to stir the listeners against the perpetrators of this victim's death, as well as a strong reminder that resistance was the only way forward.

Standing among the crowd, John Steel watched and listened to every word. He couldn't help but be impressed as well as feeling a cold shiver. There seemed to be more than a little of Lucas Brotherstone and Richard Cameron about this young stranger.

Once the committal was over the young man prayed on his own then rejoined Wylie McVee who led him among the crowd. He took his time, shaking a hand, having a word, giving a smile, being well received. When he reached John he offered a firm handshake and a direct yet friendly look. "James Renwick frae Moniaive. I've jist completed my studies in Edinburgh, noo ready tae serve my fellow man. I hear ye've been active in the cause and hae suffered much as a result. I'm pleased tae meet ye, John Steel"

"Whae tellt ye?" John sounded defensive.

"Several folk. Ye're weel thocht o." Renwick hesitated. "I'm hoping we micht hae mair tae discuss. But this is no the time nor the place."

There was a loud shout. "Troopers are comin."

James Renwick was hustled away. Everyone scattered.

John Graham had just ridden back from yet another Privy

Council meeting. This time the wrangling among their lordships, along with their show of animosity to himself, had annoyed him more than he'd care to admit.

Their lordships seemed to see Clavers as an upstart, seemed unwilling to accept that his only aim was to serve the crown as best he could. Indeed, he'd challenged them both privately and publicly, hinting how his favour with the king's brother came from real effort and honest discussion, not from any toadying. "Ye dinna like tae see onybody bar yersels receiving ony acknowledgement?" He'd thrown that at their lordships and they hadn't liked it. Unfortunately the moment's pleasure it brought was nothing compared to their continual criticism of his governance. The south-west was his domain. He knew how things were, how to maintain law and order in a particular way. The people might not like it but they understood the consequences and most were likely to try and avoid trouble for themselves or their families.

Their lordships would have none of it, couldn't see that fear of the unknown was more of a threat than direct action They were set on making examples, the more dramatic and violent the better. The votes about future policy had gone against Claverhouse yet again.

What with his instructions from the Privy Council and a rain soaked journey, he was not in the best of moods when he finally arrived at the garrison. All he wanted was a decent meal and his bed and here was one of his young lieutenants waiting to ask for a private word.

"In here Mulveen and let's hear ye."

The young man stood to attention as Clavers kicked off his boots and settled himself beside a roaring fire. The commander let him stand a few minutes then turned and nodded. "Weel?"

"It's Captain Crichton."

"Whit aboot him?"

"He's abusin his authority."

"Is he indeed?" Clavers stiffened. "That's a serious accusation young man. In whit way?"

Mulveen hesitated. Red faced he blurted out, "The captain plays wi the truth for his ain ends."

"And whaur hae ye been these past few year? He's no alane in that. If ye dinna ken that ye're a slow learner, son. Mibbe ye cud be mair precise?"

"Twa examples, sir. We went ower tae Thankerton aifter the miller as per yer orders. The captain burst intae the hoose, marched up tae the man an shot him. Nae questions asked. He did it that quick ah wisna even sure if he'd shot the richt man."

Clavers studied the earnest face. "And?"

"Yesterday at Skellyhill we gied chase aifter the rebel David Steel. He wis runnin doon the burn makin for the Nethan. The captain thocht he wis gettin awa an shouted if he gied himsel up he'd be weel treated."

"And?"

"The man believed him an surrendered. The captain didna keep his word. When we taen the prisoner back tae his farm he wis forced on his knees then shot in the heid. The captain seemed tae enjoy it."

"I see."

"Baith men are deid withoot bein arrested let alane goin afore a proper judge. Surely us troopers are no meant tae ride the land abusin folk on a whim or killin them withoot guid reason?"

Clavers turned and stared into the flaming fire. Since the vote in the Privy Council had gone against him this was exactly how it was. How could he even reprimand the likes of Crichton?

Behind him Mulveen waited for an answer.

"Weel young man, I hear whit ye're saying and I appreciate yer concern for whit micht be conseedered the niceties o keeping law and order in difficult times. I'll grant ye that Captain Crichton is no an easy man tae get on wi, nor is he a man inclined tae gie quarter. I'll also concede that his values seem tae be at odds wi yer ain. Ye seem tae be suggesting that the captain's way o going aboot whit he conseeders his duty is causing ye a problem. Aw I can say is, ye're entitled tae yer opeenion but listen tae me and listen weel. The Privy Council wants things done this way. They've jist passed a law approving sic behaviour against each and ivvery man or woman deemed tae be an enemy o the state. The vote wis decisive so whae am I or ye tae argue or dae itherwise?"

Mulveen gaped at the commander. "Whit aboot abuse thru lies? The captain said ane thing an did anither."

"Can ye prove it?"

"Ah heard the captain's words loud an clear."

"Is onybody willing tae back ye up?"

Mulveen's face went bright red.

"I thocht so." Clavers smiled. "Ane mair thing afore ye go. Conseeder whit I said and if it disna sit weel, I'd advise ye tae think aboot anither career; ane whaur ye'll hae less bother wi yer conscience."

Mulveen saluted and left.

Mary Steel wanted David's funeral to take place late afternoon. This way she hoped to escape the notice of the authorities and see her man buried without interruption.

She also asked if the young man who'd done the honours for Ritchie Wilson could be persuaded to do the same for her Davie. A message was sent to Logan House where James Renwick was said to be staying and a swift reply came back accepting the invitation.

Yet again the whole village turned out and David Steel had as fine a funeral as Mary could have wished. The fading light added to the poignancy. James Renwick certainly excelled himself. No one left the graveyard ignorant of this particular rebel's sacrifice, nor why it cried out for further resistance against a misguided king and his cruel government.

James Renwick spoke so well, so convincingly, each statement and challenge backed up with just the right Bible reading. The effect was startling.

John came away feeling much as he had when he first attended the field meetings, excited by the preacher's interpretation of the word and keen to hear more. At least he was till he reached home with time to think about the result of all that enthusiasm. Back then he hadn't known what he'd trigger off, where it would take him. He did now. It was a sobering thought.

He was wrestling with this when Wull Gemmel appeared in the yard. Close as they'd been, looking out for each other through many a scrap, particularly during the battle at Bothwell, a coolness had developed while John was trying to steer Lucas Brotherstone from his path of self-destruction. Wull thought John unreasonable and had said so. Words were exchanged, words they probably both regretted although neither had apologised. Since then they'd avoided each other.

Wull took the first step. "Ah saw ye at baith funerals an realised hoo much ah've missed sparrin wi ye."

John nodded. "It's been a while. Come awa in an ah'll see whit ah can dae."

Once in the kitchen they both relaxed. Soon they were reminiscing, tormenting each other, repairing their broken bridge. Marion smiled at their nonsense and bustled about preparing supper. It was good to have Wull back in her kitchen. She enjoyed his company and he was good for John, even if he'd never admit it.

After supper the conversation slid towards the more serious. Probably they both knew this would happen.

Wull started it. "James Renwick did weel wi they twa funerals. He's a guid find is he no?"

John nodded.

"C'mon," Wull frowned, "whit aboot a bit mair enthusiasm. It wis as guid a sermon as ah've heard since – "

"Ye listened tae Richard Cameron," John cut in. "Ah shud hae kent whaur ye wur goin."

"Ah'm only sayin."

"Ah ken fine whit ye're sayin an ye're richt. Renwick's a guid preacher. But thur's a lot mair tae it than that. He's only young wi a lot tae see an learn."

"Lik whit?"

"Lik unnerstaundin meenisters that mak grand statements aboot resistance end up on the scaffold. A guid few hae been executed in the worst possible way. Thur deaths are a terrible loss tae us as care aboot oor Kirk but as far as ah can see keepin up the resistance is jist addin mair pain an mair sufferin fur us aw. Since Cameron's death at Airds Moss back in July ordinary folk are unner suspicion an seen as potential rebels, open tae ill treatment fur nae guid reason. Ah believe Richard Cameron wis a guid man, an honest man but a mite deluded in his ambition. Ony dealins ah hud wi him it wis aye ma way or nae way. Ye cudna discuss onythin let alane argue. Ah didna like that."

"That's a bit harsh," Wull challenged.

"Mibbe so. But ah saw that same man's heid swing frae yon deil Crichton's wrist. Back an furrit lik a pendulum in front o a gawpin crowd ootside the Sun Inn in Douglas. Maister Brotherstane wis alang wi me an the sicht o his freend's deid een starin at him wis ower much. He got it intae his heid that the starin een wur threatenin him wi damnation fur abandonin his duty. He went on an on aboot it. As for his ain end he micht hae been richt aboot bein damned. Whit happened still haunts me."

Wull blinked. "Ah didna mean tae upset ye. Ah wis jist sayin hoo James Renwick micht be able tae pit fresh life intae oor resistance afore it's too late."

"Ye dinna unnerstaund. It is too late. A mere remnant o whit it wis an nivver will be again."

"It disna huv tae be. Think aboot the fire in the grate, when it dies doon it can be teased back tae life wi wee kindlers."

"See ye an yer daft notions."

They both smiled then Wull said, "We've lost twa guid men an that's a sair knock but we've jist heard anither whae believes thur is a way furrit. Wud Ritchie an Davie want us tae gie up?"

"Ah dinna ken," John admitted.

"Will ye think aboot it?"

"Will that satisfy ye?"

"Fur the meenit." Wull left it at that.

After Wull had gone John sat on by the fire.

"Ah'm gled Wull came," Marion said. "Guid tae see ye twa behavin lik freends again."

"Ay." John nodded. "Ah missed him, even if his ideas huvna improved."

Marion laughed. "At least ye're speakin."

"Ah said ah'd gang oot wi him the morn. He's takin his cairt ower tae Kirkfieldbank wi logs fur an auld auntie."

"Mibbe ah cud come tae? A lift tae Kirkfieldbank wud suit me fine. Ah need mair cough mixture fur William. Ye ken whit he's like when a cough gits a grip. Ah cud walk up the brae tae Lanark an be back doon in nae time."

"Ah'll dae it," John said.

"It's safer if ah go. Aifter whit's happened ye need tae be mair carefu."

"Ah'll be fine. Ah ken whit ah'm dain."

"So ye keep sayin. Sometimes ah wunner if ye believe it yersel."

Chapter 13

Next morning John was up extra early. Marion seemed annoyed. "Ah suppose ye're meanin tae go wi Wull this mornin?"

"Ay."

She handed him a parcel of cheese and bannocks. "Pit this in yer pocket. It'll skite the hunger aff ye. Noo mind be carefu when ye gang up tae Lanark fur that cough mixture."

"Ah will." He kissed her cheek and was out the door before she could say any more.

"Jist as weel Ritchie an Davie are safely buried afore the frost got a richt grip." Wull struggled to steer his cart over the frozen ruts in the road. "Itherwise they'd huv tae wait. Nae chance o breakin intae the earth when it's as hard as this."

John nodded. "The watter in the beasts' troughs wis near solid this mornin."

"Road's likely tae be quiet. That's ane guid thing. Suits me fine." Wull glanced at John's strained expression. "If ye dinna mind me sayin ye're no yersel they days. Is aw that's happened gettin tae ye?"

"Ay an naw. On the run's no exactly fun but ah can cope wi that. It's Marion an the bairns. Whit thur puttin up wi isna richt. No that wur alane. Laird or commoner it seems tae mak nae difference. If we dinna dae as the great an the guid decree wur fur it." He sighed. "Sometimes ah jist dinna unnerstaund."

Wull siezed his chance. "If ye come tae the meetin at Logan Hoose in twa days time ye micht chainge yer mind. Folk frae aw roond the country are comin thegither tae support ane anither an mak a difference. Thur namin themsels the United Societies."

"An then whit?"

"If ye come ye'll find oot," Wull challenged. "James Renwick seems tae be involved. Ah think that's why he's at Logan Hoose. Ye liked him, didn't ye?"

"Ay. Weel enough."

"Mibbe a word wi him wud help?"

"He introduced himsel aifter Ritchie's funeral, suggested meetin up."

"There ye are then." As he spoke Wull's cart came over the hill and down towards the village of Kirkfieldbank.

"Thank God wur here," John laughed. "Ony further an ye'd hae me signed up tae whitivver this meetin's aboot." He jumped down from the cart. "Dae ye want a haund stackin the logs?"

"Naw. On ye go up tae Lanark. Ah'll be ready tae leave in aboot twa hoors."

John saw a young man walking ahead of him. Pleased to see a familiar figure he called out, "Archie. Archie Stewart?"

The young man stopped and turned round. "It's yersel Maister Steel. Are ye fur Lanark?"

"Ay. Haud on. Ah'll walk up the brae wi ye."

They walked on together and crossed the hump-backed bridge over the Clyde. Archie stopped to look over the parapet at the frozen river and point towards the first bend. "See the ice is richt across. Luks thick enough tae skate on."

"Ay," John nodded, "the curlers will likely be oot later enjoyin themsels."

Just then a man passed them and gave a quick nod before turning onto the narrow path that led to Mousemill.

"That yin gied us a funny luk." Archie frowned. "Since Bothwell ah try tae keep oot o sicht as much as ah can."

"An here ye are heidin fur the toon." John grinned at the boy's anxious face.

"Needs must, Maister Steel."

"Ah'm shair it's naethin. Onyway, the man's on his ain. We're twa. If push comes tae shove wur mair than able. Yon path goes tae the mill. Likely he works there. Nae worries, jist listen tae they craws." John pointed to the black shapes wheeling above the tree-tops further up the brae. "Thur tellin us it's a fine day."

The miller at Mousemill was excited. He'd just passed a man he'd recognised, John Steel, a named rebel with a thousand merks on his head – and here was a chance to claim it.

He rushed into the mill where his three assistants were loading grain sacks onto the delivery platform. "Leave that be," he gasped, "ah've jist seen a rebel on his way up the brae. He's worth a thoosand merks if we catch him. Thur's a young fella alang wi him. Ah think he's a rebel as weel."

"We split the money?"

"Ay, whitivver. C'mon."

The men dropped the grain sacks.

The miller lifted a spare mill rynd from the shelf above the big grinding stone. "Ah'll tak this jist in case."

"An ah'll tak this." One of the men grabbed a length of rope hanging by the door.

The four men hurried along the path onto the road and puffed up the brae to try and catch their quarry before they reached the town.

John and Archie had almost reached the crossroads at the top of the brae and were busy talking when one of the men sneaked up behind Archie and pushed him hard.

Taken by surprise Archie tripped and fell forward.

John spun round and struck the attacker full on the face. The man yelped and jumped sideways. As he did, the other three came at John. One went for his legs. Another tried ramming him full in the chest. John rocked back, grabbed the lowered head and pulled the straggly hair till the man's face was close enough to punch.

Archie was struggling to his feet when he saw the miller behind John, about to lash out with a length of metal. "Ahint ye John. Watch yer heid."

John gasped as the sharp end of the curved metal connected then dug into his scalp. Knees buckling, he let go of the man's hair and fell to the ground.

Two of the men used this advantage to knock Archie down again and tie him up while the miller and the other man began to kick John all over his body.

They were about to start on his head when the two men holding Archie yelled, "Stoap afore ye kill him."

"Nae maitter," the miller sneered and aimed another kick. "Deid or alive we git the money."

"He luks deid." One of the men bent over the still body. "He disna seem tae be breathin."

"Weel dinna expect me tae cairry him aw the way up tae the garrison." The other man glared at the miller. "We shud hae been able tae mairch him up easy. Cairryin. Coont me oot. It's ower far. An it's yer fault."

The miller became defensive. "Ah wis jist makin sure. Onyway whit's wrang wi leavin the body here while we tak the young yin tae the garrison. Ah'm sure the troopers'll lend us a cairt fur the body. That's whit ah caw easy."

"But whit if-?" The first man didn't sound convinced.

"He jumps up an runs awa? Dinna be daft." The miller appealed to the other three.

"C'mon, the quicker we haund ower the lad, the quicker we can claim the reward."

They all laughed.

Crichton was writing his daily report when the platoon sergeant came in with surprising news. "Four men jist brocht a young man in. They say he's a rebel."

"Hoo dae they ken?"

"No sure, sir. They claim tae hae killed anither yin. They say it's John Steel frae Lesmahagow."

Crichton almost choked. "Are ye sure?"

"That's whit they said. They want a cairt tae bring in the body."

Crichton pushed back his chair and hurried out to meet the four men waiting in the courtyard with their young prisoner. "Ye've killed John Steel?"

"Ay." The miller stepped forward. "It wis me recognised him. Ma freends helped but ah brocht him doon wi ma mill rynd. It's a heavy bit metal an felled him nae bother. We gied him a kickin tae mak sure. Ye'll see fur yersel. He's lyin by the crossroads at the heid o the braes. We'll need a cairt tae bring in the body. Ah believe the reward's worth a thoosand merks."

"The sheriff will only pay oot when ah gie him the evidence." Crichton turned to the sergeant. "Fling the prisoner in a cell an fetch a cart for these men. We'll gang doon wi them an bring in Maister Steel." Crichton couldn't keep the triumph from his voice.

John felt as if he was swimming through painful darkness towards a faint mist. He tried to reach it only to slip back into the dark. It happened over and over before he reached that mist. Once there the mist became a swirling circle of blue. He closed his eyes, waited, then opened them again. The blue seemed to steady a little. He tried again. The blue held. He blinked and stared then blinked again. It's the sky. Ah'm lukin at the sky.

He tried to lift his head. Every muscle screamed in his neck against it. He stopped. The pain eased and he lay there wondering if he dared try again. Instead he moved his fingers, so stiff and cold they felt like sticks. As for his toes they seemed like a distant memory.

Maybe it was the extreme cold that revived him. Maybe he was recovering consciousness anyway. Whatever it was he began to remember men, fighting, loud shouts, some sort of warning.

He managed to lift his head, tried to see more. All he could see were stiff stalks of frozen grass while above him black birds wheeled and cried. He watched them. Craws? Last time ah saw them they wur somewhaur else. He thought about it. Ay. At the foot o the brae. Ay. Ah met Archie Stewart there an ah spoke tae him aboot the craws afore we walked up the brae thegither. So whaur is he? He lay there trying to pull those snippits together.

Each bit came. Each clear and sharp, showing how close death had come. Even now he could almost sense its fingers reaching out. He shuddered. Think man, think. Whitivver it is ye need ta git oot o here. He stared across the sparkling frosty ground to the sky with its silhouette of tall trees. They trees are at the tap o the brae. Ah ken they are. Ah've passed them often enough. If ah git masel tae the edge o the bank mibbe ah cud slide doon an hide somewhaur.

Gasping with pain he forced himself to roll onto his side. The edge of the bank seemed far away. He forced himself onto his stomach, tried to crawl. His strength was gone. He gave in and rolled again. And again. Each time he checked the edge of the bank did seem a little closer. Sometimes the pain won and he'd pass out only to wake to the sharp cawing like a warning to keep going.

Eventually he reached the edge and hung his head over to stare down through the trees and bushes, all the way to a stretch of shining ice. It was a long way, steep and sheer. There was no way he could crawl down. No way he could stay where he was.

Nae choice, he decided. Ah jist let go an slide. One more roll and he was over the edge, turning over and over, whirling faster and faster till he hit a boulder. Winded and dizzy he hung there before somehow managing to turn and face down. The slightest push and he was off again sliding face first through the undergrowth, gathering speed, skiffing past some trees, bouncing off others as he whizzed on. The freezing air and icy grass stabbed at his face, knocked the breath from him. And then it was over as he shot onto the ice itself.

Upstream he could hear laughs and shouts. Just like he'd said earlier, people were out on the frozen river enjoying a curling match. He could see round stones sliding back and forward on the ice, men following, shouting encouragement.

If ah can see them, they can see me. Palms of his hands on the smooth surface, desperation helped him propel himself towards the opposite bank. The speed of arrival meant he was already more than half way across. Within minutes he was among the rushes. He lay there then somehow found enough breath and strength to pull himself onto the bank and into a huge clump of broom.

Once among the thick fronds, he flopped down and allowed darkness to claim him again.

"Whaur's John Steel?" At the top of the brae a disappointed Crichton was beside himself with temper.

"He wis here," the miller replied. "Deid as a door nail when we left fur the garrison."

"Ah dinna believe ye," Crichton snarled and flicked his riding crop across the miller's face.

"Steel wis here, sir," the other three men joined in. "Whit aboot oor reward?"

"Ye must be kiddin." Crichton swung the length of leather again. "Git oot o here afore ah dae somethin ye'll regret."

The men stumbled away, swearing and complaining but not daring to argue.

Crichton stood watching their retreat, then glared at his men. "Whit a waste o time. Back tae the garrison. We'll hae a word wi the young prisoner an see if he can tell us the truth."

"Nae need sir." One of the troopers signalled from the edge of the bank. "Ower here."

"Whit is it?" Crichton strode over.

The trooper pointed to a patch of flattened grass and fern spattered with dull red spots. "Heavy weight been here, sir. Luk hoo the grass is aw mangled. See hoo the frost shows it up."

"And?"

"Further ower, sir."

Crichton leant forward.

Below him stretched a long, white trail, scoring through grass and fern and small bushes, all the way to the bottom. Some of the debris was scattered across the frozen Clyde.

Crichton stared at the evidence for several minutes. When he looked up his face was tight with rage. "Like I said, back tae the garrison."

"So." Captain Crichton studied his young prisoner. "The men as brocht ye in said ye were alang wi John Steel."

"We walked up the brae thegither tae the crossroads whaur we wur attacked."

"And then whit?"

"Maister Steel wis fit fur them but ane came up ahint and hit him on the back o the heid wi a bit metal. He fell lik a stane. They kept kickin him aifter that. Kept on till he wis deid."

"Are ye sure?"

"It's no somethin ah'll ivver forget."

"There wis nae sign o a body at the crossroads. Whaur is it?"

"Hoo wud ah ken, sir?"

Crichton took a deep breath. "Whit aboot yersel?"

"Whit dae ye mean, sir?"

"On yer ain admission ye've been walkin wi John Steel. Weel these days keepin sic company is a serious offence, young man. A hangin offence." Crichton turned to his sergeant. "Lock him up for the nicht. We'll send him tae Glesca in the mornin and recommend a hangin."

"He's only a lad," the sergeant dared.

"And auld enough tae ken better."

The sergeant nodded and stepped back as his captain left the cell.

The heavy door slammed shut. The key turned in the lock leaving Archie Stewart in stinking darkness. Head in his hands he sank to the straw-covered floor and whispered, "Ye wur wrang, Maister Steel. It wisna a grand day aifter aw."

An old, white horse stood by the clump of broom. It seemed to sense there was something interesting within and reached over to rustle the top of the fronds. John heard and opened his eyes to see a shape looming beyond the tight tops of the bushes. The horse snorted. John managed to sit up and peer through the branches. A white, ghost-like face stared back at him.

"Bide here," John whispered. "Mibbe ye cud help me in a wee while."

The horse eyed him, then continued to stand beside the broom. Even after dark it was still there.

The clouds cleared and a silver moon appeared. As it rose, the soft light increased to light the field.

Richt, it's noo or nivver. If ah dinna move noo ah'll freeze tae death. He managed to crawl out beside the white shape. The horse seemed to have grown in size, especially the legs. He reached out and held a back leg to lever himself up. Once upright he was dizzy, too dizzy to attempt climbing on the beast's back. He sank down again.

The horse swung its head round. Its gentle, grey eyes studied the crumpled figure. "It's nae use," John admitted to the white face. "Ah canna reach yer back."

He turned to crawl into his hiding place when heavy boots crunched on the frosty grass.

A figure came closer. "God sakes, John. Whit's happened?"

John fell into Wull's arms as darkness claimed him again.

John swam through that mist again until he managed to open his eyes. He was in a neat, wood-panelled room, lying in a comfortable bed, covered by soft blankets. More surprising, Marion was sitting beside him.

He tried to turn and smile.

"Bide still." Marion leant forward. "Jist shut yer een an hae anither sleep. Ye're safe. Ah'm here. Naethin tae worry aboot."

John allowed himself to sink back into that mist then further on to a gentle, quiet place.

When John didn't come back from Lanark Wull guessed something had happened. He'd walked up the brae himself and heard the story flying from mouth to mouth about a wounded rebel being almost captured, only to escape from the troopers by sliding down the steep bank to the river and then disappearing. Someone even pointed out where it was supposed to have happened. Wull had listened carefully then stood at the edge of that same bank and looked down. Way below, on the other side of the river, he saw a large clump of whin bushes. Beside them stood an old white horse as if staring into the bushes. *An if ah'm richt.* Wull turned and hurried back down the brae to lean over the bridge and study the frozen field and the horse. There was no sign of any footstep crushing the white grass, no trail to follow. He looked again at the whin bushes and nodded to himself. *No the noo. Aince it's dark ah'll tak a luk.*

He was right. He found John almost unconscious and badly beaten.

Once he had his cart by the gate of the field, he loaded John into the back, covered him as best he could with a smelly old tarpaulin and headed to his own home at Brocketsbrae, safer than taking him to the farm where such a badly injured man would be easy prey when Crichton's platoon next called at Westermains.

He'd left John in the care of his anxious wife and hurried off to give Marion the bad news. "He needs tae bide wi me in the meantime. If ah bring him here an thae troopers arrive, whit nixt?"

Marion nodded. "Ye're richt, Wull. Thank ye. Withoot ye guessin whit happened, weel…"

"He's ma best freend, altho we dinna aye agree. Jist the same, ah'll no see onythin happen tae him. No if ah can help it. He'd dae the same fur me."

Marion gave him a hug. "The best freend ivver. Noo can ye wait till ah fetch oor Gavin's wife Janet tae luk after the bairns an then ah'll come back wi ye."

Marion's first sight of her unconscious man had scared her and filled her with doubt. But now there were signs of progress. There was still a way to go, but no matter, now she had hope.

Two days passed. Crichton couldn't stop thinking about John Steel's escape yet again. *Again.* The word almost choked him. Next morning he made sure that his search of the district took the platoon around the Lesmahagow area, and then close by Westermains farm. After that it was easy to have the horses trot up the track and into the courtyard.

Janet Weir was waiting on the doorstep as Crichton jumped

down from his horse and walked towards her. "Whaur's Mistress Steel?"

"Nae here." Janet folded her arms.

Crichton stopped and eyed her up. "And whae are ye?"

"Her sister-in-law, Janet Weir. Marion's awa visitin." Janet held his gaze. "She's in the toun. Whit's wrang wi that?"

"Naethin. If it's true."

"Why wud it no be?"

Crichton smiled. "We had word that Maister Steel met wi an accident at the tap o Lanark Brae the ither day."

"Ah dinna think sae."

"So, ye huvna heard that Steel wis attacked. Heid staved in. Reported as deid but nae body found. Is that no strange?"

"Soonds lik nonsense tae me."

They stared at each other then Janet shrugged again. "Luk sir, Maister Steel's been on the run since yon battle at Bothwell. If he's ony sense he'll be miles awa. His wife struggles on as best she can an noo she's hud word that an auld auntie's richt poorly an needin help. She's awa tae see whit she can dae. Ah'm lukin aifter the bairns, jist tryin tae dae a relative a guid turn. No that it's ony o yer business."

"The law is my business." Crichton turned to shout across the yard to his men. "Search ivvery corner." When he looked again, Janet was watching him with the hint of an amused smile. The child in him almost had him pulling a face and sticking out his tongue. Instead he treated her to another scowl and joined his men to begin the search.

Janet was trembling as she went back into the kitchen where the two boys were sitting by the fire. They looked scared. She smiled to hide her own fear. "Nivver mind that man, actin as if he's important. He's jist kiddin himsel fur we ken he's jist a big eedjit."

"Ma disna like him," William said. "Naether dis Pa."

Janet nodded. "Naether dae ah." She went over to the window and watched the armed men scurrying about the yard, in and out the sheds, the byre, the stable, even the privy. Aware of two sets of eyes behind her she tried to keep her voice steady. "Ken whit lads, we'll hae oor breakfast an no offer thae troopers a bite. They'll be ootside hasslin aboot gettin hungry while we're inside eatin. Hoo aboot that?"

Chapter 14

A week later John was sitting up enjoying a bowl of thick vegetable soup. His appetite was improving, his cuts healing, the purple bruises beginning to fade, although the star shaped dent on his crown was still a painful reminder of the mill rynd's sharp connection.

That walk up Lanark Brae had done more than almost kill him; it had almost destroyed his confidence. Time to think hadn't helped, especially when it took him back to that first morning when Lucas Brotherstone defied the law and not only triggered off his own rebellion but managed to suck John into a situation that became a nightmare. Fur whit? Pair beggar's defiance got him naewhaur. Same as Richard Cameron an Donald Cargill an ither meenisters as weel. Then thur's ma faither, his brither, Marion's faither, her uncle, an noo cousin Davie. God kens whit's happened tae pair Archie Stewart. An whit aboot aw the rest? Hunners mair, mibbe thoosands, either deid or loaded on a boat an shipped oot tae some far awa place tae become slaves. Ay. Fur whit?

An here's me near hounded tae death. Still ah shud be gratefu. Ah'm still here, still a step aheid o auld Airlie, and Clavers, an damned Crichton. At least ah will be when ah'm stronger. He sighed. That yin's aye ther or theraboot dain whit he dis best tae mak oor life unbearable.

He was about to slide back under the covers when he heard a tap at the room door. He peered over the edge of the blanket. Another tap then the door opened a few inches to show a blonde head. "John. May I come in?"

"Ay." John sat up again.

James Renwick came into the room and stood smiling at John's surprised face. "I jist wanted tae see hoo ye are for masel. Wull said ye've been richt poorly but weel on the mend noo."

John nodded. "Ah wis lucky that Wull found me."

"Indeed. Ye micht hae ended up as anither martyr tae the cause."

"Mair lik a victim o sheer greed. Forget the cause. Ah'm worth a thoosand merks. That's whit ma attackers wur aifter. They cudna care less aboot the Kirk, or folks' richts. Siller, Maister

Renwick, that's whit moved them."

"But surely," James Renwick looked set to argue then seemed to change his mind. "Wull tells me yer escape wis quite an adventure."

"Ane ah wudna care tae repeat. Slidin heid first doon a steep, frozen bank is no tae be recommended, especially wi trees an bushes an jaggy grass in the way. Mind ye, ah wis gled o the frost. If the Clyde hudna been frozen ah'd hae drooned."

"And here ye are making a guid recovery."

"Ay, an gratefu." John gave James Renwick a knowing look. "Noo that ye've seen me is thur onythin else?"

James Renwick nodded and sat down beside the bed.

"Ah thocht as much. Is it onythin tae dae wi a meetin ma freend Wull Gemmel wis on aboot? He seems greatly taen wi it."

"I'm glad tae hear it." James Renwick hesitated. "Whit aboot yersel?"

"Ah'm no sure."

"But aifter aw ye've been thru?"

"That's why." John's voice hardened. "The past three years huv been a struggle fur ma family as weel as masel. Whit ah've seen happen tae ma freends an ithers hus made me think a kennin different. Frae noo on ah think ah'd raither keep ma nose clean an see ma way thru these ill times as best ah can."

"Whit aboot yer commitment tae the cause? Ye fought weel at Bothwell. And whit aboot the support ye gied tae Lucas Brotherstone?"

"That's by wi. Ma commitment noo hus tae be based on reality. Frae this angle it's no lukin guid. Dis that answer yer question?"

"Ye surprise me."

John stiffened. "Nae offence Maister Renwick. Ye're a young man withoot the experience tae speak lik that. Ye dinna ken me ither than whit ye've heard. As ah see it ye've still a lot tae learn."

"Indeed, and willing tae dae so. Please, I meant nae offence. At least let me tell ye a bit aboot the meeting yer freend spoke aboot?"

John said nothing.

James Renwick hesitated then said, "On Wednesday there will be a meeting at Logan House. Aboot eighty men are expected frae different pairts o the country. They come representing aboot eight thoosand ithers, aw willing tae join thegither tae develop mair field preaching as weel as continuing the resistance against oor misguided king and his unjust government. We're naming oorsels the United Societies. Oor first action will be in a few weeks time when we mak a public declaration in Lanark, much like Richard Cameron did at Sanquhar."

John held up his hand. "The government conseedered Ritchie's declaration as treason. They taen ill against it an hunted him doon. He stuck up yon declaration on the anniversary o Bothwell Brig. That wis the 22nd o June. He only lasted a few weeks aifter that. By the 20th July they'd cornered him at Airds Moss whaur he put up an awfy fight. That wis only the start o the government's revenge fur aince they killed Cameron they made sure the rest o us suffered as if it wis oor fault. They'll dae the same again or worse."

"But we must," James Renwick insisted. "The words for the declaration are being worked on richt noo. We expect the new members tae gie it their vote."

"If ye dinna mind me sayin, ah've heard this fine talk afore an then experienced the result. Richard Cameron hud his moment. Ah dare say it felt guid at the time but he didna luk sae guid when ah saw his heid swingin in front o a crowd only hoors aifter it wis cut aff on Airds Moss."

James Renwick sat up straight. "Yer reaction is different tae mine. My determination wis set when I saw Donald Cargill and four ithers executed in the Grassmarket. I felt humbled by their sacrifice."

"Ye mean ye're willin tae dae the same?" John stared at James Renwick.

"Indeed. There's nae ither way."

The silence between them lasted several minutes before John replied. "Ye an Richard Cameron hae much in common. Ah dinna unnerstaund whaur ye're comin frae but ah dinna doubt yer sincerity or bravery. But count me oot. Dae whitivver ye must but leave me alane. Ah want nae responsibility fur the pain ye'll create."

James Renwick stood up. "Ye're entitled tae yer opinion but I believe ye're wrang. I had hoped tae include ye amang oor supporters, especially aifter yer suffering. Yer signature on the declaration wud encourage ithers. But there we are." He touched

John's shoulder. "I hope yer health continues tae improve. May the Lord be wi ye." He left the room, quietly closing the door behind him.

John stared after him and had a strange feeling of history about to repeat itself. First, Richard Cameron, then Lucas, now James Renwick. Flee low an flee lang. That's whit mither aye said. He closed his eyes and pulled the blanket tight against his chin. Dinna git involved.

On Wednesday Wull Gemmel decided to attend the Societies' meeting. When he returned from Logan House he told John what had been discussed. "The Lanark Declaration is on. It'll be a big occasion."

"Did ivverybody vote fur it?" John asked.

"Ah didna," Wull admitted. "Ah said ah wisna sure aifter whit happened tae Richard Cameron. They wurna pleased wi me. Thur's mair. James Renwick's no even twenty yet but the Societies are that impressed wi him thur sendin him tae Holland, tae some university, tae complete his divinity studies and become an ordained meenister. Anither twa young men are mibbe goin as weel."

John sighed and lay back on his pillow. "Ah dinna like the soond o Lanark. An trust me, aince James Renwick is ordained an comes back here he'll be set on further resistance. He's a fine young man but he's got that luk ah've seen afore." John sighed again. "A luk that means trouble."

Monday 12th January 1682 would develop into a stormy day and not only because of the weather.

At daybreak forty armed horsemen along with twenty determined supporters on foot began the ten-mile journey from Lesmahagow to Lanark. Jamie Wilson from Logan House led the way, both saddlebags stuffed with the Declaration papers condemning king and government for their oppression of conscience and denial of basic freedom.

The contingent made a fine sight trotting along in strict order, horses clean and brushed, each man in his Sunday best as were those on foot. Wull Gemmel watched them pass his house and was almost tempted to join them. At the meeting on 15th

December, where the vote was taken, he'd held back from making the commitment. John Steel, his longest, truest friend, ever the man to react in a moment, usually with heart over head, had warned against this particular action. He'd spoken carefully and thoughtfully, especially about the possible consequences. John's change of attitude was enough to shock Wull and persuade him to hold his own enthusiasm in check although he did stare after the long line of horses and men till it was out of sight.

Back in the house, he went to the bedroom where John was just wakening. "That's the Declaration on its way tae Lanark. Ah counted aboot sixty men maistly on horseback."

John peered over the edge of the blanket. "Much guid may it dae them. Whit comes aifter will test them mair than they think."

"Ah dare say." Wull left it at that.

The United Societies men halted at the top of Lanark Brae, close by the spot where John had been left lying that freezing morning. Today was less cold. No sign of frost. Instead a blustery wind was bringing the first drops of rain.

Wylie McVee, who'd arranged that first meeting of the newly formed societies, was pleased to see his nephew Jamie Wilson up front, voted in as leader for this momentous occasion. The young man had made his plans well, had chosen this day carefully. Monday wasn't a market day. No stalls sprawled across the High Street to prevent a dignified canter towards the Mercat Cross where the Declaration would be fastened for all to see. There would be little chance of confrontation as Claverhouse and his platoons were currently based at Moffat, tasked with scouring rebels further south. They were reported as patrolling around Wigtown, well out of reach. Sheriff Meiklejon had dispatched his men to Biggar. They'd been there over the weekend, checking records on Kirk attendance and were unlikely to be back before Tuesday.

Confident of his plan, Wilson took time to explain what would happen. "We'll rest here a meenit then form up again in strict order tae mak a guid impression as we enter the toun. At the Mercat Cross ah'll fasten on the Declaration. By then we shud hae an audience so Maister Renwick will read it oot loud and clear. He'll continue wi a prayer an a Bible readin. We'll then aw sing the 23rd psalm afore heidin for the toun baillie's hoose where copies o the latest Acts o Parliament are stored. Aince we huv them we'll go back tae the Cross an burn the papers as a symbol o whit they represent. That shud aboot dae it."

Everyone nodded. No one cheered. The gravity of the occasion hung heavily on them.

As the horsemen reached the High Street the wind increased and the rain began in earnest. The street was unusually quiet. Only a few people saw the first of the horsemen approach with their blue and white flag of the Covenant, but within minutes, word spread that something strange was about to happen on the High Street.

The horsemen dismounted at the Mercat Cross. Those on foot joined them in a respectful circle. Wilson took a hammer, a nail, and the precious Declaration from his saddlebag and stepped up to the stone edifice. It took several strokes before the nail was secure enough to hold the thick Declaration paper.

He bowed before the already rain-spattered sheet of paper, then stepped back among his comrades. James Renwick took over and read the entire Declaration in a clear voice. He too bowed to the Declaration, then launched into a long and carefully worded prayer and appropriate Bible reading.

In spite of the rain, a crowd had gathered and many were moved enough to nod in agreement. The Bible reading added impact and when the men's strong voices began to sing 'The Lord's my Shepherd…' the atmosphere was so charged that most of the audience joined in. Encouraged by this, Wilson signalled for copies of the Declaration to be handed out to the crowd. People wandered off clutching sheets of paper, some beginning to wonder and worry over what they'd just witnessed or maybe been part of.

The town baillie's housekeeper was serving his dinner when they heard a commotion at the front door. "Lord sakes. Whit noo?" She slammed the meat ashet down on the table and ran into the hall to meet a surge of armed men who forced her back to her master's dining room.

"Whit's this?" Nicol Jarvie jumped up and gaped at the invasion. "Whit authority alloos ye tae burst in here?"

Jamie Wilson marched up to the table. "The authority o the United Societies, here tae remove the Acts o Parliament ye store in this hoose. Whaur are they?"

"But – " Jarvie stopped at the sight of all the set faces. He pointed to a locked chest in the corner of the room.

"Open it." Wilson stood beside the chest while the baillie wrestled with the padlock. "Richt, step back." He lifted out several rolls of paper then turned to the baillie. "Is that aw?"

Jarvie nodded. "But ye canna – " His words tailed off as the invasion turned as one and left. He stared after them and whispered. "The authorities will need tae ken aboot this."

"Indeed," his housekeeper's face burned with excitement, "an ye best be quick. Whit aboot the sheriff? He'll ken whit tae dae. Will ah stick yer dinner back in the oven for a while?"

Jarvie ran all the way to the town garrison. When he arrived he was so out of breath he could barely speak. When he did manage to blurt out the news, Meiklejon rounded on him as if he was to blame. "Whit are ye dain, neglectin yer duty by allooin sic a thing tae happen? Hae ye ony idea whit them in Edinburgh will mak o this?"

"Ah wis taen by surprise."

"A man in yer position's supposed tae hae an ear oot listenin for whit's happenin in yer ain toun. Wis there nivver a whisper?"

"Nane." The baillie hung his head.

"In that case ye best tak a guid luk at yersel an start worryin aboot losin yer position as toun baillie." The sheriff pushed past Jarvie and ran down to the courtyard to muster his men, only to remember most of them were still in Biggar. "Damn and blast." He hurried out of the garrison and looked up the High Street to see a large group of men and horses milling about the Mercat Cross. As he watched, he saw smoke begin to rise through the driving rain. Only later would he discover it was a rather damp bonfire trying to consume the country's laws.

After a few minutes the men remounted, shouted for those on foot to form up behind and then the contingent came back down the High Street at a slow pace.

Meiklejon glimpsed a sheet of paper flapping against the Mercat Cross. It reminded him of Sanquhar not so long ago. "Chris sakes." He groaned. "It luks lik anither declaration. Same as Richard Cameron's defiance." He stood waiting; as the line passed he recognised the leading horseman and he'd seen the fair young man somewhere before as well. A few men doffed their caps, even smiled at the angry figure. For once, Meiklejon was nonplussed. But a moment later he was racing back into the garrison.

As he came through the gate, he roared for his clerk. "Thrum, whaur are ye? We've an important report tae write."

Thrum darted out from his pokey room to join the sheriff and try to make some sense of his master's garbled muttering.

An hour later he'd managed to draft a report.

Meiklejon reached out for the paper.

"Wait sir, the ink's nae dry. Ah need tae dust it or thur lordships will nivver be able tae read a word." Thrum kept his master waiting another minute before handing over the report.

"Richt." Meiklejon signed along the bottom and began to roll up the document.

"Sir." Thrum held out the tin of powder. "Anither wee dust tae mak sure."

"God's sake, man. Hurry up. I want ye doon thae stairs tae find the best man ye can find. Ane that rides weel. Ye can promise twa extra merks in his pay and the use o ma ain horse, for ivvery meenit counts in reachin Edinburgh. Noo mind he's tae gang straight tae the parliament building and seek oot George MacKenzie in the Privy Council. This report is for his haund only. Naebody else is tae touch or hae sicht o it."

"Ay sir." Thrum stumbled downstairs. Mention of extra pay and the use of the sheriff's own horse helped him find a willing recruit. Minutes later the man was galloping out of Lanark on his mission to Edinburgh.

Task complete, Thrum returned to his work but couldn't concentrate on the columns of figures, not when he thought how today's event might affect the town.

Meiklejon sat down by his usual roaring fire and downed a glass of best claret. It did nothing to ease his agitation. He downed another, then spat into the flames. "Whae's fault will this be? Whae will the Privy Council turn on, askin hoo sic an act o treason cud tak place in the middle o the toun, in broad daylicht wi naebody tryin tae stop it?" He spat into the flames again and poured another glass.

The United Societies' men stopped at the top of Lanark Brae and looked back at the quiet town. Behind them was the evidence of a successful venture, or so they believed. Resolve had been strengthened. Resistance was still possible.

Tired but satisfied, sixty men followed Jamie Wilson down the steep hill and on towards the Lesmahagow road.

"Weel, Meiklejon." John Graham jumped down from his horse and ran up the Lanark garrison steps towards the sheriff's bulky figure. "Whit dae ye want first, the guid news or the bad news?"

Meiklejon gave an anxious smile. "Oh it's yersel, commander. Guid tae see ye. I tak it ye're on yer way back frae the Privy Council. Can I offer ye a meal and a rest aifter yer journey?"

Clavers bowed. "Why thank ye. But are ye no anxious tae ken whit the Privy Council thocht o yer report?"

"Whitivver it is can wait. Come awa in." Meiklejon turned and shouted across the courtyard to the kitchen. "Get some dinner ready for the commander, and bring a bottle o claret. The guid stuff."

Clavers allowed himself to be steered upstairs to the sheriff's private quarters and settled by the fire. He removed his cloak and feathered hat, then sat back to enjoy the blast of heat. "A cauld wet day tae be sittin on the back o a horse for hoors on end."

The sheriff nodded. "We're pleased ye've stopped by."

Clavers gave Meiklejon a side-on glance. This seemed to create an uneasy silence, which lasted till the garrison cook appeared with a tureen of tender chicken pieces in a medley of roasted vegetables. He sniffed the tempting smell. "Ye dae weel, sir. We dinna hae fare lik this in oor billet at Moffat."

"It's nae mair than oor usual." Meiklejon ladled out a good helping and offered the commander a plateful. "Tuck in."`

Clavers cleared his plate and accepted a second while Meiklejon pushed his food round his plate and kept glancing at the commander.

Eventually the commander pushed back his chair. "Richt. Time tae put ye oot yer misery. But first I'd appreciate anither glass o yer fine claret"

"Nae sooner said." The sheriff held out the bottle. "If I mind richt ye said somethin aboot guid news and bad news?"

Claverhouse laughed. "Ay. But ease up, man. The Privy Council wis grateful for yer report, although it didna mak pleasant reading. Mair tae the point, they're no luking in yer direction, especially since ye gied them some names tae work on."

Meiklejon looked relieved. "Whit's the verdict?"

"Lanark is held responsible for this unfortunate happening. The toun's disloyalty is condemned in the strongest terms. Their lordships want tae ken hoo as mony rebels cud arrive bold as brass and commit a treasonable act at the Mercat Cross nae less withoot ony attempt being made tae question whit wis happening let alane stop the rascals. Whaur were the councillors and magistrates? Yer report said some o the citizens even saw fit tae join in."

"I said there wis an audience. I nivver said – "

Clavers flapped a hand. "Nae maitter. They were there." He grinned at the sheriff. "It's raither unfortunate ye'd sent yer men awa tae Biggar jist afore this happened."

Meiklejon thumped the table. "Hoo wis I tae ken?"

"Ay weel." Clavers smiled. "Things happen."

"Indeed they dae. If ma men had been here things wud hae been raither different. There wudna hae been ony declaration pinned up on the Mercat Cross, nae ceremony in front o the tounsfolk, and ivvery last rebel wud be sittin in the tolbooth richt noo waitin for a hangin."

"So ye say." Claverhouse seemed amused. "Anither thing. The Privy Council are mair than disappointed that naebody saw fit tae follow the rebels and see whaur they went. Their lordships believe this shows a serious lack o civic duty in this toun. Apart frae yersel, naebody did or said onything."

"Will this merit punishment, a fine mibbe?"

"It will. Tae the tune o six thoosand merks."

"Whit? Thur's no that kinda money in the toun coffers."

"They've nae choice but pay." Claverhouse held out his empty glass.

Sunlight shone on the water of the duck pond behind the

Gemmel house. A busy duck bobbed and dived for its breakfast and sent ripples across the smooth surface. The fields beyond were dusted with frost and snow. The sky was blue with the sun reflecting on the dark water of the pond. It was a fine morning. A morning to enjoy. John Steel smiled. This was his first outing since his walk up Lanark Brae. He limped to a nearby log and sat down.

At the end of the garden he admired the stark skeleton of an ancient oak, on past the first field to a jaggy line of pine trees, then more fields, one after another, stretching towards Tinto hill with a thick white hat on this morning. The familiarity of it all seemed to reassure him and chase away some of the doubts and fears he'd wrestled with while confined to bed. Ay, he thought, it's anither day an time tae think aboot whit nixt.

Later on he suggested it might be time to think about going home.

Wull shook his head. "An when Crichton's platoon comes by lukin fur ye, whit then? Ye'd be a sittin duck, as easy caught as ane o the ducks in ma pond oot there. But first things first. Ye need tae show me hoo weel ye can move aboot. Mibbe ye cud try runnin roond the garden." Wull held the door open. "On ye go. Ah'll watch."

John sat still.

"Jist as ah thocht. Fur the time bein ye need tae dae as ye're tellt an content yersel. Aince ye're weel enough ye can dae whit ye like. But nae afore. An nae arguin."

Chapter 15

James Renwick and Wylie McVee were riding along the last stretch of rutted track to Logan House. Backs aching, clothes sodden, hands and faces stinging with cold their journey back from Lanark was a miserable experience after such an eventful day. Ahead was a lighted window with its promise of warmth and food. McVee pointed towards the long, dark shape of his house and the flickering pinpoint of light. "I canna wait tae be oot o this rain. It's been a lang day. But worthwhile. Ma nephew Jamie did weel." He turned to James Renwick trotting by his side. "As did yersel. It's a pity John Steel didna come. Wi his support Lesmahagow village wud hae been oot in force. Lanark wud hae seen an invasion."

"Maister Steel isna very weel. His attack near killed him. But he wisna for comin onyway, tellt me he wanted naethin tae dae wi oor plan, wudna even sign the declaration."

"Weel that's a surprise. I had him doon as a stalwart for the cause."

"He's suffered a lot since Bothwell but I suspect whit happened tae Lucas Brotherstone is at the back o it."

"If whit I heard is true it haurly bears thinkin aboot."

James Renwick nodded. "I've been praying aboot it since visiting him. I'll wait a wee while then go again. Mibbe he can still be brocht roond."

Wull Gemmell had gone to Lanark to fetch the medicine John was supposed to collect that fateful day. He didn't stay long for the news in the town had him rushing back home.

John was sitting on his usual log by the duck pond watching the birds' antics. He frowned at Wull's flustered face. "Whit's up?"

"Whit ye said is happenin. Lanark's in an uproar. Everybody's on aboot the fine slapped on the toun fur allooin yon declaration tae tak place."

"Ah canna see hoo they cud hae stopped it."

"The Privy Council dinna agree. Thur sendin mair military tae roond up ony culprits an mak an example."

"They'll need tae catch them first."

"Haud on. Jist listen. When thur lordships found oot aboot Lanark they ordered the Edinburgh councillors tae pit on thur official robes then walk in procession ahint the hangman tae the Grassmarket. He wis cairryin copies o the declaration papers in a big basket. When they reached the gibbet they'd tae staund an watch while he set fire tae the lot. It wis supposed tae be a serious warnin tae the rebels but the crowd didna see it that way. A few wur heard tae laugh. They say the howfs an taverns are still ringin wi jokes an sangs aboot the event. Tae mak maitters worse the Societies are supposed tae hae murdered a trooper oot by Lanark. The Privy Council's in a richt lather aboot that so we'll aw suffer."

John sighed. "Whit's new?"

"It's stertit aready. A man's been arrested, tried an sentenced fur bein pairt o the Declaration. He's bein brocht tae Lanark Cross fur a public hangin. Except onybody ah spoke tae say he wisna even there. He's a weaver, bides oot by Carstairs an wis seen at his loom maist o that day. But thur Lordships are no listenin."

"As far as ah can mak oot they only listen tae themsels."

Six weeks after the declaration at Lanark William Harvie, a weaver from the nearby village of Carstairs, was hanged at the very spot where Jamie Wilson had fastened that contentious piece of paper. Harvie protested his innocence to the last but it made no difference.

By then the town was swarming with the military and no one dared argue. Meiklejon himself was under pressure with his garrison bursting for several more weeks as platoon after platoon arrived from the capital to scour the district. The jail was soon full and many who came before the judiciary would find themselves shipped out to Carolina plantations as slaves. A few would survive and eventually return. Most didn't make it across the Atlantic, dying in filthy, airless holds with little or nothing to eat or drink. Being in the wrong place at the wrong time then giving the wrong answer was enough to be found guilty. Justice was served under a dark cloud as the Privy Council tried to control every dissenting thought or action with their own brand of authority.

When James Renwick made his second visit to Wull Gemmel's cottage he found John Steel almost back to full health.

John seemed surprised to see him. "Why Maister Renwick. Whit can ah dae fur ye?"

Renwick smiled. "Cud we talk. By oorsels?"

"Come oot by the duck pond. It's fine an private except fur quackin birds."

Renwick followed John outside to settle on the log John had adopted during his weeks of recovery. Neither spoke for some time then Renwick said, "I'm pleased tae see hoo weel ye are."

"Ah've much tae be gratefu fur."

"As we aw shud be." Renwick hesitated. "In spite o whit's happening around us."

John gave him a side-long glance. "A guid bit is doon tae yersel an yer freends."

"Depends whit ye're referring tae."

"Sufferin, Maister Renwick. Injustice. Whit aboot yon pair man hung at Lanark fur bein pairt o yer declaration? They say he wisna even there."

"Unfortunate things happen."

"Tell that tae the man's family."

"I did." Renwick held John's stare. "They received me kindly, listened, then tellt me that although William Harvie hadna been part o this Declaration he did support us and believed in the cause. He'd been a drummer at the Hamilton Declaration afore Bothwell. He fought there lik yersel. His family seemed tae understand ma feelings o guilt and wanted tae reassure me when I tellt them that oor cause is aw aboot preserving and spreading the word. Allooing oor fellow man the chance tae understand and experience the truth as the Lord intended. Because o the government's stance the only way is by field preaching. Folk oot there hanker aifter the truth and God willing I intend tae gie them it."

"Back at the beginnin ah went tae a guid few a meetins an heard some grand sermons."

"I'm glad tae hear it."

John sighed. "Whit followed wisna guid. Ah found masel lukin aifter a meenister, hauf daft wi his ain guilt alang wi ither notions that didna help. It got worse when he got involved wi Richard

Cameron. Yon man wis a force tae reckon wi. A guid preacher an ah nivver doubted his sincerity. But he wis a tad radical an convinced he wis richt. It hud tae be his way or nae way an nae arguin."

Renwick frowned. "Ye didna agree?"

"Hoo cud ah? As fur Lucas Brotherstone his grand ideas an intentions got the better o him. Whit happened in the end wis the stuff o nichtmares."

Silence fell between them again before Renwick said, "Tae yer ain sel be true is no an easy road."

"Tell me aboot it. Richt noo ah'm strugglin."

"Whit if I offered ye a wee challenge? Something that micht help?"

John blinked.

"Let me explain. The United Societies are sending me tae Holland tae finish my studies at Groningen University, and hopefully be ordained. Aince in Holland I need tae send back a full report. The Societies had aready decided on Alexander Gordon o Earlston tae dae the honours but he has a wide remit. They expect him tae visit Scottish congregations and ministers across Holland and attend meetings. Alang wi that he's tae hear a variety o proposals then write aboot them. He'll be struggling for time tae check my progress let alane report back. This is the first time Scotland has reached oot in this way tae anither country. I'm keen tae get it richt for the Societies mean tae send ither students. I want them tae get the same chance and then come back here tae spread the word. I've explained my concern. We discussed it fully at oor last meeting and the delegates agree I shud hae my ain messenger. He'd only bide a wee while then bring back my words tae the United Societies while Alexander Gordon gets on wi ither important work and negotiations. I wis hoping that somebody lik yersel micht consider the task."

John flushed and looked away. There was a long silence then he said, "Whae's payin fur aw this?"

"The United Societies and the Dutch Kirk are prepared to share this burden. Think aboot it, ye'd be daing something worthwhile, spending time in a new place, meeting new people, seeing new things. An opportunity lik that micht help ye see things mair clearly and feel better aboot yersel and yer unfortunate position."

"Ah'd need tae think aboot it."

"Of course. Either way thank ye for listening." Renwick touched John's shoulder then rose to leave. "Guid day, Maister Steel."

John didn't answer. He was staring in the direction of the swimming ducks without seeing any of them.

"Whit wis that aboot?" Wull was at John's side before James Renwick reached the garden gate.

"He wants me tae go wi him tae Holland."

"Ye're kiddin?"

"That's whit ah thocht."

"Stert again. Tell me richt."

John did and Wull listened. Finally he asked, "Did ye gie him an answer?"

"No aforet thinkin it thru. Ah worry aboot Marion runnin the farm on her ain when ah'm oot on the moor. That's hard enough withoot sufferin they troopers forivver hasslin her an the bairns."

"Ah cud see tae Westermains an gie Marion support tae fend aff the likes o Crichton."

"Whit aboot yer ain work?"

"Ma joinerin can fit roond ony farm work. Ah'd hae ma Helen wi me. She'd help Marion. They twa git on weel an the bairns ken us fine. Onyway, ah've aye wantit a farm, so has ma Helen. She'd enjoy spendin some time there."

"Ye nivver said."

"Ye nivver asked. Why shud ye? Mair tae the point dae ye want tae go? Be carefu ye're no takin on anither yin as needs lukin aifter. Maister Brotherstane wis hard work."

John made a face. "Maister Renwick seems mair content in his skin, shair o himsel an his intentions. Onyway, ah'd only be a messenger, awa fur a month or twa an then back hame. Tae tell the truth ah raither fancy the idea."

"An nae Crichton on yer tail fur a while."

"That tae. But ah need tae soond oot Marion."

Marion gave a shrug then a nod but made no comment as John told her about James Renwick's invitation. She still said nothing when he mentioned the possibility of Wull and Helen coming to stay while he was away. John began to sound defensive. "Ah'll mak sure thur's enough siller tae keep ye goin. Ah'll organise it wi Maister McAvoy. If ye need onythin Gus McPhail can tak word. An ah'm sure the maister cud see aboot ma berth on a boat fur Holland."

"It's fine John." She looked away and fiddled with her apron strings. "It's jist."

"Jist whit?"

She looked up. "Did it nivver occur tae ye that ah micht want tae go on this trip?" The apron strings were almost in a knot. "But ah ken ah canna. Thur's the bairns an the farm tae luk aifter. An of course ah'm jist a wummin."

"Ah suppose Wull cud see tae the farm but ah dinna think the bairns wud be happy. They like Wull an Helen weel enough but if ye're no there – " He leant forward to free her fingers from the apron strings. "Ah'm sorry."

"So ah'm ah. But ye're richt the bairns put up wi mair than enough aready withoot me disappearin fur a while."

"Ah nivver thocht fur a meenit ye'd want sic a thing. It's no that lang ago ye wur diggin in yer heels aboot bidin on nae maitter whit."

"Ah meant it. Disna mean ah wudna enjoy a chainge fur a wee while. It's temptin."

John flushed. "Aifter aw this bother's feenished ye'll git yer wish. Onywhaur ye like. Jist keep it in mind."

"An pigs micht flee."

John's flush deepened. "Ah've jist said."

"Ah hear ye." She almost smiled. "On ye go. Jist mak shair Maister Renwick disna demand ower much. Ye ken the bother that caused afore."

"Nae fear. Ah'm dain this fur masel. It's a chance tae see an hear ither ideas, ways o dain things."

"Whit's no tae like aboot that?" Marion leant over to kiss his cheek.

John Steel and James Renwick stood together at the back of a tall rigged ship and stared into the distance till all sign of land had gone.

Eventually John said, "Ah'm gled we came this way. Maister

McAvoy suggested we shud leave frae Leith raither than Glesca. It's supposed tae be a shorter route but ah wisna keen fur it meant passin yon Bass Rock afore we got oot intae the open sea."

James Renwick nodded. "A bad memory. But dinna let it haud ye back. Try tae leave yer dark shadows ahint and luk forward tae landing in Holland. I understand this ship is named *The Sweet Hope*. Is that no a promise for us baith?"

John smiled at the eager face. "Ah'm sure it is."

The journey was more or less storm free. This allowed the travellers to spend time on the open deck, fascinated by a myriad of ropes stretching from the deck to the top mast, marvelling how the crew could climb such dizzy heights, adjusting groups of sails, allowing them to billow in the prevailing wind. Few orders were given yet each man seemed to understand what was needed to keep *The Sweet Hope* on her course.

This was the opposite of how John felt, and had him remembering that one defiant step which had led him in a direction he'd never intended, ending up on the wrong side of the law, hunted and harried by the government. He'd survived so far but many others had been less lucky.

Guilt took over yet again until his first glimpse of land triggered off a new curiosity.

As *The Sweet Hope* edged along the narrow inlet to Rotterdam she passed many different ships. Tall masts, short masts, full rigged, single sail, no sail, slim and elegant, aggressive looking as well as chunky, all crowding either side, so many that John hardly knew where to look.

When they dropped anchor only yards from a busy quay they were shocked by the sudden noise and frantic activity laced with unfamiliar smells. In every direction something was happening with giant hoists swinging heavy boxes and bundles on and off the anchored ships while lines of men scurried up and down narrow gang planks carrying sacks aboard or unloading them onto waiting carts.

The ship's captain joined the two travellers. "A busy place tae be sure. Much tae see."

John nodded. "Vera interestin but hoo dae we find oor guide amang aw that?"

"I think I've spotted him. Ower there, ahint yon carts." The captain took off his cap and waved it at a young, stockily built man who was staring intently at *The Sweet Hope*.

The man waved back then hurried to the edge of the quay and shouted up to the watching faces. "Are ye for Groningen?"

"They twa." The captain pointed to John and James Renwick. "Ready and waitin."

John Steel and James Renwick stood on the solid, stone quay which felt strange after so many days learning to walk along the open deck of a ship.

Their new guide gave a quick bow. "Jonas Hawthorn. Here tae see ye safely on yer way tae Groningen."

James Renwick grasped the outstretched hand. "James Renwick alang wi ma freend John Steel."

Jonas studied James's face. "If ye dinna mind me sayin ye're a kennin young fur a man sae highly thocht o."

James stiffened. "I hope I'll prove worthy."

Jonas flushed. "Ah'm sure ye will. Nae offence meant."

This time James smiled. "And none taken."

"Jist so. Ma faither's keen tae meet ye. He's meenister at the Scots Kirk in Groningen."

"Is it far awa?" John cut in.

"Aboot twa days. A hunner an fifty miles. Easy enough though wi nae hills tae climb. We'll mak fur Utrecht first tae the Scots College. They ken we're comin. We'll git a guid meal an a decent bed."

"Shud we no jist press on?"

"We need tae gie the horses a rest."

"Of course." James nodded. "Where are they?"

"At a stable ahint yon warehouse." Jonas pointed towards a huge building beyond the busy quay.

"Richt." James lifted his heavy bag and began to push his way through the crowd.

"He's quick aff the mark," Jonas winked at John.

John smiled. "An single minded."

The three horsemen moved slowly through the busy streets of Rotterdam. Many had canals running alongside with barges going about their business much like the people on the streets above. On either side of this rose tall, narrow houses, some little more than two windows wide and painted in a variety of colours, almost gaudy in comparison to the grey Glasgow buildings.

Further along they came to a large square with a beautiful golden-coloured tower at one end. In front of it stretched a sea of brightly striped canopies. This was John's first glimpse of a Dutch market where stalls offered everything from pails of glistening silver fish, small mountains of round cheeses, baskets of vegetables, trays of crusty bread and sweet-smelling cakes, to patterned plates and bowls and jugs, and bunches of beautiful fresh flowers alongside rows of black jackets, neatly stacked leather boots, wooden clogs, and much more. Among all this people in unfamiliar clothes bartered and argued and John had no idea what they were saying. He stopped to watch and listen but James Renwick pressed on as if none of it was of any interest.

Jonas turned and winked at John again. "Ah see whit ye mean aboot single minded."

Out in the countryside John saw a flat and well organised landscape with regular shaped fields full of healthy looking crops. Every inch was put to good use. The grass in the meadows was lush and dotted with wild flowers where well-rounded cows seemed perfectly content. He was even more impressed by the number of windmills, working away as their great sails slowly turned in the soft breeze.

Jonas explained how the farms were organised, why everything seemed to work so well. "Yer problems in Scotland are haudin ye back. We dinna hae that here."

John nodded. "A settled life maks a difference." Suddenly he felt depressed at what was waiting for him back home.

"It'll no last forivver." Jonas seemed to sense John's mood. "Tak back the best o whit ye see an tell folk aboot it."

"Mmm." John glanced at James Renwick trotting along, engrossed in his own thoughts which probably involved more resistance against the government.

Daylight was almost gone when they reached the outskirts of Utrecht and followed Jonas along streets and canals very similar to those in Rotterdam.

Almost in the centre was a paved square dominated by a huge, stone tower like a guardian. Jonas crossed the busy square, past traders dismantling their stalls for the day, then turned into a narrow alley that ran alongside this hulk of a building. "The college stable is at the end o this wee lane. It's richt narrow so raither than fricht the beasts jump doon an lead them alang an thru yon archway up aheid."

Minutes later they were in a neat, cobbled yard bounded by a high, white-washed wall. Above this loomed a tall building with a pointed roof and rows of narrow, shuttered windows overlooking the courtyard which was lined with red-painted half doors. "This is the back o the college," Jonas explained. "Thur's a wee gate in yon corner that taks us thru tae the main door."

A boy was sweeping up loose straw. When he saw the strangers he seemed to guess who they were. *"Zijn jullie de bezoekers die wij verwachten?"*

James and John gaped at the string of strange syllables. They gaped again as Jonas nodded. *"Wilt u alstublieft vanavond onze paarden verzorgen?"*

"Geen probleem meneer." The boy smiled and nodded.

"Whit wis that aboot?" John asked.

Jonas looked amused. "The boy asked if we're the expected visitors. Ah said ay an asked him tae luk aifter the horses."

"Weel done."

"Not at aw. Ah wis born here. Ma mither's Dutch. Ah'm as much that as Scots. It's a funny auld language but ah'll pit ye richt wi a word or twa. Folk like that. Richt then, gie yer horses tae the lad an we'll awa in an see if we're in time fur dinner."

The master of the college met them in the entrance hall. In spite of his sombre expression he seemed pleased to see them. He politely shook hands, asked about their journey then led them through to a large dining room where masters and students were seated at long trestle tables. "Yon table at the far end. Sit yersels doon gentlemen. We're aboot tae eat and maist likely ye're hungry. Aifter that we'd appreciate some news aboot oor beleaguered country." He took a small silver bell from his jacket pocket and rang it.

Three women in starched, white caps and wrap-round aprons appeared, each with a steaming tureen which they set down on a great sideboard alongside baskets heaped with crusty bread.

Jonas smiled. "Thank guidness. Ah'm starvin."

The master rang the little bell again. Every chair was pushed back and the whole room stood with bowed head while the master said grace. At a further signal everyone sat down again while the women began to pile stew and dumplings on large china plates and quickly serve each man in turn. Within minutes everyone had a steaming plate in front of them then the baskets of bread were laid along the centre of the tables along with ashets of cooked vegetables. The meat, swimming in dark gravy, smelt delicious, the dumplings were large, white and fluffy. The three travellers could hardly wait.

"Gled we made it," Jonas sat back and wiped his mouth. "That wis guid. Tellt ye we'd git a decent meal." He pointed towards one of the women who'd begun to clear away the plates. "Yon's the college cook. The maister's real pleased wi her. She arrived frae Scotland a while back wi her man an a bairn. Nice family."

John watched as the woman organised the tidying away. Something about her seemed familiar. As she turned to check if the tables were now cleared she looked in his direction. My God. It's Meg Gillon. Hoo did she git here?

The woman hesitated, seemed to catch John's eye. He smiled. Her expression froze then she turned and hurried away with a stack of plates.

John said nothing to the other two and waited to see what would happen next but Meg Gillon didn't come back into the room.

The master stood up and smiled at his guests. "I hope ye're feeling better aifter yer meal. Noo lets awa thru tae the sitting room. There's a guid fire and if ye're no ower tired mibbe ye can gie us some o yer news." He led them through to a wood-panelled room filled with many chairs. It obviously doubled as a teaching space as well as somewhere to relax or read. The master lit his pipe and turned to the other men already in the room. "Oor visitors hae some news aboot back hame. I'm sure ye want tae hear so gaither roond and listen."

Chairs shuffled and soon the visitors were surrounded by eager faces. Questions came thick and fast and the faces grew ever more serious as James Renwick answered each one with care, leaving no one in any doubt about the current situation.

Jonas nodded to the master. "If ye'll excuse us sir, we'll leave Maister Renwick tae dae the talkin. He's best placed tae answer yer concerns. If ye dinna mind us twa will sit in a quiet corner an rest."

At the far end of the room John sat and thought about his day, the two strange cities, the landscape, the people in different dress, carts and carriages, that busy market, all very different from home. Much tae luk at an think aboot. Closing his eyes he leant back to visualise it all again when a hand lightly touched his shoulder.

He jumped and saw Meg Gillon's anxious face only inches away. "Ah thocht it wis ye. Ye're the last person ah'd expect tae see here."

"Ah cud say the same fur yersel."

Meg's frown deepened. "Hae ye a meenit?" She glanced at Jonas. "Private like. Wud ye come oot the back till ah explain?"

Jonas grinned. "On ye go. Dinna mind me."

John rose and followed her along a narrow, stone corridor, through the kitchen where piles of plates were being washed and huge iron pots scrubbed.

"This way." Meg lifted the bar of an outer door and opened it. Only feet away was a narrow path bordering a canal. On the other side a row of tall houses, some with lit windows, stared back at them, their twinkling lamps reflected in the still water. To John it seemed almost magical and he stood a moment enjoying the scene till Meg interrupted. "Sit doon here Maister Steel." She sat down on a bench by the door.

John turned and joined her. Neither spoke for a moment then Meg blurted out, "Ah've a favour tae ask, Maister Steel."

"Aboot a curate mibbe?"

"My ye're quick on the uptake."

"It wisna hard tae guess. An lik ah said the last time ah saw ye, yer man an yer bairn, it's nane o ma business."

Meg looked relieved. "Ay weel. Ah dare say ye've hud yer ane problems since then."

"Ye cud say that."

"We've been lucky. It's aw chainged fur the better. But let me explain. If ah mind richt the last time we saw ye it wis the middle o the nicht."

John nodded.

"That nicht we wur drivin oor trap awa frae the manse tae escape frae the sheriff. Ma Sandy wis terrified o him an when the ither grand gentleman suggested that Sandy micht like tae spy on the village, we'd nae choice but go."

"Ah tak it ye mean the military gentleman. The ane that stopped Sandy's hangin yon day in the village square?"

Meg nodded.

"He's Claverhoose. Richt important an worth the watchin."

"Tell me aboot it. The sheriff wis set on a hangin. He'd found oot hoo Sandy wis sittin wi an empty kirk an no lettin on. He wis hoppin mad when the gentleman led ma Sandy back intae the hoose. Ah wis greetin wi relief but when ah heard whit wis whispered in his ear ah wis terrified. Sandy wud nivver mak a spy. No that he wantit tae dae it onyway."

"So hoo did ye land here?"

"When we reached Glesca we thocht it wud be safe. Sandy went back tae his trade an we wur dain fine till – "

"The sheriff caught up wi ye."

"We only got awa wi meenits tae spare. Ah'll no bore ye wi it aw. Aifter that we managed tae git passage on a boat. Best thing we ivver did. It's grand here an safe. Sandy's a guid shoemaker an buildin up a decent business."

"He's gied up wantin tae be a curate?"

"He kens better than mention the word ivver again. That's why ah'm askin a favour. Wi me workin here amang aw they meenisters an students ah wudna like them – "

"Tae ken aboot Sandy's previous occupation? Nae worries. Not a word."

Meg went back to the kitchen and John sat on watching the dark water. Funny hoo things work oot. He thought about Meg making a new life for herself and family then he thought how his

Marion struggled with the troopers forever pestering her when they visited the farm. Mibbe she'd like it here. Nae worries, nae Crichton hasslin her, me no on the run.

He was quietly dreaming when Jonas appeared. "So this is whaur ye disappeared tae." He sat down beside John. "Whitivver ye said tae yon cook she's awa intae the kitchen singin lik a lintie. Ah tak it ye kent her back hame?"

John nodded but offered no explanation.

Jonas stared at the dark canal as if its water held some threat. "When ah heard whit Maister Renwick wis sayin aboot aw the trouble an sufferin it made me gled tae be here. Whit's happenin in Scotland soonds terrible. Mind ye he seems tae think there is a way furrit."

John sighed. "So did a wheen ithers afore him."

After that neither spoke.

Next morning the college master was waiting in the stable-yard to see his visitors off. Most of the college was with him, lined up to shake hands with James Renwick and wish him well with his studies.

As Jonas and John watched the bowing and smiling Jonas whispered, "That yin's mair than weel thocht o. Ane o they days he micht walk on watter."

"Wheesht," John tried not to laugh. "Ye shudna talk lik that."

"Hoo no? Ah micht be a meenister's son but ah can see fur masel hoo things are an work oot whit's whit."

"Maister Renwick's no seekin ony fuss. He's here because he wis specially selected. Ah'm shair he'll dae weel."

"Ah ken," Jonas cut in. "Nae need tae defend him. Ah've heard ivvery detail. Ma faither's fair cairried awa wi the plans tae mak sure Maister Renwick fulfills his mission tae become a meenister."

"Whit's wrang wi that?"

"Naethin," Jonas admitted. "He tellt me it's aw aboot goin back hame tae spread the word an stop folk driftin awa frae the truth."

John sighed. "Ah've heard an seen it aw afore. A while back anither yin wis much thocht o. He wis young lik Maister Renwick, same fair hair, same starin een, that guid wi words he hud ivverybody wantin tae listen. If onythin he seemed mair single minded, definitely mair fiery if onybody dared tae argue."

"Soonds lik a student we hud ower here. Richard Cameron." Jonas shook his head. "He wis somethin else. Ye cud hear a pin drap when he spoke. Best ah ivver heard. He wis a great organiser as weel but lik ye said everythin hud tae be done his way. Ah met him in Rotterdam jist afore he wis ordained. Aifter that he wis straight back tae Scotland, determined tae keep the cause alive. Did ye ken him?"

John nodded. "He ended up deid wi his heid on a pike above the Netherbow Gate in Edinburgh."

"Ye dinna soond as if ye approve so whit are ye dain ower here wi this yin?"

"Weel micht ye ask." John frowned and turned away to lead the horses across the yard to the group of black-coated men still milling round James Renwick. No one seemed to notice so he called out, "Time we wur awa, sir"

"Of course." James Renwick bowed to his admirers. "Thank ye all. I appreciate yer support. God bless." With a happy smile he took his leave and walked towards the waiting horses.

John's expression forbade any conversation. Not that James Renwick seemed to notice, lost in his own thoughts as they began their journey in silence.

Gradually the landscape itself had an effect. The almost too neat fields and tidy looking farms dotted along the way, some bordering the network of canals with the many working windmills. John was impressed and began asking questions.

Relieved by the change of mood Jonas enjoyed answering and explaining. Soon he and John were arguing about Dutch methods of agriculture. When they arrived on the coast John's mood lifted even further at the sight of so many high masted ships anchored in the huge bay.

"This is Lelystad." Jonas pointed to the town close by. "We're on the edge o the Zuiderzee. It's a grand safe anchorage. Ah came this way so ye cud see they ships. Best in the world in ma opeenion. Maist work fur the East India Company an are built here. The toun's surrounded wi woodland, the richt kind fur boats. An of course thur's nae shortage o men wi the skill tae dae it richt."

John stared at the elegant ships with their tall masts and

fluttering sails. "Whaur dae they sail?"

"Hauf way roond the world an back again wi things ye'd haurly dream aboot."

"An makin money?"

"That's whit it's aboot." Jonas smiled. "Yer Scottish merchants are catchin on an dain the same." He turned to James Renwick. "Whit dae ye think?"

"A fine sicht." Renwick nodded. "Beautiful ships." He drifted back to his own thoughts.

Jonas winked at John. "That yin's no in the real world."

John stiffened. His frown slid back and he didn't answer.

Jonas turned his horse. "Richt gentlemen we leave the coast an heid north fur Groningen." Under his breath he whispered, "Somethin's no richt here."

Chapter 16

Tobias Hawthorn stood at the front door of his church and watched three weary looking travellers come up the road towards him. The horses were dusty and looked as if they'd be glad to stop.

Tall, almost gaunt, with an expression to match his sombre dress he looked every inch a Kirk minister with fine woven breeches and matching jacket finished off by a row of silver buttons down the front edge. Legs encased in white stockings and a pristine silk cravat round his neck provided stark contrast to his matt-black outfit while a pair of highly-polished shoes with heavy metal buckles completed the impression of an imposing figure who issued orders and expected obedience in return.

Or so it seemed.

When the travellers drew near Tobias was down his kirk steps, running forward, arms outstretched to pull Jonas from his saddle and give him a huge hug. His son returned the greeting then turned to grin at the two watching faces. "Yer host, gentlemen. Reverend Tobias Hawthorn, meenister o the Scots Kirk here in Groningen, ma esteemed faither."

James Renwick and John Steel jumped down to shake hands and found themselves crushed in a double hug.

"Welcome tae oor toun." Tobias gave James Renwick a second hug. "Yer studies await young man. May ye dae as weel as yer reputation seems tae suggest."

James Renwick drew back. "Sir, I'm weel aware o the honour afforded me and appreciate the opportunity tae fulfill my responsibilities and return hame tae carry forward the Lord's work."

"Ay. The Lord's work. Rest assured this community is pleased tae support yer aspirations." Tobias blinked twice then smiled again. "Ay. We'll talk mair aboot that later. Come awa thru tae the manse. Ye'll be aifter a bite tae eat and a freshen up afore I tak ye tae yer lodgings. Ye'll hae twa rooms wi Monsieur Aupetit at 54 Folkerdingestraat. Richt place under the circumstances. It means the street o the strangers."

Renwick looked puzzled.

"Och, dinna heed me." Tobias flapped a hand. "Me and ma daft notions. No that ye'll be a stranger for lang. No in this toun. We're a freendly, God fearin lot and keen tae mak ye baith feel welcome. Monsieur Aupetit's a Huguenot. Ye'll get on jist fine."

"Huguenot?" This time John looked puzzled.

"A French Protestant wi beliefs much lik oorsels. Unfortunately the French king taen ill against the Huguenots and tellt them tae tak on Catholic ways or else. And he meant it. Thoosands resisted and were killed, or tortured, or baith. Aupetit wis lucky tae escape. He's settled here and established himsel as a watchmaker, does weel wi plenty customers and has a reputation for guid work. A few years back he married my sister Lisa. They hae twa fine sons. Lisa runs a tidy hoose for students at the university. She's a guid cook and weel able tae gie ye plain Scottish fare if that's whit ye want. Folkerdingestraat's maist respectable, under the shadow o the Aa Kerk and close by the Martinitorn. We're prood o oor buildings here. If ye git a chance tak a luk at them baith. Best o aw ye're only a meenit's walk frae the university."

"Thank ye." James glanced at John. "We're baith grateful. Ye've gone tae a lot o trouble on oor behalf."

"Ay." John shuffled his feet. "But ah'm jist a messenger. Nae important lik Maister Renwick, an nae expectin ony special treatment."

"John's a farmer lik me," Jonas cut in. "Ah thocht ah'd tak him oot tae see Grootvader. Show him the farm. Ah'm there maist days an cud show him hoo we dae things, mibbe even persuade him tae gie a bit haund aboot the place while Maister Renwick's at his studies."

Tobias nodded. "I'm sure yer grandfaither wud like that. But richt noo gang roond the back an gie yer horses tae the stable lad. He'll see tae them while ye bring oor guests in tae meet yer mither. She has a guid spread ready. If ye're onythin lik ma Jonas ye'll soon dae it justice so come awa thru."

John woke in a tiny attic room, at the very top of the steepest, narrowest, wooden stair he'd ever climbed, so close to the slates he could hear rain drumming only inches above his head.

In spite of morning light filtering through the little roof window the room seemed in constant shadow. Not that John minded. He had it to himself. The first night for weeks that he hadn't had to share a space with James Renwick. It was a good feeling. His own privacy away from the quiet but insistent solemnity that seemed to pervade every bone of that young man's body then transmit itself to everyone he met.

John lay there listening to the rain, the familiar rhythm reminding him of the times he'd sheltered under a bush with raindrops pattering through the leaves, tucked into a moorland hollow where tight clumps of heather could stop most of the rain from filtering through, or best of all a tiny cave at the bottom of some gully, hiding from the ever searching troopers. And then there was that special time when he'd sheltered on the edge of the Duchess of Hamilton's wood, watching the rebel camp go about its routine, hating it, wishing it could all wash away with the rain. But it hadn't. Hours later the sun was shining. That's when that battle to save the covenant began. And the sun kept smiling as the bonny blue banners faltered and fell as the enemy came on, ever on, warning those who wanted to fight, to defend their beliefs, that it was all a waste of time. Defeat swarmed around them, closing in like a trap. Only a few would manage to turn and flee before it was too late.

It was still there in his head, the noise of cannons and muskets and clashing steel, the acrid smoke billowing across the frantic scene where men lunged and roared with hate or fear or pain. And all the time the sun kept on shining, even when the man who was supposed to be their leader galloped off and left them to it. All so wrong, so strange. And here he was in a strange bed, in a strange house, in a strange town, in a strange country, accompanying a strange young man he suspected would take him further on this awful journey.

This'll no dae. He sat up abruptly and rubbed his eyes.

John stood at the kitchen door and nodded towards the man sitting at the kitchen table. "*Goedemorgen.*" He spoke slowly and deliberately.

Monsieur Aupetit looked up and grinned. "Ye tae, Maister Steel. But there's nae need fur ony Dutch. Ah hae a Scots born wife wi a guid Scots tongue in her heid that taught me hoo tae speak the way she wants. Aince upon a time ma language wis French, noo it's a bit o Dutch but maistly Scots."

"Ye soond Scots."

"Ah'll tak that as a compliment. Here sit doon, ma wife will be thru in a meenit."

A slim, sharp-featured woman with bright eyes and a ready smile bustled into the room. "Guid mornin Maister Steel. Ah see ye're gettin acquainted wi ma man. Hoo aboot some breakfast? Mibbe a bowl o porridge an then a bit ham?"

"Perfect." John sounded pleased.

"Has it been cheese, cheese, an mair cheese they past few days?" John nodded.

"Weel forget aboot that. This mornin ye'll git a richt breakfast. By the way yer freend's up an awa tae the university. He wis anxious no tae be late meetin his professor. An weel he micht. He's highly honoured bein allooed tae study wi the rector, Johannes Marck himsel. But whit aboot yersel? Hoo are ye meanin tae pit in yer time? Ah unnerstaund ye've been sent here as some kind o messenger."

"Ay. Ah'm charged wi takin back a report on ma freend's progress. Them as sent him are keen tae ken hoo he's gettin on. Thur maist anxious fur him tae dae weel."

"Jist so." Lisa Aupetit smiled. "Ah'm shair he will, sic a serious young man an raither pre-occupied. No that he's ocht but polite."

"His mind's fu o worry aboot hame an whit's happenin."

"An that's nae guid." Lisa frowned. "Ah hear aboot it frae ma brither Tobias. Maks me gled tae be safe here in the Netherlands."

"Dae ye ivver miss Scotland?"

Lisa shook her head. "Ah came here wi Tobias tae be his hoosekeeper an then ah met Aupetit. Nixt aff Tobias marries a Dutch lassie so ah'd nae worries aboot him bein luked aifter. This is ma hame noo, wi a guid man an ma ain family. Whit mair cud ah want? Whit aboot yersel?"

"Here, here," Aupetit cut in, "whit aboot the man's breakfast?"

"Ay richt." Lisa blushed and turned towards the huge range that almost dwarfed the kitchen.

Aupetit smiled fondly as she bent over the porridge pot then whispered, "A tongue as wud clip cloots an repair auld shin. But ah luv her dearly an wudna hae it ony ither way."

This time John blushed but didn't dare nod.

John had just finished breakfast when Jonas Hawthorn appeared. "Mornin Uncle Jake. Mornin John."

John glanced at Aupetit who laughed. "Ma richt name's Jean-Pierre. At least it wis till Lisa got haud o it an turned me intae Jake."

"An Jake ye'll bide." Lisa pushed past Jonas and began to clear the table. She frowned at her husband. "Shud ye no be in yer workshop? Ye best move yersel. Thur's a wheen clocks waitin fur attention."

Aupetit pushed back his chair. "As ye say ma dear. Ah'm on ma way." He winked at John as he left the room.

Lisa Aupetit bustled through to the scullery and began clattering the dishes.

Jonas called after her, "Ah'm showin oor veesitor the university an the twa towers. Faither's insistin ah show him oor kirk as weel. Aifter that ah'm takin him ower tae Grootvader's. Ah think that's mair in his line."

Once in the street Jonas turned at a sign saying Prinsenhof. "This way." He walked past neatly cut boxed hedges bordering a raked gravel path. A long row of red-roofed, white-washed houses guarded the way towards the university building with its soaring, sandstone walls and shiny slate roof. Behind this impressive sight loomed the Martinitoren itself.

There was no shortage of money here. No shortage of ambition on show. Suddenly John felt jealous, almost angry.

His expression seemed a giveaway and Jonas smiled. "Ah ken wur lucky compared tae yersel. Jist mind we dinna hae yer troubles. Settled times mak a difference. Scotland needs this afore real progress can be made."

"It'll no be ony time soon."

"Ye nivver ken." Jonas smiled again. "Ah'm sure it's no fur the want o tryin. But nivver mind, this is neither the time nor the place fur sic thochts. Come on, ah'll show ye faither's kirk. Ah'll nivver hear the end o it if ah dinna. Aifter that we'll gang on tae the farm."

John followed Jonas through the door of the Scots Kirk and into a great barn of a space well filled by row on row of wooden pews. The whole place was lit by clear, sparkling windows and every corner danced with bright light. In the centre stood a massive oak communion table with a huge, black book carefully placed on its polished top. Behind this stood a high carved pulpit like a sentinel on watch. Directly above hung a gleaming brass candelabra.

"Hoo mony come in here?" John stared round at it all.

"Near a thoosand on a guid Sunday."

"Whit?"

Jonas laughed. "Ye heard faither say wur God fearin folk. Dis this no prove it? But come on. Ah think ye've seen enough an Grootvader's waitin. Ah tellt him we'd help wi the milkin."

The time at the farm was exactly what John needed, milking, feeding the pigs, fresh straw in the stable, all done with a will and real enjoyment. Jonas's grandfather was impressed with the visitor's skill and the way he fitted in so easily. At the end of the day he asked, "Wud ye like tae come back again?"

John grinned. "Ah'd happily bide here insteid o hangin aboot Groningen lik a knotless thread waitin tae be usefu."

And so a routine began. Most mornings John headed for the farm after breakfast and returned late in the evening after a day at the kind of work he understood and wanted to be part of, learning some new ways that might be useful back home, sharing his own knowledge with Jonas and his grandfather. Best of all the very nature of the work gave him space to just be himself.

Apart from eating and sleeping James Renwick spent his time attending lectures or studying, his head forever bowed over his books or his pen scratching away, filling page after page with notes, and corrections, and suggestions on divine interpretation. He was loving every minute while time stood back, waiting to see if this eager student would emerge from his chrysalis with everything he'd need for the role he was desperate to play.

This bothered John and had him worrying how all this might unravel once Renwick was back home facing the government's determination to quash what they considered treason. Cargill and Cameron had both given resistance a good go, defiant to the last, or maybe just a bit too willing to become a martyr for the cause.

When John mentioned his concern Jonas surprised him by

saying his father believed quite the opposite and was filled with hope that Renwick would be the one to make a difference. "In fact he's keen tae see yer freend ordained as soon as possible an makin a richt stert."

"But thur's months yet afore his course is feenished."

"Mibbe so." Jonas nodded. "But accordin tae faither Renwick's mair than ready. He's been writin tae ither meenisters sayin so as weel as speakin tae the professors at the university. They seem tae be listenin. Mair than that thur agreein, an seekin further council. Letters huv been fleein back an furrit on the maitter an nixt week thur's tae be a big meetin whaur the presbytery meenisters mean tae mak some decision about maister Renwick's future."

"Dis Renwick ken aboot this? He's nivver said a word tae me."

"Ay. He seems on wi the idea, tellt faither it seems lik divine intervention is allooin him tae move furrit wi the Lord's work."

John sighed. "He wud say that."

Jonas gave him a sidelong look. "Mibbe ye'll be takin back a report aboot yer freend sooner than ye thocht."

"Whitivver. Ah'm only the messenger. Only tellt whit ah need tae ken."

"Ah wudna be annoyed. Sometimes it's the best way." Jonas grinned. "The less ye ken the less trouble ye git intae."

"If only," John laughed. "Ye dinna ken the hauf o it."

"Ah hear ye're the centre o attention these days." John was waiting for James Renwick when he came back from his university lecture. "Ah heard aboot the professors, the meenisters, the letters, the proposals."

Renwick smiled but didn't answer.

"Weel?"

"I didna seek it John. It came to me."

"Nae doubt. But nivver a word frae ye. Whit aboot the trust atween us?"

Renwick's mouth twitched. He looked uncomfortable. "Of course I trust ye. Wi ma life if need be. The truth is – " He hesitated. "It seemed best tae wait till I kent whit wud really happen. The possibility o being ordained sae quickly is a big step for these meenisters tae consider let alane support."

"And whit aboot yersel? Are ye sure aboot this? Jist mind ye belang tae anither kirk, anither country. Wi the best will in the world they meenisters ken nocht aboot ye. Dae they hae the richt tae ordain ye? Sic a thing's nivver been done afore."

"They ken aboot oor problems and terrible suffering back hame. Oor sad condition troubles them. They seem tae think that my ordination is needed tae further oor aspirations. I believe it will for I've prayed ivvery day asking the Lord tae tak me as I am, summon up whit must be and live in my heart. Does that no reassure ye?" Renwick held out his hand. "My apologies. Nae slight wis intended."

John returned the handshake but said nothing. Later he'd lie awake most of the night, staring into the dark, wondering, and not really wanting an answer.

The day of the meeting arrived. Black robed ministers and professors gathered in the university chapel and prayed for a good hour before beginning a long and intensive debate about James Renwick and his capability of becoming a fully-fledged minister with no need for further study.

Eventually they emerged. Tobias Hawthorn led the procession, grinning with pleasure as he conducted his esteemed colleagues down the long gravel path and into the Scots Kirk hall for a special meal before summoning James Renwick to attend and hear the result of the great men's deliberations.

John and Jonas accompanied him as far as the door then stood watching the formal assembly's reception of this unusual student as he walked in to stand in their midst.

One figure caught John's attention. He stared. Blinked. Stared again. No fancy hat with a long-plumed feather, no curly wig, just hair scraped back and tied at the nape of the neck with a slim strip of black leather. The face neither primped nor prepped but clean-scrubbed and smooth-shaved. A simple, white cravat sat above the tightly-buttoned jacket of a black suit. Everything spoke of discretion, sobriety, the perfect picture of a strict-living Presbyterian except for the expression. John remembered that only too well. It hadn't changed, still as haughty and defiant, and those eyes flicking here and there as if searching for some advantage. But it couldn't be. Not here. Not looking like that. Not this man.

Sir Robert Hamilton of Fingalton and Preston was in his element. The hours of debate and argument had delighted him, the best he'd had since those far away days before that unfortunate battle at Bothwell. As the commander he'd been determined to make sure his men understood the full importance of their cause. That way their resolve would remain firm. All this took time and he'd made time by fixing camp on the banks of the Clyde and inviting ministers to come and speak to the men on a daily basis. Early one morning his ambitious plan had been cut short by the enemy's pre-empted strike, so unexpected he'd been forced to withdraw and flee from the battlefield, even flee further to keep his own head on his shoulders. Finally he'd no choice but board a boat, put the sea between him and danger and head for Holland where he treated many an audience to his opinion on the disastrous failure he'd left behind. Not that everyone seemed sympathetic to all his criticisms and condemnations. This had caused him to travel further seeking some way to redeem himself and force his critics to eat their harsh words and give him back his rightful place as a respected leader for the covenant.

James Renwick was that opportunity. He could feel it, sense it. Best of all, Renwick seemed to believe it.

Hamilton had worked hard on this venture, encouraging Renwick, agreeing with his plans, nurturing the young man's confidence, seeing it increase. He'd also sat with many a minister, nurturing them, persuading them of Renwick's ability to keep the cause alive and see Scotland return to her true beliefs. And then he'd sewn the seed of bringing everything forward. He'd kept at it and his efforts seemed to be paying off. The ministers were now in agreement that Renwick should be ordained sooner rather than later and given full authority before God. Back in Scotland he'd re-kindle that tiny, remaining spark of resistance, allowing the remnant of believers to re-group, and grow, and prove themselves for Christ and the Covenant. And who'd be remembered for making it happen?

John studied the figure mingling through the black-robed crowd, watched the smiles, the nods, the handshakes, the back clapping, all signals of acceptance and respect from those devout men, perhaps even trust.

The more he watched the angrier he became. Eventually he made to step forward as if meaning to join the throng in the kirk hall.

"Naw John." Jonas grabbed his arm. "This occasion's only fur those and such as those, no the likes o us. Onyway, whit's wrang? Ye luk as if ye're ready tae murder somebody."

"Indeed." John pointed. "See that yin standin near the centre. Dae ye ken him?"

"No tae speak tae ither than sayin guid mornin."

"Keep it that way." John clenched his fists. "He's a danger tae himsel an onybody he meets."

"Hoo come?" Jonas sounded surprised.

"If ah'm richt he wis ma commander afore the battle at Bothwell. Useless disna begin tae describe him. But he luked different then, dressed lik some fancy doll, aw lace and velvet, wearin high-heeled shoes wi fancy silver buckles, forivver prancin aboot lik a cockerel on tap o the midden. As weel as that he wis the maist unbearable man ah ivver met."

"Ye didna like him then?"

"Like him? Ah despised him. If ye'd seen whit ah huv ye'd feel the same. First aff he mairched us tae Glesca, richt intae the toun an ordered new recruits tae storm a locked garrison bristlin wi cannon an lines o muskets pokin ower the walls. Ye can imagine whit happened. No jist that, he repeated the order three times afore he wis stopped. An then he taen the huff at bein defied. He didna care a jot fur aw they men lyin deid, jist flapped his haund an denied ony responsibility. Aifter that he made us sit aboot on the banks o the Clyde fur days on end, wastin time debatin scripture or listenin tae the meenisters' sermons wi nivver a thocht aboot the enemy gettin ready tae attack. Mony a man's deid or taen prisoner because o that eedjit's stupidity an selfishness."

"Are ye sure that's the same man? He's tidy dressed and sombre as ony meenister. Naethin lik ye described. Tell ye whit ah'll gie faither a signal. Git him tae come ower then ye can ask him yersel."

Tobias Hawthorn came towards Jonas and John. He looked at John's scowling face then at Jonas. "Whit's up?"

Jonas pointed into the crowd. "John thinks he kens that man.

Can ye pit him richt?"

Tobias nodded. "He's Robert Hamilton. Came here aifter yon battle at Bothwell. He's brither-in-law tae Alexander Gordon, the man sent by the Societies tae visit the Scots congregations and gauge whit support micht be forthcoming.

When he arrived in Rotterdam he had a bit altercation wi the meenisters in the college there. Aifter that he tried Amsterdam. He wisna much welcome there either and decided his spiritual hame micht lie elsewhaur. He journeyed on till he landed here and met James Renwick. He's much taen wi that young man's ability and impressed wi his intentions. In fact he's been the first tae suggest bringing furrit Renwick's ordination."

"Whitivver Hamilton's ahint will be proved wrang, or doomed, or baith."

Tobias Hawthorn drew back. "I hope ye can justify sic harsh words."

John nodded. "Sir, if ye can spare me time later ah'll gie ye it aw, chapter an verse."

Robert Hamilton noticed his host deep in conversation with two men at the door. Ever curious he left the chattering ministers and approached them. "Is there a problem Maister Hawthorn? Can I be of assistance?"

"Not at aw," Tobias pretended. "I wis jist having a word wi ma son and his freend here."

Before Hamilton could say any more John burst out with, "Dae ye mind a man cawed Gumsy?"

Hamilton blinked at John. "Why shud I?"

"Ye hud his ears cut aff fur laughin at ye."

Hamilton's face went white. He hesitated then snapped, "Utter nonsense." He turned on his heel. "Gentlemen. If ye'll excuse me."

John looked from Tobias to Jonas. "Ay he did. An later on that same Gumsy wis responsible fur the death o ma freend in circumstances that haurly bears repeatin."

Tobias Hawthorn stared after Hamilton's retreating back. "I luk furrit tae yer story John. Ivvery last word."

Chapter 17

Tobias Hawthorn listened carefully as John rhymed off the huge list of Robert Hamilton's faults and misdemeanors. He'd nodded, frowned, then looked shocked, sighed, sucked in his teeth, once or twice he'd even wiped away a tear. Afterwards he sat for a long time staring out the window of his study.

Unsure what next John wondered if he should say more. Finally he said, "Ah hope ye believe me sir. Ivvery word is true. Ah'm only tellin ye whit ah saw. Trust me, it gies me nae pleasure tae condemn ony man lik this."

Tobias sighed again and reached out to touch John's arm. "Nae worries on that score. By the soond o things it needed saying. A sorry tale." He stopped and looked away.

"Mibbe ye hae mair questions?" John sounded anxious. "Somethin ye're nae clear aboot? Whitivver it is Maister Hawthorn, oot wi it. Guid or bad, ah'd raither ken."

"Vera weel but ye'll no like it. In ma opinion we need tae be mindful o Maister Hamilton's ither side. It needs tae be conseedered as weel."

"Whit ither side? Thur isna yin. Whit dae ye no unnerstaund, sir? The man's oot fur himsel. Naethin else maitters. Worse than that he canna be trusted. Shairly whit ah've jist said proves that beyond doubt?"

"Whit happened back at Bothwell Brig wis bad, very bad. But tae be honest a man can learn frae experience and chainge as time passes. In this instance for the better."

John's eyebrows almost disappeared into his hairline.

"In his favour Maister Hamilton has done guid work here. Encouraging James Renwick, promoting his commitment tae the cause. In truth John, if it wisna for Hamilton's efforts and persistence these past weeks yer freend wud nivver hae been conseedered for an early ordination."

John clamped his teeth together although his eyes spoke loudly enough.

Tobias Hawthorn continued, "We're at a crucial stage in yer freend's progress towards his final test. Aince he passes that, and

I fully expect him tae dae weel, he can be fully ordained. That means he'll hae approval frae a number o weel respected men tae ignite that dying spark o resistance in oor beleaguered country. Think aboot it John. He needs that authority. "

"Richard Cameron went doon that road and failed. Things huv gotten worse since then. James Renwick has nae chance o success. He micht believe it but he's wrang. Ah ken. Ah saw whit happened tae Cameron. Worse than that ah saw hoo the government reacted; hoo mony a body suffered fur bein in the wrang place at the wrang time an giein the wrang answer. The Societies seem tae think James Renwick can dae somethin special. That's why they've sent him here. But ah'm nae convinced. Whit ye're proposin will simply mak anither martyr fur the cause. The thocht o it is terrifyin."

"Ye need tae show mair understanding o the bigger picture John. Thru oor Lord we're aw forgiven. He gied us the word and shows us the way. His work must tak precedence ower everything else.'

"Hoo can it wi Hamilton at the back o it? Can ye nae see hoo flawed he is? Judgement. He disna ken the meanin o it. Gang doon that road aifter a man lik that an ye'll live tae regret it. So will James Renwick when he mounts the scaffold at the Grassmarket in Edinburgh."

Tobias flinched and turned to look out the window. "We're living in a testing time wi challenges we haurly dare face. But oor Lord moves in mysterious ways. He brocht that young man here tae show us hope, ability, conviction. I cud see it the meenit I met him and my prayers for guidance are telling me this man is the way furrit. As my Lord's servant I hae nae option but obey his will."

"An dismiss whit ah've tellt ye? Hamilton wisna mindin the Lord or his will yon day back at Bothwell. It wis aw aboot his ain importance an then savin his skin. Hoo can ye even listen tae a man lik that?"

"That's unfair John. The thocht o that disaster pains ma heart. But ye need tae accept it's in the past. Maister Renwick is the future. We need tae grasp this chance. If it means supporting Robert Hamilton in his efforts tae alloo James Renwick's ordination sooner raither than later, weel, I conseeder it ma God gien duty."

"Ye're no seein the truth. Ye jist think ye are."

"Can we no agree tae disagree?"

"An gang furrit wi Hamilton?" John stood up. "Nae way. Aw ah can dae is ask ma freend tae pen an early report aboot his progress an alloo me tae tak it back tae the Societies."

"Whit aboot the ordination? Wud it no gie ye pleasure tae be pairt o it?"

"No unner they circumstances, sir. Ah'm best oot o here an miles awa frae the likes o Hamilton."

John hurried back to 54 Folkerdingestraat, rattled up the narrow stairs and burst into James Renwick's room to find him on his knees, deep in prayer.

Undeterred John crossed the room and touched the young man's shoulder. There was no reaction. This time he shook the shoulder. It still took a moment before Renwick realised he was being interrupted. He turned to see a pair of hard eyes and a tight expression warning him that something was terribly wrong. He blinked at John. "Whit's wrang?"

"Aw this toadyin tae Robert Hamilton that's whit's wrang. Ye're playin a dangerous game mixin wi that yin. Ah tellt ye aboot him aready, hoo mony a man ended up deid at Bothwell Brig because o his stupidity. As weel as that he caused the final push fur yon guard Gumsy whae did in ma freend Lucas Brotherstone on the Bass Rock. Granted Gumsy wis bad enough tae stert wi but hain his ears cut aff on the orders o yon grand gentleman wis lik openin the door fur evil tae tak ower. An it did. Pair Lucas micht no hae suffered the way he did, micht still be alive."

Renwick blinked again then closed his eyes as if shielding himself from this onslaught. Finally he said, "I dinna ken whit'll happen next but I believe Christ walks aheid reassuring me that he kens the richt way. If nane are willing tae come wi me I still must go."

"Dis that include associatin wi the likes o Hamilton?" John sounded more hurt than angry.

Renwick shook his head. "I must be prepared tae venture intae dark and difficult places as weel as working wi unlikely folk if it gies me the chance tae help the hurt and the damaged. Shairly they deserve that?"

"Ay. An ah commend ye're intentions. But it disna justify takin up wi a fraud."

"There's aye a bigger picture. Can ye no see it?"

"Weel enough tae tell ye that ah canna bide here an watch this deception. Ah'm still willin tae tak yer report back hame but dinna expect me tae tell the Societies that aw is weel wi yer studies."

"John please, I must. It's my only way forward."

"In that case sit doon an write oot yer progress report then gie me it in the mornin; aifter that ah'm oot o here."

When Jonas Hawthorn heard John's decision he insisted on seeing John safely back to Rotterdam as well as promising to help him find a berth back to Scotland.

John didn't argue. In truth he was glad to have the young man's company.

James Renwick and John Steel parted with a handshake but no word was exchanged.

When John Steel and Jonas Hawthorn rode out of Groningen neither spoke till several miles were behind them. Jonas began with, "Whitivver ye said tae faither had him on his knees aw nicht."

"Serves him richt." John glared at Jonas. "Ah tried tae pit him richt but he wudna listen."

"Ah tak it ye're referrin tae Maister Hamilton?"

"Whit's said is said an whit'll come o it ah shudder ta think."

"That bad?"

"Ay. Dinna git me wrang, ye're faither's a fine man."

"But whiles willin tae duck an dive tae git his ain way."

"Seems like it. In ma book it's mibbe mair aboot wearin blinkers."

Jonas nodded. "Whit aboot yer freend Renwick? He didna seem best pleased wi ye?"

"Him an yer faither thegither. But enough aboot them, whit way did ye suggest comin wi me? Ah appreciate yer effort but ah'm shair ah cud manage masel."

"Ah'm sure ye cud but ah'd guid reason tae want tae come. Ah've a wee bit personal business needin attention in that toun; business ah'd rather keep tae masel."

"An if yer faither kent he wudna be pleased wi ye either?"

Jonas nodded and they rode on again in silence.

By the time they reached Rotterdam John and Jonas were more relaxed in each other's company, finding it easier to talk, even joke, without James Renwick's serious face riding alongside. Their companionship loosened Jonas's tongue, had him testing John's reaction to what was on his mind. He began with, "Can ah tell ye aboot ma horse? He's ma pride an joy but mibbe a mistake. He's costin me mair than ah huv."

"Hoo come?"

"Ah taen oot a loan tae meet the askin price."

"As lang as ye can afford it thur's nae harm."

"That's the problem. The moneylender keeps addin tae the interest ah owe. Ah canna see masel ivver payin aff the debt."

"Shairly ye hud an agreement?"

"Ah thocht ah hud but he seems tae think different."

"Remind him then."

"It's no sae easy wi his minders aye there an thereaboots. Ah'm due tae mak anither payment this week. If ah slip up the auld deil's threatenin tae send ma faither a bill fur the fu amount."

"Soonds lik blackmail tae me. Mibbe ah shud come wi ye an hae a word? Mibbe atween us we can persuade him tae be a bit mair reasonable?"

"Wud ye?" Jonas looked relieved.

"Ay. Whaur dae we find this man?"

"Maist o his business is done in the Green Dragon; a big inn ahint the storage shed at the end o the harbour road. It's only five meenits awa."

The Green Dragon looked impressive; every inch freshly painted with sparkling windows enhanced by pots of red geraniums and trailing ivy. Clean-scrubbed trestle tables lined the pavement outside with most seats occupied by well-dressed citizens enjoying a beer or the latest fashionable drink, black coffee. Above their heads swung a beautifully painted bright green dragon sign, its glass eyes glinting in the sun. Everything about the place warned the down at heel they'd find no welcome here.

John frowned. "Yer moneylender must dae weel if he can afford dain business in there."

Jonas nodded. "Disna seem tae be a problem. Thur's nae shortage o folk lukin fur a loan. Eedjits lik masel." Jonas pointed to the open door of the inn. "That's him, the wee yin alang wi they twa big, rough lukin tikes. Dinna be fooled tho, thur's nae doubt whae's the maister."

John studied the group in the doorway. "My God." He turned to Jonas. "Ye nivver said he wisna Dutch."

"Ah didna think it maittered. Dis that mean ye ken him?"

John kept staring. "Ah'm sorry tae say ay. Hoo he's got here is a mystery. In fact ah nivver thocht tae see him again. Mind ye they say the deil luks aifter his ain. Whit did ye say his name wis?"

"Henry Wylie. But ye must ken his name aready."

John frowned. "That yin's hud mair than ane name. He stertit aff as Sam Galbraith, kent as Gaby afore he chainged tae Davie Shaw. God kens hoo mony ither names he's hud since then. Ane thing fur sure, he's still the same tinker; still lik a bad smell whaurivver he goes."

"Tinker?"

"Ay. He often brocht his pack tae ma farm an persuaded ma saft hearted wife tae tak peety on him. She nivver turned him awa, aye gied him a bite tae eat. In the winter ah'd whiles let him sleep in the barn. An whit did he dae but clype tae the sheriff when ah tried tae help oor meenister in his hoor o need. It caused the awfiest stramash. Ah wis arrested, flung in the tolbooth fur a week then gied a heavy fine. He kept oot ma way fur a few weeks but his nose got the better o him an came snoopin roond the village again. Ah got haud o him an locked him in a cousin's cellar while we decided whit tae dae wi him. Early in the morning this cousin decided tae tak him a bite tae eat. She wis carefu, shouted in afore she opened the door then stood at the tap o the stairs, weel awa frae him. She didna ken he'd a sling in his pocket, didna ken he wis a dab haund wi it, cud kill a rabbit nae bother, so pingin a stane up at the pair wummin wis nae problem. Got her atween the een an she fell richt doon the stairs. That's aw Gaby needed an wis up an awa afore the rest o us kent onythin. Nixt aff he visits an auld farmer an steals a pile o money aff him. The auld man wis found deid. We dinna ken if the auld man wis aready deid when Gaby grabbed his chance or jist helped him on his way."

"My God, he's dangerous."

"Tell me aboot it. Aifter he stole the money he disappeared. Twa months later ah wis in Glesca an happened on him by chance. Ah caught him unawares but he wis quicker than ah thocht. Ah ended up wi a knife atween ma ribs while Gaby made aff again." He smiled at Jonas. "This time ah'll mak nae mistake."

175

"Whit aboot his minders?"

"We jist wait till he's on his ain."

As John spoke the three men disappeared inside.

Jonas groaned. "He'll no be on his ain fur hoors. Aifter dain business he aye bides fur a meal an a few glesses o wine."

"If that means waitin, we wait." John sounded determined. "Trust me, we'll git oor chance. Ah'll keep an ee oot here an ye can tak oor horses an git them stabled. Whit ah huv in mind will likely mean jookin alang in the shadows an bein discreet."

Jonas looked doubtful as he led the horses away.

It was almost dark before the three men left the inn and began walking back towards the city. John and Jonas followed at a careful distance, all the way to a grand, cobbled square bounded by tall, expensive looking houses. The three men crossed to the largest house and stood a few minutes together. The small, ornately dressed man seemed to be giving his minders precise instructions before he turned and went up the wide steps to his front door. The two men stood and waited till the door closed behind their master then wandered off together.

"Whit noo?" Jonas asked.

"We tak a luk roond the back."

"Thur's only a path ahint they hooses, runnin alangside a canal."

"Jist show me."

Minutes later they were staring up at the back of the high building. A light flickered in a downstairs window and in one directly above.

"That's mibbe a kitchen," Jonas suggested. "Maist like Wylie hus a servant lukin aifter him."

"We'll see. Patience."

Jonas had almost given up when the ground floor light went out. A minute later the outer door opened and a short, shadowy figure stepped out, turned the lock and started to walk along the path towards them.

"Must be his servant goin hame fur the nicht," Jonas whispered. "Luk, it's jist a wee lass."

John didn't answer. He stayed in the shadow till the slight figure drew level then he stepped forward, blocked the path and had the girl in a tight grip before she realised what was happening. She made to scream. John covered her mouth. In desperation she bit into his hand. He winced but held on. "Tell her no a word or else."

Jonas translated.

The girl gave a slight nod but John didn't release his grip. "Tell her we want the key tae her maister's hoose. Tell her we want a word wi him, private like."

Jonas repeated this.

The girl's eyes swivelled between the two men then her hand slipped into her pocket to pull out a large key.

John nodded, took the key with one hand, released his captive with the other then grinned as she took off along the dark path.

"Done this kinda thing afore?" Jonas sounded impressed.

"Ye cud say that," John admitted. "Richt, in we go an no a soond."

Once inside they stood in a dark corridor and listened as a pair of light feet pattered back and forward across the floor above.

After a while they stopped. Everything went quiet.

Gaby, who was now Henry Wylie, snuggled under the soft blankets and feather quilt of his comfortable bed.

Escaping to Holland after his unfortunate encounter with John Steel had been a desperate move but necessary. And it had worked out. Life was better than it had ever been. The Dutch needed loans as much as the Scots. So many of them willing to accept his terms. Once he had them signed up his minders made sure they kept paying. It was a true saying that money makes money. Soon he'd be in a position to merit an introduction to the diamond merchants. And then? He smiled at the thought and felt content as he snuffed out his bedside candle.

Gaby was snoring loudly, his mouth open when a huge hand slipped under the quilt to find his throat and squeeze hard.

He woke up gasping for air, arms flailing against his satin topped quilt. Above him a large figure leant closer as a soft voice, a pleasant voice, a voice he'd heard before whispered, "Weel met ye auld deil." The hand pushed him further up the bed till his head banged against the wooden headboard. "Dinna move. Nae a word. Jist listen." Strong fingers gave an extra squeeze. "Ay, it's me. Aifter whit ye did ah shud throttle ye. Mibbe ah'll dae it yit."

Gaby didn't struggle. He stayed perfectly still while his fingers crept towards the edge of his pillow.

"No ye don't. No this time." John struck Gaby hard then pulled out the slim blade he'd been trying to reach. "This time ye'll dae as ye're tellt. Paper. Ink. Whaur dae ye keep it?" He turned to Jonas. "Licht a candle till we see whit wur dain." He held Gaby rigid till the candle flickered. "So whaur's the paper?"

"Desk," Gaby croaked. "By the windae."

"Pu the shutters ower," John ordered.

Jonas obeyed then watched as Gaby was trailed over to the desk and dumped in the chair beside it.

"Richt," John's voice remained soft and calm, "stert writin whit ah say then sign an date." John went on to dictate the completion of an agreement between Henry Wylie, moneylender of Rotterdam, and Jonas Hawthorn, farmer of Groningen.

Finally Gaby signed as instructed, dated and dusted the letter.

John smiled. "Ye're no feenished yit. Noo ye'll write a wee confession. Ah'll help ye mind aw yer misdemeanours then ye'll sign wi aw the names ye've been kent by. Ye'll gie Maister Hawthorn yer agreement. Ah'll haud on tae the ither yin."

"Ye're goin a bit far," Gaby dared, "breakin in here tae molest a defenceless auld man ower a past grudge."

"Ah dinna think so." John grabbed Gaby's throat again. "Ye're gettin aff lightly but dae onythin, onythin at aw an a magistrate gits yer confession. Ah dae believe the guid Dutch folk wud tak ill against a thief, mibbe even a murderer, masqueradin as a respectable moneylender. Ye cud end up wi a rope roond yer neck or locked up forivver. Dae we unnerstaund ane anither?"

Gaby blinked.

"Ah'll tak that as ay." John turned to Jonas. "Tak the candle frae the bedside an hae a luk aboot, see if ye can find some rope or strong twine tae mak oor freend mair comfortable fur the nicht."

While Jonas searched the house John stood over Gaby without saying a word.

Eventually Gaby tried another challenge. "Cat got yer tongue, big man?"

John continued to stare but said nothing.

After that Gaby said no more.

Jonas returned with enough twine to tie Gaby up like a parcel. This done the two men carried him back to the bed. "Jist a meenit." John tore a slim length from the fine, linen sheet. "Noo open wide." He placed the length of cloth across Gaby's open mouth, pulled it tight then tied a knot at the back of the scrawny neck. Satisfied he patted Gaby on the head then pulled up the blankets and quilt. "Noo mind an behave yersel."

The candles were snuffed out then the two intruders left.

Footsteps faded downstairs and Gaby could do nothing but lie there waiting for morning when Marina would bring up her master's breakfast.

After they left Gaby's grand residence Jonas led John back to the harbour area, to a small inn almost hidden at the end of a narrow lane beside a packing shed. "This is whaur ah come fur news o ships comin an goin. Maist information passes thru here. We've a guid chance o findin whit berths are available. If thur's nane an we need tae bide the inn's clean an weel run wi decent food an disna charge the Green Dragon's fancy prices."

The inn was indeed small, almost like someone's house. It seemed a friendly place and late as it was the place was packed. The air was full of smoke floating among a variety of languages as the multi-national customers enjoyed each other's company.

They found a corner at the far end and sat down. "Whit noo?" John asked. "Ah wis in charge dealin wi Gaby, noo it's yer turn."

"Jist gie me a meenit," Jonas scanned the many faces. "ah'm lukin fur ony folk ah micht ken." Suddenly he jumped up. "Ah think ye're in luck. See ower there." He waved towards a group in the middle of the room. "Man wi the whiskers an the black cap. He's a captain, back an furrit aw the time. Oot o Glesca nae less. Cudna be better. If he hus a space ye're awa. An he's sympathetic."

"Whit dae ye mean?"

"Thru the years he's brocht mony a meenister here tae safety. His maister's Walter Middleton, a weel kent Scottish ship owner. He has a decent fleet that travels the world. Twa o his ships, the *Elizabeth* an the *Marianne*, come here aw the time. He's been a great supporter o the cause, bringin men an supplies at risk tae himsel. A fine man."

John sat up straight and peered through the crowd. This was

good news; the very man who'd helped Lucas Brotherstone make his first journey to Holland, and that second time John had met him when they arranged the fateful second journey which never took place.

The man across the room saw Jonas and waved back.

Jonas signalled for him to come over.

The man nodded, lifted his mug, and began to push his way across the crowded room.

Jonas stepped forward and shook hands. "Guid tae see ye Captain Scoular. Are ye comin or goin?"

Scoular grinned. "Aye tae the point Jonas Hawthorn. Tae answer yer question ah'm aboot tae go. Whit way?"

Jonas turned to John. "Ye micht be in luck aifter aw." He turned back to Captain Scoular. "Ah hae a passenger fur ye, wantin tae gang hame in a hurry."

"Huv ye noo." Scoular studied John. "Micht ah ask why?"

John glanced at Jonas.

Jonas nodded. "Nae need tae haud back. Ye're amang freends."

John hesitated then said, "If ye hae a space fur me ah'd be gratefu. Ah'm a messenger fur the Societies takin back important information. Ah unnerstaund ye're ane o Maister Middleton's men. He's been guid enough tae help a freend o mine afore, an masel if it comes tae it. Ma name's Steel, John Steel."

Scoular nodded. "In that case ah'll mak space. Ye'll need tae share a cabin. It's a ticht squeeze."

"Nae problem."

"Scoular held out his hand. "A deal then. Onyway, ye're better aff wi me. The ither ship aboot tae leave is frae Newcastle an ye dinna want that, no aifter whit happened tae a messenger lik yersel on the way oot."

"Did the captain tak against him?"

"Naw. Nature did."

"Whae wis this messenger? Ah micht ken him." John was already guessing who it might be.

"Somebody cawed Earlston. He'd been hame wi word frae the Dutch kirks an passin on news aboot some special student in Groningen."

John and Jonas looked at one another and frowned.

Scoular hesitated. "Ye ken whit ah'm on aboot?"

They both nodded then asked, "Whit went wrang?"

"Lik ah said, nature hud a haund in it. The ship wis settin oot, wis jist aff the mooth o the Tyne when it ran agroond on a sand bank. Richt stuck so ivverybody wis taen aff tae mak it lighter when they'd try tae refloat it. Mibbe ye dinna ken but the English huv gotten awfy suspicious aboot traffic goin or comin frae Holland. A wheen customs officers wur waitin on the quay ready tae interrogate the passengers. When Earlston saw them he must hae panicked. He flung the box he wis cairryin intae the sea. Daft eedjit shuda kent it wud float an draw attention. An it did. When it wis hooked oot the watter an opened it wis fu o incriminatin papers. No jist frae the Societies but Earlston hud been in touch wi folk in London as wur plannin against the King an his brither.

That did it. Earlston wis clapped in irons then sent back tae the Privy Council at Edinburgh. He'll git a richt grillin an ah wudna haud oot much hope on him keepin his heid."

"Whit aboot Glesca?" John looked concerned. "Are customs officers on the luk oot there as weel?"

"Oh ay. Nosin aboot ivverywhaur. Been dain it fur weeks." Scoular tapped his nose. "But dinna worry. Ye'll be lang gone afore we dock. Ye'll be rowed ashore at the tail o the bank afore we sail up the river. They'll nivver even ken ye wur a passenger."

"Soonds lik ye've done this afore." John looked relieved.

"Ye cud say that. Needs must."

"When dae ah need tae be ready?"

"Early mornin wi the tide. Aifter ah've hud ma meal ah'll walk ye doon tae the ship."

Dawn was breaking when the *Elizabeth* cast off. Jonas Hawthorn stood on the quay watching and feeling sorry to see his new friend sail away so soon.

John waved to Jonas. He'd miss this young man who reminded him so much of his younger self. He was glad he'd been able to help with the money problem. As for Gaby, would he really keep to his agreement? Because of that the confession paper had been left with Jonas. John's last words had been, "Use it if ye huv tae an dinna haud back." John guessed it might come to that. Ay, he thought, mibbe ah did let the auld deil aff ower lightly.

Chapter 18

"This way, Gentlemen." The Lord Advocate George Mackenzie ushered his fellow members of the Privy Council into one of the sitting rooms at the back of Holyrood House. "I thocht this wis a guid chance for a private discussion afore oor official meeting next week."

Their lordships made themselves comfortable and called for the claret decanter before they were inclined to comply.

Jamie Douglas, recently appointed colonel of the Foot Guards, looked round the assembled group. "Whit aboot Clavers? He's nae here yet. Shud we no wait a meenit?"

The Marquis of Queensberry raised his glass of claret as if making a toast. "He's no coming. Ower busy preparing for his nuptials the morn. Ye must hae heard. The word's ivverywhaur, even folk in the alehooses are joking aboot it."

His brother-in-law, the Duke of Hamilton, joined in. "Ay. June 10th micht turn oot tae be the day Clavers maks his biggest mistake."

"Whitivver dae ye mean?" Clavers' friend Lord Balcarres demanded.

Hamilton smiled. "When he ties the knot wi ane o the finest frae a rebel hoose. No that I dinna conseeder the lady in question ither than a maist worthy lass; and no that I hae onything ither than respect and admiration for John Graham. I'm jist saying."

Balcarres scowled at Hamilton. "There's nae need tae comment on a private maitter."

"Is that so?" Hamilton's smile tightened. "Even when the lady in question is Jean Cochrane? We aw ken whaur the Cochrane sympathy lies. Her faither's a runaway in Holland wi a price on his heid, her mither's strong for the so-cawed cause, nivver mind the rest o the family, aw they cousins, uncles and hingers on." He sucked in his breath. "I'm jist wondering whit his Majesty will mak o it."

Queensberry shook his head. "I'd be surprised if Clavers even thocht tae tell his Majesty or his Royal Highness."

"Why shud he?" Hamilton's smile became a sneer. "Him wi sic a grand opinion o himsel."

Queensberry grunted, "That's as may be but I'm mair concerned hoo Clavers has gotten raither close tae his Royal Highness. Smooth governing o this country is difficult enough withoot his Excellency hearing reports that wud benefit frae mair carefu wording afore reaching the royal ears."

"Ay." Aged eighty-five, the oldest member of the Privy Council, General Tam Dalyell made his feelings plain. "It's aboot time that young man realised whae's in charge aroond here. Yesterday he came tae my hoose demanding tae see me. I had my servant tell him I wis indisposed for I wanted tae avoid ony confrontation. Undeterred he left a note stating he'll be at the Cochrane hoose for the nixt week and only available if his Majesty requires his service. The cheek o it. And me his commanding officer. But ken whit." Dalyell tapped his nose. "It micht jist happen."

"Shairly no," Balcarres protested. "No on the man's wedding day."

"Dinna git sae het up, sir." Dalyell leant back in his chair and looked smug. "I said it micht happen. I didna say it wud."

Several faces looked amused, one or two remained impassive. Balcarres stood up as if to protest.

"Enough." Mackenzie signalled for Balcarres to sit down again. "This is neither the time nor the place for tittle tattle, we need tae conseeder Alexander Gordon o Earlston and whit he's been up tae. At his trial the ither day ye heard clear evidence o his treachery but somehoo yer lordships didna think it merited a hanging. In my opinion the man deserved it. Nae doubt aboot that. I wis mair than disappointed at yer decision but as always I must bow tae yer collective will. Mind ye, if ye'd made the effort for a proper read o the papers rescued frae yon box the daft eedjit flung in the sea afore he wis arrested ye micht hae thocht itherwise insteid o sending him tae the Bass Rock tae cool his heels. Whit kinda sentence is that for treason? Mony a man's been hanged for a lot less. Nae wonder I shook my heid at ye. If they letters are no a warning that the Covenanting cause is rallying again I'll eat ma hat."

"I voted wi ye," Queensberry gave his usual grunt and looked displeased.

"Ay." Mackenzie nodded. "But the ithers didna. That's why I suggested this meeting; tae clarify whit we're up against. We aw ken the bother they mad Presbyterians hae caused aready wi their challenge tae the crown and legal government. Hae nae illusion they're at it again. Reading the words and suggestions in they letters made my blood run cauld. Gie folk lik that an inch and they'll tak a mile and we'll be left regretting oor generosity. We need tae dae whitivver it taks tae maintain law and order."

Queensberry and Hamilton both nodded while Jamie Douglas studied his feet and looked uncomfortable. The others simply stared at Mackenzie like a pack of confused owls.

"Weel micht ye luk ashamed." Mackenzie's voice rose. "Dinna say I didna warn ye at the trial. Ye didna listen then so I'll tell ye again. Maist o the letters are frae some organisation cawing itsel the Societies, claiming tae speak for the people while condemning oorsels as usurpers o the truth. And no jist that, they traitors are reaching oot tae ither countries, seeking support for their plans tae undermine the crown and chainge oor way o life. A guid few o the letters are signed aff by a James Renwick. I havena see the name afore and this worries me. Dis ony o ye ken ocht aboot him?"

Every head shook.

"So whae is this man? And whaur is he? Mair tae the point, whit's he up tae? We need tae be thinking aboot that insteid o wasting time discussing the likes o Clavers and his matrimonial arrangements."

The *Marianne* had almost completed her journey. As dawn broke she slid past the Isle of Arran into more sheltered water. On the opposite coast spirals of smoke began to rise from the town chimneys of Ayr as well as villages strung along the coast. The shapes of trees and buildings stood out in the clear sky, the sea calmer than it had been for days, the sky blue with the promise of a fine day to come.

So it seemed till the ship crept round what was known as the Tail of the Bank and into the Clyde Estuary. Here a soft mist was waiting, hovering above the water to shroud ship from land and land from ship.

Captain Scoular came over to where John Steel was leaning over the rail peering into nothing.

"This is whaur ye leave us. Ye'll be picked up in a meenit. The man comin fur ye will hae seen oor ship approach afore the mist stertit."

A few minutes later a voice called up. "Davie Scott here. Is ma passenger ready?"

"Ay." The captain lifted John's bag and fastened it to a long, curled up rope. "Comin ower." The bag was lowered to a small boat bobbing far below. As it dropped a rope ladder unravelled alongside.

"Richt, on ye go." The captain shook John's hand.

"Ay. Thank ye. Let Maister Middleton ken ah'm back safe an gratefu fur the help."

"Ah will. An tak care. Glesca's a dangerous place these days."

John climbed over the rail, grabbed rough ropes and began the long descent. Eyes tight closed he felt his way, counting each swaying rung till a pair of strong hands grasped his waist and held firm. "Step back," a soft voice ordered. "Aince in the boat turn roond and sit doon nice an slow."

A moment later the little boat backed away from the ghostly ship and the stranger began to row steadily through the mist. After a while he nodded. "Name's David Scott, aye cawed Davie. Ah'm tasked wi seein ye safely on yer way."

"John Steel. Gled o yer help."

"Nae bother." Davie nodded. "Wur lucky wi the mist. Whit naebody sees dis them nae harm. Sit back it'll nae tak lang."

"An then whit?" John asked. "Can ye direct me tae a stable?"

"Nae need. Ah'll be takin ye intae toun. Aifter that ye're on yer ain. Ma horse an cart's waitin close whaur we land."

"Hoo dae ye ken whaur we are nivver mind whaur tae land?"

Davie laughed. "Ah jist dae."

Half an hour later John climbed into the waiting cart and off they trundled, out of the mist into a beautiful morning again.

Davie turned to John. "Ah'm a carrier aboot here; pickin up folk frae a ship noo an again is a wee extra. This is jist me goin aboot ma usual business. Naebody's likely tae gie us a second luk so dinna worry, we'll be fine."

"Ay," John nodded. "Lik ah said ah appreciate yer help." He smiled at the road ahead. "Ken whit, it's guid tae be back."

Davie Scott's cart had reached the outskirts of Paisley when the road was suddenly filled with carriages, elegant traps, men on horseback, all heading for the town.

Davie didn't seem bothered and simply pulled into a narrow

space in front of a rundown cottage. "We best let this lot pass afore we move on. Naethin tae worry aboot."

John frowned. "Whit's happenin?"

"It's a weddin party heidin fur Lord Dundonald's hoose. We passed the gate a few meenits ago."

"Seems lik a big affair."

"Ay. But no the happiest. Dundonald's grandochter is mairryin the very man as harasses her family."

"Can they no sort oot thur differences?"

"Ah doubt it. The bride's folk are staunch fur oor cause, her faither hus a price on his heid an bides in Holland lest he gits arrested. The bridegroom represents the king, the government, the very anes as wud arrest ony lik oorsels. No jist that, he's a force tae reckon wi, a man wi a reputation tae scare ye."

"So hoo's ony marriage possible?"

"They say the bride's cairried awa wi her suitor. Seems tae care mair fur him than onythin. Her mither refused tae gie her permission for a weddin but the young lady's the apple o her grandfaither's ee so whit she wants she gits. He's gied her his blessin, so hus the grandmither. This mornin Lady Jean Cochrane will become Lady Jean Graham."

John stiffened. "Wud the bridegroom happen tae be John Graham?"

"If ye mean Clavers, ay. Dae ye ken the man?"

"Ye cud say that. Lik ye said, he's a force tae reckon wi."

Davie gave him a sidelong glance. "In that case ye best pu doon yer bunnet an hide yer face. Here he comes."

Riding towards them John saw a grand officer in a scarlet coat with a short cloak slung over his shoulder. The finest lace circled his throat, an officer's scarf knotted round the waist below a protective steel corselet. His sword was looped up for riding while the long jack boots, the stirrup irons, the curb chain, the engraved pistols in their holsters on the saddle all gleamed with constant polishing and confirmed the importance of this officer. On his head was the final giveaway, the commander's famous black hat with its long white plume fluttering in the breeze.

Jist as ah mind ye. John Steel dipped his head and hoped the grand figure wouldn't look in his direction.

The beautiful black horse trotted past, its rider accompanied by two other officers. No-one seemed to notice the horse and cart or its occupants. Other carriages followed and John breathed a sigh of relief.

That wis close he thought and tried to look less anxious than he felt.

John Graham was riding to marry the woman he loved, who loved him so much she was prepared to defy her family's hostility. What not to like on such a fine morning?

Permission had to come from Lord Dundonald, her grandfather. Fortunately the old man had taken a shine to Clavers, agreeing to the marriage without much persuasion, although he did express concern over the problems the pair might face in the future. "If the trouble atween Covenant and King grows worse ane o ye will be expected tae tak strong action against it while the ither worries aboot kinsfolk on the ither side."

John Graham had shrugged. Lady Jean had simply looked sad and squeezed her grandfather's hand.

"Ay weel," Dundonald had sighed, "Dinna say I didna warn ye."

Once committed he'd done his best, making sure the ceremony took place in his house instead of the usual kirk, gladly paying the twenty shillings fine in the poor box for such a privilege. It seemed a small price to avoid any possible offence to the bridegroom and spare his own kinsfolk any more embarrassment than was necessary.

Invites were dispatched and food bought for the wedding feast which would require cooking for several days beforehand. Once this was underway Dundonald still had a huge list to attend to; the house was cleaned from top to bottom then decorated with flowers and greenery, pipers and fiddlers hired, wine cellar checked and much of it replenished, tapestries cleaned and re-hung, china and silver cleaned and polished, tablecloths and napkins washed and starched. Finally each servant was issued with new livery. Nothing was forgotten, no detail overlooked.

It all seemed set fine except the guests travelling to this grand event were all Cochranes, unlikely to show any friendship, seeing their attendance as a duty to their lord.

Not that the commander cared. Not on so fine a morning.

Lady Jean Cochrane and John Graham stood before the black-clothed minister and smiled as he pronounced them man and wife. Around them their guests watched in silence, no smiles, no sign of approval.

Lord Dundonald stepped forward and held up a glass of best claret. "Guid health tae the newly weds."

The guests hesitated then obediently followed the old man's gesture before he led them through to the dining room where tables groaned with an array of food; everything from a side of beef, roast pheasant, venison, a whole salmon both hot and cold along with ashets of vegetables to suit all tastes, to the most delicate and sweetest of desserts, all washed down by the best of wine and spirits.

The bride and groom were conducted to the top table. Dundonald had settled them both then turned to wave his guests forward when a burly figure in a scarlet uniform pushed through the crowd.

The Cochranes glared and muttered when the soldier reached his commander and announced, "Sir, ah bring a message frae General Dalyell. His Majesty requests yer presence tae deal wi a conventicle reported tae be takin place oot by Black Loch."

John Graham stood up and nodded to the embarrassed looking trooper. "Gang intae Paisley, tae the garrison, caw oot the Life Guards and warn them tae be ready tae ride within the hour."

The trooper saluted and hurried away. John Graham turned to grip his wife's hand and gently ease her from her seat. She seemed to understand and together they walked the full length of the room, past all the glaring faces and out to the flower bedecked hall where they'd been married only a few minutes ago. Here he held her in his arms and whispered, "Be strong Jean, please. This is oor first challenge thegither."

Eyes wet with tears she clung to him. "Shairly ane day wisna too much tae ask? Ye dinna need enemies John; no when ye hae freends as dae this tae ye."

Within minutes John Graham had cast off his wedding finery for his official uniform, was out the front door and away while a tearful bride stood between her shocked grandparents and watched her new husband gallop off to do his duty for his king.

When General Dalyell heard of Clavers compliance he pulled

a sad face. "And this his wedding day. Whit a peety His Majesty's needs come first."

John Steel sat beside Davie Scott as the slow-moving cart covered the seven miles into Glasgow. He paid little attention to his surroundings for the sight of John Graham had taken him right back to the start of it all when a simple farmer had dared to confront and torment the commander's lieutenant. The price he'd paid for that indulgence had been a salutary lesson with a week in the tolbooth at Lanark and then brought before the commander to be tried for his crime. Clavers had been clever, allowing his victim space to condemn himself with his own rantings about the lieutenant. The resulting fine had been heavy, a mixture of money and beasts. The commander himself had come to John's farm to collect and count it all. That had been bad enough but the suggestion the great man made had been worse; discreetly, almost secretly, he'd suggested his admiration for John Steel, wondered if changing sides was a possibility. This had left John unsettled for days.

Weeks later at Drumclog things had seemed different when John had helped see off the bold commander and his troopers, preventing them from enforcing the ill law against field preaching meetings. That day ordinary folk had stood against the government for meddling in their way of life and chosen style of worship.

As it turned out none of it had mattered, not with that terrible defeat at Bothwell where the disgrace of it all had left those of the Covenant to years of harassment or worse.

John Graham's name seemed to run through each thread of John's own suffering yet he'd never felt outright hate for the man; what he did yes, how it was done yes, but never the man himself. This was reserved for his lieutenant, now Captain John Crichton.

Davie Scott seemed to understand John's preoccupation and left him be.

Finally John seemed to come to and ask, "Whaur are we?"

"Ootskirts o the toun. Ye've been sittin there lost in thocht fur the past six miles. It seemed best tae let ye git on wi it. Wis it the sicht o Clavers that set ye aff?"

John nodded but didn't explain.

"Ay weel, that yin seems tae affect maist folk he meets, or so ah'm tellt. At least he didna see ye this time."

"He'd be a busy thinkin aboot his bride. Onyway it's a lang time since ah hud onythin tae dae wi him direct."

Davie grinned. "Ye mean ye're nae an aince seen an nivver forgotten kinda man?"

They both laughed then Davie said, "The city gate's up aheid. Is thur onywhaur parteeclar ye want tae git aff?"

"Ah'd appreciate goin further in. If it disna pit ye oot yer way?"

"Wud takin ye up by the High Street dae? Aifter that ah need tae stert ma deliveries."

"Perfect." John nodded. "Ah want tae visit an address there."

"Posh freends, shairly?" Davie looked curious.

"Weel enough," John agreed and thought about James McAvoy.

Captain John Crichton was in a bad mood. Instead of appearing at his commander's wedding here he was filling his day with stupid errands.

When Clavers had said his captain was required to accompany him to Glasgow Crichton had assumed it was for the forthcoming occasion. How wrong he'd been. He was only wanted for pushing his way through Glasgow's busy streets, delivering worn boots for repair at the foot of Argyle Street then collecting three maps from Clavers' favourite cartographer. This meant trudging through countless lanes to a musty shop in the Old Vennel then taking the rolled-up parchments back to the little garrison by Glasgow Green. Too much walking. Worst of all he'd still to visit a moneylender and pay some of the interest due on a loan Clavers had been forced to take out for feeding and stabling.

He'd watched his master ride off with two other officers while the one who tried the hardest was ignored as usual.

Clavers' relationship with his captain veered between controlled patience, impatience, open irritation, sometimes anger, and often amusement. But never a hint of respect. Crichton was well aware of this and longed to change things. Ane o they days, he promised himself. Ane o they days.

By now he was fed up trailing through the stinking streets on foot. Up there on a horse gave a different view of things, forced people to step aside, brought power, which he liked; down here among the sweating bodies was very different.

The moneylender lived on the High Street. When the captain reached it he was surprised to find a grand building, no hole in the wall as he'd expected. Three storeys high, well maintained with a pillared entrance and a brass plate by the door announcing James McAvoy Goldsmith; the whole place spoke of wealth and quality. An nae doubt high payments Crichton thought as he rang the bell and waited till the door opened.

"Ay?" A liveried servant looked the immaculately uniformed officer up and down.

"Captain Crichton. Here on behalf o Colonel Claverhouse."

"An yer purpose?"

"Tae mak a payment." Crichton almost choked saying it.

"Richt. In ye come." The door swung open and the servant signalled for Crichton to follow him across the black and white chequered floor of an immense hall to an ornate, inlaid desk where a young man sat behind a neat pile of papers and books.

"Anither customer, sir." The servant nodded to Crichton and left.

"Morning." The young man looked up at the scowling face.

Crichton stood to attention. "Captain John Crichton. Here tae mak a payment on behalf o Colonel John Graham o Claverhoose."

The young man nodded and began to flick the pages of a huge black book. "Ah, here it is." His finger ran down a particular column of figures.

Crichton lost patience and dumped the small leather bag on the table. "It's aw here, as agreed."

"And twa weeks late." The young man frowned.

"We're military men wi demandin duties tae attend tae, keepin law and order in difficult times. Is that no mair important than makin payment at a specified time?"

"That micht be yer opeenion sir, but Maister McAvoy relies on cooperation frae his clients. He's maist parteeclar aboot prompt payment."

"Whit dis that mean?" Crichton snapped.

"By richts yer colonel shud be charged extra."

"But ah tellt ye." Crichton's voice rose.

"Indeed ye did, sir." The young man stood up. "Jist wait a meenit till I consult Maister McAvoy aboot this."

"Be quick aboot it. Ah'm a busy man."

The young man hurried up a flight of stairs at the end of the hall. At the top he disappeared behind a pair of double doors. After a few minutes an old man in a long tapestry coat appeared and leant over the balcony. He stared down at Crichton. "On this occasion, and this occasion only, I'm prepared tae waive the extra due for late payment. Please convey this tae Colonel Claverhouse. I understand he's being married the day. Under the circumstances he may consider this as a freendly gesture. But as I said, on this occasion only." Something about the gentle voice held as much authority as when Clavers was barking out orders. Crichton found himself clicking his heels and saluting then feeling ridiculous.

The young man returned to his desk, emptied the leather bag, counted the gold coins, slipped them into the top left hand drawer of the desk, marked the date and amount in the ledger page, wrote and stamped a receipt then handed bag and receipt to Crichton. "That's aw sir. Please gie yer commander oor guid wishes for a happy future. Guid day." He lifted his pen and began to write again.

The liveried servant appeared by Crichton's side. "This way, sir."

Crichton was led back to the outside door and made to wait while the door was unlocked.

"Guid day." The servant bowed, ushered him out then quickly closed the door again.

Crichton stood on the pristine steps of the McAvoy house and slipped receipt and bag into the safety of an inside pocket. Thank God that's ower. He breathed a sigh of relief. Whit a palaver in there. Noo for a drink. He looked up and down the street for a likely tavern. Further down the Gallowgate he saw a brightly painted inn sign swinging above the heads of the crowd. Ay, that'll dae.

He was about to duck under the low lintel of the tavern when something made him stop and turn round. A loaded cart was passing. Above the heads of the crowd he could see the driver and passenger. Weel ah nivver. He stiffened as he recognised the passenger. This micht be ma lucky day aifter aw. That yin has a thoosand merks on his heid, deid or alive. Suit me nicely as weel as settlin a few auld scores.

He began to follow the cart as it made its way towards the crossing with the High Street.

The cart stopped by the vintner's shop. The two men sitting

up front stayed there talking.

That's the way, Crichton smiled. Mak it easy for me. He edged past three narrow shop fronts and then stepped into the shadow of a close mouth. Perfect. Ah can see fine while bidin oot o sicht. Naebody's likely to notice whit ah'm up tae.

Eyes fixed on the cart and its two passengers he took his Murdoch pistol from his thick leather belt. No need to prime. Powder, ball, paper were all in place, ready. He'd done that before leaving the garrison that morning. Dangerous as it was to walk about with a half-cocked pistol in his belt it helped him face the demons he imagined might be lurking in the dark city vennels. He'd felt like this since that night in Lanark when he'd been attacked in just such a vennel, stripped of his clothes then tied to the mercat cross. He'd shivered there till early morning when the garrison washerwoman found him and laughed at the sight of his quivering body. He still dreamt about the embarrassment. The whole town had laughed about it. He'd never proved who'd been responsible but John Steel's name had to be in there. He thought about this and smiled a tight smile.

The frizzen was in place, tight over the pan. All he had to do was fully cock the hammer. Holding the pistol steady he took careful aim at the broad backed passenger on the cart. An inch either way would make little difference to the result. Index finger resting against the trigger he held his breath, took one more look to be sure. Perfect. His finger obeyed. There was a bright flash and explosion as the pistol fired. At the same time a knot of a fist crunched into the middle of his own back. His arm jerked up directing the lead ball high in the air before it dropped harmlessly into the cover on the back of the cart.

Swinging round to face his attacker Crichton glimpsed a short, stocky man with a fierce expression, then felt a sharp sting between his ribs, so sharp the shock made him drop his pistol. As he did something very hard met his brow and closed off his world.

"Jeezus." A man about to turn into the close saw the falling soldier, took one look at the figures standing behind him and ducked back into the street.

Alex and Pete Jamieson lifted the unconscious Crichton and carried him through the close to dump him in the darkest corner of a tiny courtyard.

Pete dusted his hands and grinned at his brother. "Lucky we happened tae be in the vintner's or we'd nivver hae seen a thing."

"Ay," Alex agreed, "funny hoo we aye manage tae be in the richt place at the richt time. But we best move. Git John Steel aff yon cairt an tak him tae the maister's hoose. If ane trooper's aifter him thur micht be ithers close by."

John Steel had heard the gun shot above the street noise and automatically ducked. He was still like that when two Jamieson faces appeared at the side of the cart and signalled for him to climb down at once.

Davie Scott leant forward and peered down, seemed to recognise the men, and pushed John from his seat as he clicked the horse forward. The horse was already on its way as John's feet touched the ground.

"Whit's up?" John asked as the Jamiesons grabbed his arm and steered him through the crowd.

"Trooper in yon close across frae whaur ye wur sittin wis aboot tae shoot ye. We stopped him. He's lyin in the back yaird sleepin lik a baby. Noo come on. Oot o here afore onythin else happens."

John didn't argue and was soon crossing the back yard to James McAvoy's grand house and into the safe warm kitchen.

When Crichton opened his eyes he was in the garrison infirmary. His head pounded, he wasn't seeing too well, and his chest was warning him not to breathe too deeply. He lifted his head slightly, saw the thick, white bandages across his chest and groaned as he realised that something had gone terribly wrong.

"Ye wur lucky." The garrison surgeon leant over him and pointed at his bandaged chest. "Anither inch tae the richt an ye'd had it. Mind ye, ony siller aboot ye is awa, so's yer sword and yer dress dagger. Yer boots are gone as weel."

"Ma pistol. Whaur is it? Did ah manage tae shoot John Steel?"

"Thur wis nae pistol, nae Steel. Ye wur on yer ain, got attacked and left for deid."

The surgeon offered him a sip of water. "Lik ah said, ye wur lucky that somebody found ye an summoned a constable afore it wis too late."

"Lucky." Crichton almost choked and closed his eyes again.

Chapter 19

John Steel sat beside a roaring fire in James McAvoy's fine sitting room and smiled at the old man. "Only hauf a day back frae Holland an hud a narra escape. Ah wis lucky the Jamiesons were close by."

McAvoy nodded. "A lead ball in yer back wud hae been worse than the last time when Maister Shaw, or whitivver his richt name is, stabbed ye in this very hoose."

"An guess whit, ah met up wi that very gentleman ower in Holland. Came across him in Rotterdam jist afore ah left."

"So that's whaur he disappeared tae."

"Seems so. Yon money he stole frae the auld farmer ah tellt ye aboot must hae helped him set up as a moneylender. He's still fleecin folk, dain weel tae, bides in a big hoose, wears the best o claes, has a servant lukin aifter him, an walks aboot the toun as if he's richt important wi twa minders coverin his back. Ah managed tae git him on his ane an gied him a fricht but aifter ah left he'd be back tae his auld ways. Aince a tinker aye a tinker."

"If the Jamiesons had gotten haud o him it wud hae been different. Is that no a warnin?"

"Aboot whit?"

"Ye're accumulating a wheen folk as hae a grudge against ye an letting them awa wi it. If ye dinna watch oot ane o them'll git ye. Luk whit happened oot there in the street this morning. Yon trooper cud hae killed ye."

John sat up straight. "Trust me. Ane way or anither ah intend tae see ma way thru they unfortunate times an come oot the ither end."

"I hope so." McAvoy sat back and stared at the flaming fire. "Ye've been awa a while in Holland. Wis it worth it?"

"Ay an naw. Wi the benefit o hindsicht it wisna the maist sensible thing tae dae."

"So why did ye?"

"Jist bein selfish. Ah fancied gittin awa fur a wee while, seein new things an no feelin lik a huntit animal. It happened aifter ah met a young man cawed James Renwick. He's connected wi the

Societies. Ah tak it ye've heard aboot them?"

McAvoy nodded. "They seem tae hae a deal o support."

"Ay. An determined tae tak on the government. They want meenisters oot field preachin again an believe James Renwick is the man tae mak it happen. When ah met him they wur aboot tae send him tae a university in Holland. Somehoo he persuaded me tae go wi him an then bring back word aboot his progress. It seemed lik a guid idea at the time so ah agreed. He's done weel. The Dutch meenisters are ower the moon wi him, even prepared tae ordain him withoot the need tae feenish his course at the university in Groningen. Ah dinna think that has happened afore."

McAvoy frowned. "The Societies are dangerous folk tae be involved wi John. The government has them marked as traitors since they got haud o Alexander Gordon frae Earlston."

"Ay." John sighed. "Ah met him aince or twice. He wis travellin aboot Holland on behalf o the Societies, meetin Scots congregations an collectin support fur back here. Ah heard aboot his wee adventure frae the captain as brocht me back frae Rotterdam, hoo he wis caught wi a box o letters frae the Societies alang wi ither suspicious papers. The Privy Council jist sent him tae the Bass Rock so somebody amang their lordships must hae a soft spot for him or else he kens something aboot them."

"Maist likely," McAvoy agreed. "An noo that the Privy Council has aw they papers James Renwick's name has come tae their attention. They seem tae think he micht be intendin mair resistance against the King."

"Thur richt." John sighed. "He canna wait tae git stertit. Dae ye mind Richard Cameron?"

McAvoy took a deep breath. "He wis a force tae be reckoned wi."

"This ane is ivvery bit as determined an as guid a preacher. He'll hae been ordained since ah left. Micht be on his way back by noo."

"Ye dinna soond ower happy aboot it?"

"Ah'm no. The hale thing's nae richt an nae guid will come o it. Ye see Robert Hamilton's at the back o it. He wis supposed tae be oor leader at Bothwell Brig except he wis worse than useless. Tae add insult tae injury he ran awa durin the battle an left us tae it. Ah met up wi him in Groningen. God kens hoo he ended up there, an still the nasty wee tyke he aye wis while kiddin on he's pure as the driven snaw. Whit yon deil did at Bothwell sticks in ma craw. No that he'd admit ony fault; he's still fu o himsel, moothin his opeenions, struttin aboot as if he's somebody as maittered insteid o a liability. Worse than that, James Renwick listens tae him, taks his advice."

"Did ye no put him richt?"

"Ah tried. It wis nae use. Renwick wisna pleased when ah warned him aboot gettin involved wi Hamilton. Ane word borrowed anither especially when ah suggested his so-cawed freend wis naethin but a fraud. The eedjit wudna listen, kept sayin hoo a man can chainge fur the better, hoo Hamilton really hus the country's best interests at heart. That did it. Deil mend him if he believes onythin yon man says. Aifter that ah hud tae walk awa. Onyway, ah'd been awa a while an wantit hame tae ma wife an weans. Ah've missed them somethin terrible. Frae noo on ah'll be keepin ma heid doon an bidin oot o sicht. Aince ah deliver James Renwick's letter tae the Societies ah'm done."

McAvoy gave John a long stare. "So ye say John. But whit ye've tellt me aboot this Renwick and his plans is worrying. We've trouble enough richt noo withoot the likes o him stirring up mair."

There was a light tap on the door. McAvoy turned his head and smiled as both Jamiesons appeared. Pete nodded to his master then spoke to John. "We've been doon tae the garrison an hud a word here an there withoot drawin attention. Yer wud be assassin is a Captain Crichton. He wis in the toon alang wi Commander Claverhoose but somehoo he didna git an invite tae the great man's weddin itherwise he'd nivver hae seen ye let alane tried tae attack ye"

"There's a surprise."

"Ye ken him?" Alex stepped closer. "Yon captain's richt poorly aifter his dunt on the heid. They say somebody stuck a knife in him as weel. Micht no survive."

John shook his head. "Trust me, the like's o him is indestructible. He'll be on ma tail afore ah ken it. Him an his maister."

Alex laughed. "Ah dinna think sae. We heard that auld General Dalyell has sent Claverhoose aff on a wild goose chase aifter supposed rebels at some field meetin."

"No on his weddin day?"

"Oh but ay. The auld general disna seem tae git on wi Claverhoose, cudna resist the chance tae tweek his tail. Likely be hell tae pay when the commander finds oot he's been set up. They say he's got some temper."

John nodded. "Ah've been on the receivin end an lived tae regret it. Mind ye, if he's busy chasin rebels elsewhaur and Crichton's at death's door mibbe ah can gang hame an bide in peace fur a wee while."

"Mibbe." McAvoy looked doubtful. "But ye need tae mind whit I said aboot being careful."

"So ah will." John reached out to squeeze the old man's arm. "Dinna worry."

An hour later John hired a horse from the stable at the top of the High Street and headed home. The two Jamiesons insisted on coming with him to the outskirts of the city. "Richt then." They solemnly shook hands. "Tak care lest yon captain recovers an comes aifter ye again."

John laughed. "He's aye aifter me. Bane o ma existence."

"We cud mibbe sort him oot?" Pete winked but didn't smile.

"Ah thocht aboot askin ye," John admitted, "but he's ma problem an ah need tae deal wi it in ma ain way. Onyway, ye've plenty tae dae lukin aifter yer maister's needs withoot botherin aboot me."

The Jamieson brothers watched John Steel's horse trot into the distance. Pete shook his head. "That yin's his ain worst enemy. Ower saft hearted. Hauf o whit he's suffered hus been his ain dain, giein in tae ithers or jist tryin tae dae whit he thinks is richt. Luk at the cairry on wi yon meenister, an as fur yon tinker. The way he passed himsel aff as a businessman an ended up stabbin pair John in the maister's hoose itsel is a disgrace. As fur gettin awa wi it. John needs tae think mair aboot himsel an let ithers mak thur ain mistakes."

"Ah doubt if that'll chainge noo," Alex smiled. "He canna help it. C'mon. Time we went back tae the maister."

John turned onto the Waterside farm track. He'd decided to leave the horse at the farm then cut across the fields and part of the moor on foot to Westermains. Safer to have the horse stabled with the Weirs and not draw attention.

Gavin was clearing muck from a corner of the yard. He dropped his shovel and gaped at John. "Whit on earth?"

"Ah'm back early. Lang story."

Gavin grinned. "Nae doubt. Let me stable yer horse then come awa in fur a bite tae eat."

"Ay tae stablin the horse but naethin else, ah'm fur hame. Come ower an see me the morn. We can talk then."

Gavin waited while John jumped down from the horse then took the reins and led the beast towards the stable. He turned at the door to say something but John was gone. He smiled. Back safe but no happy by the luks o things. Nae doubt ah'll find oot the morn. He stroked the brow of the tired, mud-spattered horse. "Ah think ye deserve a wash doon afore a feed an a rest. C'mon."

John came out of the little birch wood on the edge of the moor and stood a minute staring at the roof of his own farm. No smoke here, no sign of life, no beasts in the fields. It was a sad reminder.

In the distance the smoke rising from his father's house told a different story, as did the cows waiting by the yard gate to be milked. Everyday life was here, meaningful life, worthwhile life, the life he wanted and had been born to.

Beyond the two farms stretched mile upon mile of heathery moor. He smiled and almost hugged himself. Instead of walking on he sat down and closed his eyes, listened to the swish and rustle of the leaves, the slight moan from the swaying trees along with tiny hidden scuttles in the undergrowth and occasional bird chirps here and there around him. His fingers crept across the fronds of damp grass, touched the daisy stalks, the buttercup heads, even the twisting tangles of purple vetch beside a tiny clump of sweet smelling thyme. Ah've missed ye. He lay back, opened his eyes to stare at the scudding clouds, moorland clouds, clouds wilder and more alive than any he'd seen in Holland. Ay. Guid tae be back.

Feeling better he turned to sit up again and saw a tiny ladybird crawling along a buttercup leaf beside his left hand. He smiled at the shiny red back with its three black spots then frowned. Just before the battle at Bothwell he'd sat on the edge of an oak wood feeling desperate and worried about the future. Like now he'd seen just such a ladybird, climbing up the stalk of a flower, determined, knowing where she was going. Was this one giving him the same warning? He sighed and stood up. Aifter ah deliver this letter tae the Societies ah'm done. As fur James Rewick, he can dae whit he likes, ah'm bidin weel clear.

Maybe it was the way the sneck clicked on the outside door that warned Marion. Anyway, she knew, flung the wooden dolly in among the steaming clothes she'd been wrestling with and was out the scullery, through the kitchen, down the dark hall and into John's waiting arms.

They clung together in the shadows, both faces wet with tears, no need for words. Eventually she drew back, took his hand and led him into the kitchen where he hugged her again.

"Pa." Both boys appeared from the scullery where they'd been playing among the buckets of clear water waiting to rinse the soapy clothes. John was almost knocked over as the two boys flung themselves at him, forcing him to let go of Marion and give them his full attention.

"Are ye bidin?" William demanded.

"We want ye tae bide," Johnnie added.

John gathered them both in his arms, struggled over to the big settle by the fire and sat down with a thump.

"Are ye bidin?" William's voice rose.

"Ay." John almost choked. "But luk at ye. Hoo big ye are. Maks me realise hoo lang ah've been awa."

"We countit ivvery day, marked it on the kitchen wa." William pointed to rows of chalk marks along the wall beside the dresser. "See. That proves it." He jumped off John's knee and ran into the scullery. "C'mon Bella. Pa's hame."

A tiny blonde whirlwind appeared clutching a carved wooden doll and pushed her way into the centre. "See Pa this is Polly. Maister Peat made her for me." She held up her treasure.

"My she's bonny." John admired the beautifully carved face of the doll

"Ay." Marion wiped away her tears. "Jo Peat has taen a lot o care ower Bella's wee doll. He's gotten richt fond o the wee rascal since he helped her intae the world that day. Trust Bella tae decide tae come at the worst possible meenit. If Jo's dug hudna heard her whimpering ah dinna ken hoo ah'd hae managed. Since then he's made a habit o comin by. Ye'll see fur yersel. He comes by maist days. Ye shud hear the conversations they huv."

"He's mair than welcome." John smiled at the bobbing blonde head. "Lik ye said withoot him – "

"But he wis. An she is. An it's by wi. Onyway, it wisna yer fault ye wurna here. Hoo cud ye be aifter Gaby stabbed ye in Maister McAvoy's hoose? Whit if the maister hudna gotten a doctor sae quick? It disna bear thinkin aboot. If onybody's tae blame it's yon tinker. If ah ivver see him again."

"Ah did see him," John admitted.

"Whaur?" When?" Marion gaped at him. "Whit happened?"

"In Holland. Ah gied him a fricht an a warnin aboot his evil ways."

"An let him be ah suppose." She shook her head. "Some day ah'd like tae shake some sense intae ye."

"But ye prefer me as ah am."

They grinned at each other and three confused little faces stared from one parent to the other then seemed to realise that everything was fine and back to normal.

John didn't sleep a wink that night. Being able to hold Marion and love her over and over, feeling her urgency as fierce and demanding as his own made a night he'd always remember for its reaching out and responding. Most of all her forgiveness of his selfishness made him feel guilty, seemed to drive him even more, to try and disappear within such pleasure.

Finally they lay curled together, watching the pale slivers of dawn appear through the shutter cracks. He stroked her hair and gently kissed her brow. "Us an the bairns. Naethin else frae noo on."

Marion's finger touched his lips. "Ay mibbe. Dinna forget that ah ken ye better than yersel."

John kept his word, delivered James Renwick's report to Logan House, declined the invitation to join in the Societies next meeting and rode back to the farm whistling with a new sense of freedom.

As the weeks passed Westermains farm had few visits from any government platoon. When they did appear the troopers were usually led by Captain McCann, always polite, almost respectful when he asked the dutiful question, "Hae ye seen Maister Steel?"

Marion suspected the soldier guessed the answer but each time she'd shake her head then stand back as the uniformed invaders began their usual search through every corner of the farm. Now it was tedious, inconvenient, annoying but not scary as when Crichton strutted and threatened.

Sometimes John had time to retreat up the hill, to the little birch wood where he'd watch the performance till the troopers left. If there was little warning he'd sit in the airless hidey-hole in the hall. It had almost become an accepted routine.

And then one morning Gavin arrived with the dreaded news. "Crichton's back. Him an his maister. Ah saw them baith in the village, baith wi faces lik thunder."

John Graham was not a happy man. General Dalyell's ruse had rattled him more than he cared to admit. As for the way his loyalty had been challenged, the insinuation that his love of Jean Cochrane compromised his status as a law enforcer. Upstart. That's hoo they see me. Resent hoo my record speaks for itsel. Whitivver the crown requires I dae it willingly. His Majesty kens that. I ken that. We share a trust so jist let their lordships try tae undermine ma authority.

He turned to Crichton riding by his side. "I hae word aboot somebody ripe for a lesson. It means a rough ride across the moor. Are ye up for it aifter yer wee mishap? Or shud I wait for McCann?"

Crichton scowled. "Nae need, sir. I'm perfectly able and mair than willin tae dae ma duty."

John Steel saw the flurry of red leave the Lesmahagow road, edge down the steep bank and cross the Logan Burn to begin the long climb towards the open moor. No need to hide. On this occasion the troopers were heading further afield.

Later that day Gus McPhail would stumble into the kitchen at Westermains, his face grey with terror, eyes full of what he'd witnessed after John Graham's platoon arrived at Priesthill farm to question his partner John Brown about loyalty to his king.

From now on the Privy Council would have no reason to question Clavers' efficiency in dealing with suspected rebels.

John Brown and his nephew Jo had been out cutting peats since before daylight. They were about to take a break when John Graham's platoon trotted out of the heather. Jo pointed at the approaching horses. "Mind the last time troopers cam by?"

John Brown nodded. "They wur lost in the mist an wantit directions. It micht be different this time."

"But wur only cuttin peats. That's haurly a crime."

"Indeed no. But whit we think, whit we believe, whit we micht dae worries them."

Jo began to look worried.

Clavers pulled up his horse alongside the two men. "I'm luking fur a man by the name o John Brown, bides at Priesthill. Wud this be the place?"

"It wud. Ah'm John Brown. Can ah help ye?"

"Indeed. I'm here tae ask if ye're a faithful servant tae his majesty."

"Whit majesty wud ye be referrin tae, sir?"

"I wudna jest if I wur ye." Clavers stared down at the weather-beaten face. "A new law's been passed that demands ivvery citizen's allegiance tae the crown. Maist folk agree wi the need for it but ane or twa seem tae think itherwise. I've heard a wee whisper that ye micht be sic a man. Of course, I cud be misinformed."

John Brown's expression remained impassive. "My maister is Jesus Christ. No ony earthly king."

Crichton turned to his commander. "I heard him. Ye heard him. The law states only twa witnesses are needed before summary execution. The man is clearly a traitor against the state as weel as his majesty."

Clavers frowned at his captain. "But we must mak sure he understands the law and the consequences o disobedience."

John Brown stared up at his questioner. His questioner stared down at him. Eventually Clavers said, "Dae ye understand whit I'm asking?"

John Brown nodded but said nothing.

"Weel?" Clavers seemed to lose patience. "Are ye willing tae swear the oath o allegiance and disavow rebellious behaviour?"

John Brown shook his head.

"If that means whit I think ye've jist put yer ain life in jeopardy."

John Brown bowed his head but still said nothing.

"Sir?" Crichton reached for his pistol.

John Brown's nephew dropped to his knees. "Sir, ah'll gladly swear the oath fur us baith."

"Will ye noo? And whit aboot my intention tae search Maister Brown's property. Whit micht I find I wonder? Will ye still answer for baith o ye?" Clavers smiled at Jo's ashen face. "I thocht so." He leant forward and hauled the boy upright. "C'mon. I'm keen tae see if the property in question is hiding onything it shudna."

John Brown and young Jo led the platoon along the narrow track to the little farm.

The horses clattered into the tiny courtyard and surrounded the two captives.

John Brown held up his hands. "Whit ye find in the cellar belangs tae me. The boy kens nocht aboot it."

Minutes later the troopers carried out a bundle of swords, muskets and pistols. A terrified woman followed them and watched as they laid the weapons at John Brown's feet.

Clavers pointed at the pile of metal. "No the sort o thing I'd expect tae find on a law abiding farm. A stash lik this maks me wonder if ye're planning yer ain rebellion?"

John Brown remained silent.

Clavers shook his head. "No that I need an answer. The evidence speaks for itsel and condemns ye. Ye're guilty o treason and must pay the price as the law demands." He signalled for the troopers to line up in front of John Brown. "Tak aim. When I signal, fire at the captive."

The woman ran forward.

Clavers wheeled round. "Git that woman inside and see that she bides there."

John Brown still didn't speak. He stood straight, eyes wide open staring at the musket barrels.

Clavers waited till the woman was back in the house and the door shut. He lifted his hand and barked out, "Fire."

Jo screamed and covered his face.

Clavers glanced at the crumpled figure then at the quivering boy. "Yer uncle seemed singularly unbothered aboot throwing awa his life. Noo whit aboot yersel?"

Jo dropped to his knees again. "Ma uncle said ah kent naethin. Ah didna. An mind ah offered tae swear the oath. Ah'm still willin."

"Indeed ye did." Clavers turned to his captain. "Strap this ane across yer horse. We'll tak him tae Muirkirk and let the justiciary decide whit nixt."

"But sir," Crichton dared.

Clavers held up a gloved hand. "The boy is willing tae tak the oath. We aw heard his uncle say he kent naething. By law we can only mak an arrest and hand him on for mair questioning."

"Sir." Crichton grabbed the boy and threw him over the broad back of his horse then jumped up himself.

"That's better." Clavers smiled then signalled to the troopers still standing beside John Brown's bleeding body. "Saddle up. We've a captive tae deliver."

The platoon had barely left the tiny courtyard when Isabel Brown opened the house door and crept out to kneel beside her dead husband. Two hours later she was still there, still kneeling and cradling the bloody head when Gus McPhail arrived with his horse and cart.

On the other side of Cumnock Sandy Peden was in a shepherd's cottage about to baptise a baby. As he leant over to make the blessing his eyes filled with tears and his hands trembled. "A happy day here wi this new life. No far frae here it's a sad ane for ah see ma freend John Brown lyin wi his heid ablo a wee rowan tree."

The shepherd and his wife glanced at one another. From experience they guessed that the old minister's words had a special meaning. In a few days time they would hear of John Brown's execution and understand why old Sandy had been so upset.

"Whit's tae be done?" Marion gaped at Gus. "Whit aboot pair Isabel? Is she still at Priesthill?"

Gus nodded. "She'll no move frae John's side. Ah said ah'd git help an then we'd bury him proper like."

John Steel stood up. "Ah'll gang ower tae Waterside an fetch Gavin. Ah'm sure he'll want tae help."

Marion grabbed his arm. "Ask ma mither if she'll cam ower an watch the bairns while ah go wi ye."

Later that day John Brown was buried in his own garden with a young rowan tree planted alongside to mark the spot.

"Whit noo?" Marion asked Isabel. "Will ye come back wi us? Ye canna bide here yersel. Whit will ye dae if the troopers come back?"

"Whit's done is done. They huv nae interest in me. It's pair Jo ah'm worried aboot. No that ah can help the lad. Best thing ah can dae is heid fur Strathaven. Back tae bide wi ma mither. She'll tak care o the bairns while ah find some work tae keep us aw goin."

"Wud ye no be best tae gie yersel time an think aboot it a bit mair?"

"Naw. Lik ah said, whit's done is done. John's awa an thur's nae way back frae it."

John, Gavin and Marion helped Isabel pack up her possessions and load everything onto Gus's cart. They then watched the cart lurch away down the rough track towards the Strathaven road, taking the new widow and her two small children towards an uncertain future in that town.

John, Gavin and Marion trudged back across the moor in silence. Each was angry, sad and confused as they tried to make sense of what had happened.

When they reached the Lesmahagow side of the moor and John saw their farms he was close to tears, especially when Marion stopped and stared through the darkening towards a tiny flickering light in one of the windows. "See yon wee licht? That's whit wur like. Whit if it gits snuffed oot as weel? First it wis ma faither at Drumclog, then yer ain faither at Bothwell, then Richard Cameron, yer cousin Davie, ma uncle Ritchie, an noo oor freend John Brown. An that's only the anes ah ken. As fur Maister Brotherstane. He lost his wife at the stert then whit an end he hud."

John nodded. "Whit happened at Douglas didna help. The sicht o Richard Cameron's heid pued oot a bag tae swing back an furrit lik a wean's toy. Ah jist managed tae git him awa afore he drew attention tae himsel. Aw the way back across the moor he kept mutterin an prayin an blamin himself. An nixt mornin his precious conscience hud him sittin at oor kitchen table readin ane parteeclar line frae his Bible ower an ower.

When ah asked him whit wis wrang he jist drummed his fingers lik somethin dementit then pointit at the words.

"No that ah unnerstood. 'Lovest thou me more than these?' is no the easiest question tae be confrontit wi first thing in the mornin an try tae answer." John's face tightened. He looked away. "Ah still struggle tae mak sense o it. Noo ah jist tell masel the morn's anither day. Things micht chainge. An mibbe fur the better." He put his arms round her.

"But back there."

"Ay weel," John sighed. "That wis an awfy business but think aboot it. John Brown made his choice."

"An paid fur it," Gavin added. "Paid the price fur bein sae radical."

John nodded. "Ah blame Richard Cameron. Aifter he cam on the scene John Brown wis cairried awa wi the thocht o rebellion. That kinda extreme behaviour attracts attention. Ah shudder tae think whit he wis plannin wi as mony muskets and swords. Ane thing fur sure Richard Cameron wud hae approved."

Marion gaped at them both. "Cameron's deid an gone."

John frowned. "Ay. But thur's anither yin. Huv ye forgotten aboot James Renwick?"

Marion shook her head. "Ye left him in Holland. Ye said so yersel."

"Fur the time bein but rest assured he'll be back."

There was no answer to that and they all walked on in silence.

The End

Historical figures appearing in Desperate Times

The Steel Family

John Steel of Loganwaterhead farm: Bonnet laird with three farms. Lived near Lesmahagow. Fought at Battle of Drumclog and Bothwell Bridge. Declared a rebel with 1000 merks on his head for capture dead or alive. All his property was confiscated, spent next ten years on the run but never caught. After what was known as the Glorious Revolution, when William of Orange became King, he accepted Captaincy in Cameronian Regiment in 1689 to oversee ousting of English curates without bloodshed. Buried in Lesmahagow Old Parish Churchyard under a plain thruchstane. Date unknown but after 1707.

Marion Steel, wife of John Steel of Loganwaterhead Farm: Dates unverified. After Bothwell Bridge she was named as a rebel's wife, thrown out of her farm and forced to live rough on the moor with her young family. Bravely endured ill treatment from government troops. Eventually dared to return to the farm.

David Steel, Cousin of John Steel: Lived at Nether Skellyhill farm near Lesmahagow. Fought at Drumclog and Bothwell Bridge. Fugitive till 1686 when he was caught and shot.

Other Figures

Andrew Bruce of Earlshall: Dates not verified. Military man on Loyalist side. Led troops at Airds Moss to kill Richard Cameron. Appointed Claverhouse's lieutenant in 1682. Very active in pursuing Covenanters throughout south of Scotland

Reverend Richard Cameron, 1648-1680 Radical Covenanter: Ordained in Holland before returning to Scotland to try and revive resistance against government. Known as the Lion of the Covenant. Great preacher. Fearless adversary. Drew up Sanquhar Declaration denouncing king. 5000 merks reward for his capture dead or alive. Four weeks later killed during skirmish at Airds Moss near Cumnock. Short but meaningful ministry. The 26th or Cameronian Regiment named in his memory.

Reverend Donald Cargill, 1610-1681: One of the main ministers and rebel preachers of the Covenant. Minister of Barony Church Glasgow till 1662 when he was expelled for refusing to celebrate the king's birthday. Fought at Bothwell Bridge. Long career of rebel preaching. Colleague and stout supporter of Richard Cameron. After Cameron's death he published a paper excommunicating king and government. As a result 5000 merks reward for his capture. Caught at Covington Mill near Biggar on 12th July 1681, tried and hanged in Edinburgh Grassmarket 27th July 1681.

Lady Jean Cochrane: Married John Graham on 9th May 1684. Granddaughter of Lord Dundonald. She was 16 years younger than her husband. It was a love match not an arranged marriage as her family were strong Covenanting supporters. Immediate family much against marriage but grandfather gave his consent. Members of Scottish Privy Council made mischief of this match to do down Graham at every turn. After Graham's death in 1689 she survived him only another 7 years before dying herself after an accident while staying in Utrecht. She was brought back to Scotland and is buried in Kilsyth.

Lieutenant John Crichton or Creichton: Dates not verified. Served in His Majesty's Regiment of Dragoons. He did rise to rank of captain. Well known for his brutality to prisoners or any rebel on the run. One infamous incident involves the shooting of David Steel of Nether Skellyhill farm on 20th December 1686. Imprisoned in Edinburgh Tolbooth after change of government in 1690. He is remembered in Jonathan Swift's book in 1731 titled *Memoirs of Lieutenant John Creichton* where the account of his exploits are somewhat at odds with recorded fact.

Thomas Dalyell of the Binns, 1602-1685: Long serving Royalist. Earlier in career was Lieutenant General in Russian army. Very individual, fierce, uncompromising, eccentric character. Given special privilege of raising regiment known as Royal Scots Greys, paid for it from his own purse. Determined persecutor of Covenanters. Member of Scottish Privy Council.

Lord George Douglas, 1st Earl of Dumbarton: 3rd son of William, 1st Marquess of Douglas. Served in French army then recalled to Britain by Charles II who made him Earl of Dumbarton.

When James VII came to throne he was made commander in chief of Scottish forces. An adversary of John Graham.

John Graham of Claverhouse, Viscount Dundee, 1648-1689: Faithful supporter of Stuart Kings who relied heavily on his ability to keep order in the south of Scotland. One of the most successful Scottish soldiers of his time. Considered a ruthless opponent by Covenanters, earned title of Bluidy Clavers. Administered justice throughout southern Scotland, captain of King's Royal Regiment, member of Scottish Privy Council, created Viscount in 1688. Killed at Battle of Killiekrankie, 17th June 1689 where his men won the battle.

Sir Robert Hamilton of Preston and Fingalton: A poor leader of the Covenanters at Bothwell Bridge. Almost first to leave the field and flee to the safety of Holland. In Holland he met and befriended James Renwick then encouraged Renwick to return to Scotland and begin field preaching. Returned to Scotland after 1689.

George Mackenzie of Rosehaugh 1636-1691: King's Advocate. Main member of Scottish Privy Council. Sentenced many Covenanters to transportation, imprisonment, or death. After what was known as the Glorious Revolution in 1689 he wrote two books justifying his action. A power-hungry man.

John Maitland, 1st Duke of Lauderdale, 1610-1682: Secretary of State for Scotland. One of King Charles II's advisers. Another power-hungry, unethical man prone to plotting against colleagues. Fierce prosecutor of Covenanters.

James Ogilvie, Earl of Airlie and Strathmore: Stout royalist supporter. Cavalry leader at Bothwell Bridge. During final stage of battle he tried to capture John Steel. John Steel fought back, knocked Airlie off his horse then escaped. Airlie then tried to hunt down Steel. Unsuccessful. In revenge he claimed the Steel farm and land.

Reverend Alexander Peden: One of the most significant Covenanter ministers. Inspirational preacher. Outed from his parish at New Luce in Wigtonshire, he spent most of his life living rough and taking secret religious meetings. Famous for wearing a leather mask. Credited with second sight and described as Peden the prophet.

Ambushed in June 1672, sent to the Bass Rock for four years then ordered aboard the *St Michael* for transportation to America. The ship put in at Gravesend in England where the captain set all the prisoners free. Returned home then wandered between Scotland and Northern Ireland. Died at his brother's house, 26th January 1686 aged sixty. After burial troops dug up the corpse with intention of staging a hanging. Local laird intervened and corpse was buried at foot of the gallows. Subsequently dug up again and buried in Cumnock.

Reverend James Renwick, 1662-1688: One of the most inspiring Covenanting ministers. Last martyr at age of 26. Supporter of Richard Cameron and Donald Cargill. Ordained in Holland which caused problems when he returned to Scotland. Involved in Lanark Declaration, 12th January 1682 and 2nd Sanquhar Declaration, 28th May 1685.

Helen Spreul: Wife of John Spreul who supported him during his imprisonment on the Bass Rock. She visited him on several occasions but never managed to persuade him to pay the fine of £500. She died before he was released.

John Spreul, Apothecary: Wealthy business man arrested on false charge of being at the Battle of Bothwell Bridge. Refused to confess and demanded apology from Privy Council. Given fine of £500 which he refused to pay. Sent to Bass Rock till he would pay. Was there for years but still refused. Eventually order given for cell door to be left open. Spreul took the hint and left. By this time he'd lost his businesses but he somehow started again and became an important merchant once again. A very determined man and clever apothecary.

Logan House: A remote farmhouse beyond Lesmahagow where Covenanters met after death of Richard Cameron to form the Societies with an allegiance to field preaching. This meeting took place on 15th December 1681 and led to the publication of the Lanark Declaration in January 1682. They remained active till 1689.

About the Author
Ethyl Smith

Ethyl Smith is a graduate of the University of Strathclyde Novel Writing course and the Stirling University MLitt Creative Writing course.

Smith has had numerous short stories published in a range of publications, including, *Scottish Field*, *Spilling Ink*, *Stirling Collective Anthology*, *Mistaken Identities Anthology* (edited by James Robertson) and *Gutter Magazine*. Ethyl is also winner of the Dragon's Pen for *Mixing The Colours*, from Glasgow Women's Library.

Ethyl has also been a finalist three times, and winner once, in the Dragons Pen competition, and a Finalist in the Wigtown Book Festival Short Story Competition.

Ethyl Smith says, "I have always liked stories, always admired a good storyteller, longed to become one. As a child I told my stories through pictures. Later as an illustrator I interpreted the words of others before daring to link my own words with my own pictures. In this series of novels I have worked to portray the images of turbulent 17th century Scottish lives in words, and give them their voice."

Changed Times
Ethyl Smith

ISBN: 978-1-910946-09-1 (eBook)
ISBN: 978-1-910946-08-4 (Paperback)

1679 – The Killing Times: Charles II is on the throne, the Episcopacy has been restored, and southern Scotland is in ferment.

The King is demanding superiority over all things spiritual and temporal and rebellious Ministers are being ousted from their parishes for refusing to bend the knee.

When John Steel steps in to help one such Minister in his home village of Lesmahagow he finds himself caught up in events that reverberate not just through the parish, but throughout the whole of southern Scotland.

From the Battle of Drumclog to the Battle of Bothwell Bridge, John's platoon of farmers and villagers find themselves in the heart of the action over that fateful summer where the people fight the King for their religion, their freedom, and their lives.

Set amid the tumult and intrigue of Scotland's Killing Times, John Steel's story powerfully reflects the changes that took place across 17th century Scotland, and stunningly brings this period of history to life.

'Smith writes with a fine ear for Scots speech, and with a sensitive awareness to the different ways in which history intrudes upon the lives of men and women, soldiers and civilians, adults and children' – James Robertson

Dark Times
Ethyl Smith
ISBN: 978-1-910946-26-8 (eBook)
ISBN: 978-1-910946-24-4 (Paperback)

The summer of 1679 is a dark one for the Covenanters, routed by government troops at the Battle of Bothwell Brig. John Steel is on the run, hunted for his part in the battle by the vindictive Earl of Airlie. And life is no easier for the hapless Sandy Gillon, curate of Lesmahagow Kirk, in the Earl's sights for aiding John Steel's escape.

Outlawed and hounded, the surviving rebels have no choice but to take to the hills and moors to evade capture and deportation. And as a hard winter approaches, Marion Steel discovers she's pregnant with her third child.

Dark Times is the second part of Ethyl Smith's sweeping *Times* series that follows the lives of ordinary people in extraordinary times.

'What really sets Smith's novel apart, however, is her superb use of Scots dialogue. From the educated Scots of the gentry and nobility to the broader brogues of everyday folk, the dialogue sparkles and demands to be read out loud.' – Shirley Whiteside (The National)

The Bogeyman Chronicles
Craig Watson

ISBN: 978-1-910946-11-4 (eBook)
ISBN: 978-1-910946-10-7 (Paperback)

In 14th Century Scotland, amidst the wars of independence, hatred, murder and betrayal are commonplace. People are driven to extraordinary lengths to survive, whilst those with power exercise it with cruel pleasure.

Royal Prince Alexander Stewart, son of King Robert II and plagued by rumours of his illegitimacy, becomes infamous as the Wolf of Badenoch, while young Andrew Christie commits an unforgivable sin and lay Brother Brodie Affleck in the Restenneth Priory pieces together the mystery that links them all together.

From the horror of the times and the changing fortunes of the characters, the legend of the Bogeyman is born and Craig Watson cleverly weaves together the disparate lives of the characters into a compelling historical mystery that will keep you gripped throughout.

Over 80 years the lives of three men are inextricably entwined, and through their hatreds, murders and betrayals the legend of Christie Cleek, the bogeyman, is born.

'The Bogeyman Chronicles haunted our imagination long after we finished it' – iScot Magazine

The False Men
Mhairead MacLeod

ISBN: 978-1-910946-27-5 (eBook)
ISBN: 978-1-910946-25-1 (Paperback)

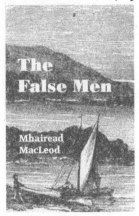

North Uist, Outer Hebrides, 1848

Jess MacKay has led a privileged life as the daughter of a local landowner, sheltered from the harsher aspects of life. Courted by the eligible Patrick Cooper, the Laird's new commissioner, Jess's future is mapped out, until Lachlan Macdonald arrives on North Uist, amid rumours of forced evictions on islands just to the south.

As the uncompromising brutality of the Clearances reaches the islands, and Jess sees her friends ripped from their homes, she must decide where her heart, and her loyalties, truly lie.

Set against the evocative backdrop of the Hebrides and inspired by a true story, *The False Men* is a compelling tale of love in a turbulent past that resonates with the upheavals of the modern world.

'...an engaging tale of powerlessness, love and disillusionment in the context of the type of injustice that, sadly, continues to this day' – Anne Goodwin